Mary Gardner, Karl Wied

A Short and Easy Modern Greek Grammar

with grammatical and conversational exercises, idiomatic, proverbial phrases, and

full vocabulary, after the German of Carl Wied

Mary Gardner, Karl Wied

A Short and Easy Modern Greek Grammar
with grammatical and conversational exercises, idiomatic, proverbial phrases, and full
vocabulary, after the German of Carl Wied

ISBN/EAN: 9783337387747

Printed in Europe, USA, Canada, Australia, Japan

Cover: Foto ©Andreas Hilbeck / pixelio.de

More available books at **www.hansebooks.com**

A SHORT AND EASY

MODERN GREEK GRAMMAR

WITH

GRAMMATICAL AND CONVERSATIONAL EXERCISES,
IDIOMATIC, PROVERBIAL PHRASES, AND
FULL VOCABULARY.

AFTER THE GERMAN OF CARL WIED

BY

MARY GARDNER

WITH A PREFACE BY

ERNEST GARDNER, M.A.

FELLOW OF GONVILLE AND CAIUS COLLEGE, CAMBRIDGE,
AND DIRECTOR OF THE BRITISH SCHOOL OF ARCHAEOLOGY AT ATHENS

London
DAVID NUTT 270 AND 271 STRAND
1892

RICHARD CLAY AND SONS, LIMITED,
LONDON AND BUNGAY.

TRANSLATOR'S PREFACE.

My very hearty thanks are due to all who have so kindly helped me in my slight task. First I must thank Mr. Wied, and take the opportunity to ask his pardon for the amount of alteration and rearrangement of his text which I have found it impossible to avoid. Mr. Legrand has also my gratitude and thanks for his invaluable dictionaries—French-Greek, and Greek-French; their ample information and clear arrangement were a great help.

To Mr. Noel of Euboea I am indebted for his kindness in putting an extensive knowledge of the vernacular idioms to use in looking over and correcting those cited, and to Mr. William Loring for similar help with the vocabulary; while Dr. Walter Leaf has completed the tale of my indebtedness by looking over the proofs. Others who have helped me I need not mention by name; but it is not out of place to acknowledge here my thanks to my husband, Mr. Ernest Gardner, to whose constant help alone the book owes its existence.

I hope that the book will be useful to all who visit Greece; I should have been glad of something of the sort myself some years ago.

MARY GARDNER.

ATHENS, Nov. 1891.

PREFACE.

It is hoped that this translation of a Grammar of the Modern Greek or Romaic language, as it is spoken in the Levant, will supply a need in England. The condition of the language presents innumerable difficulties even to Greeks themselves, much more therefore to foreigners who would learn to speak and read Modern Greek. And the absence of any fixed and recognised standard of grammatical accuracy, of accidence, of syntax, of vocabulary, or of style, has led many to make the assertion that there is no such thing as a Modern Greek language at all. Strange to say, it is among the Greeks themselves that this assertion has found the strongest supporters. Their method is to ignore the Modern Greek or Romaic tongue as dialectical and hybrid, and to fix on some arbitrary standard of past times, say the Greek of the New Testament or even of Xenophon; they admit indeed that the future, the infinitive, and perhaps the dative, have fallen out of use; but even these they are anxious to restore, and, with these exceptions, they would make a professedly Modern Greek Grammar identical, to all intents and purposes, with a grammar of the Ancient Greek κοινή. And it must be admitted that many newspapers and books are published in Greece which are intelligible to any scholar who is familiar with Ancient Greek, and has learnt some few idioms and periphrases which even the strictest imitators of Classical Greek

find indispensable in modern usage. For the student who wishes
to learn this artificial language the present Grammar is not
intended. But he must not imagine that he will find his
knowledge of much use to him in travelling in Greece, or in any
other part of the Levant. He may be able to converse with an
educated Athenian who has learnt this same artificial tongue—
and who is sure also to be able to speak French, Italian, or
English. But with shopkeepers and servants, muleteers, boat-
men, and peasants—all indeed with whom he will wish to speak
in his travels outside the pale of European languages and
civilisation, he will find himself quite unable to communicate.

This Grammar, on the other hand, endeavours to teach Modern
Greek as it is spoken by the common people. The attempt is a
difficult one; there is, as has been said, no fixed standard of
correctness, and the dialectical variation from place to place is
considerable. But a peasant of the Morea would not really
have a difficulty in making himself understood if he found
himself in Smyrna or Cyprus, though his speech and pronunciation might seem peculiar; and if this book can give some
notion of the common and living basis which underlies the whole
spoken tongue of Greece, it will not be useless. Doubtless the
student will notice small variations from the forms or rules here
laid down in almost any place where he may find himself; but these
will seldom prevent him from being understood when he speaks, or
from recognising the meaning of what he hears. Thus, if he requires the simplest necessaries of life, say bread and wine, the
words ψωμί and κρασί will find them for him wherever there are
Greeks to hear; but the ancient words ἄρτος and οἶνος, which he will
find in some books and newspapers, will certainly not be understood, even though he may ask in an Athenian shop with ἀρτο-
ποιεῖον or οἰνοπωλεῖον written in 'archaic letters' over the door.

This Grammar, in its English form, is intended to be useful
especially to classical scholars who possess already some famili-

arity with Ancient Greek, and are anxious to learn the modern language either for the sake of facility in travelling, or from interest in the historical development of the language and its modern literature. At the same time no knowledge of Ancient Greek is assumed except in dealing with forms, usages, or idioms which properly belong to the classical language. Thus the Grammar may be used also by those who, without a previous knowledge of Ancient Greek, wish to acquire a practical acquaintance with the modern tongue.

A few words may be added as to the relation of the study of Ancient and Modern Greek. It has sometimes been asserted that a conversational acquaintance with Modern Greek would be useful as a basis for the acquisition of Classical Greek, or at least as a help to its study. But it must in the first place be remembered that by Modern Greek those who adopt this view do not mean the language as spoken by the common people, but that artificial semi-classical dialect written by some, and spoken by a few. Still, even this dialect might be taught. But the fact is that the whole tendency of Modern Greek is so different from that of Ancient that it is much to be doubted whether a knowledge of one would greatly facilitate the acquisition of the other. Modern Greek, with its compound tenses and resolved cases, is an analytical language just as English is. And even those who are most careful in the selection of a purely classical vocabulary cannot escape the influence of French and German idioms, which destroy the character of the language, and are most difficult to avoid if once become familiar. Thus there is little left of that exquisitely perfect inflexional instrument of expression, the Ancient Greek language ; and the intellectual training offered by its accurate and scientific acquisition completely disappears, if it be taught merely as an analytical language in a transitional stage : to the student of the history of language such a stage is most inter-

esting and instructive ; but not so to a beginner whose mind is
to be trained in a new and accurate method of expression.

The future of the Greek language will be watched with the
utmost interest ; it is exposed to most serious danger ; for there
is some doubt whether it is strong enough to survive the attempt
at a classical and artificial renovation that is now being made—
an attempt not only to reject all words of foreign origin, but to
return to the accidence and the idiom of classical times. Such
a rude amputation of the growth of 2000 years cannot safely
be performed. Should the advocates of classical revival attain
their object in Greece, then Greeks will cease to be mutually
intelligible throughout the Levant, except in an artificially
constructed dialect ; and no people has ever yet consciously
invented a language, or restored a dead one to the life of popular
speech, after it had followed the ordinary course of decay and analytical regeneration which has produced nearly all the languages
spoken in Europe at the present day. Many of the best educated Greeks are fully aware that any reform and purification of
the Romaic tongue must start from the language now learnt by
the people at their mother's knee, and enrich its vocabulary
without altering its essential nature ; and it is to be hoped that
the more moderate counsels of this body may prevail over the
rash experiment of the extreme purists.

The analogy of another language that has passed through the
same stage is instructive. In the days of Dante there were
many purists who despised the vulgar tongue of Italy, and
thought that ancient Latin was the only language fit for an
educated man to speak or write. Had not the monumental
work of the great Florentine at once raised the vernacular to a
literary language, it is even possible that a frigid pseudo-classical
Latin might have first strangled the popular tongue and then
died a natural death. In Greece there are many songs and
ballads, and even some prose works written in the true language

of the people; and the influence of all is needed to strengthen that language in the dangers it is now passing through. There are already many indications that the popular tongue is beginning to prevail in the struggle. If its development, which has been retarded during the last fifty years by the classical mania, be once again allowed its free course, there is little doubt that it will be very rapid; Modern Greek only requires a little organisation and academic acknowledgment on the part of educated Greeks to take its due place among the analytical modern languages of Europe: and then its position will be unique, bearing as it does almost the same relation to Ancient Greek which the Romance languages bear to Latin.

The difficult question of pronunciation cannot here be entirely passed over, especially as those who advocate learning Ancient Greek by means of Modern often assert the identity of pronunciation between the two. In the pronunciation of consonants the divergence in principle is not so great, though the weakening and assimilation that has taken place in Modern Greek involves considerable changes, and is very confusing to a learner, when *e.g.* he finds he must pronounce Βέμπερ as the German name Weber or that Byron's name is represented by Μπαίρων, or when he recognises in the modern δέντρο (tree) a familiar word, of which the first δ is a soft th, while the second has only saved its sound by changing its written symbol. But it is two points chiefly that are matters of controversy; the pronunciation of vowels and the pronunciation according to accent.

That any should seriously assert that the Modern Greek pronunciation of vowels, in which η, ι, υ, ει, οι, υι, are all absolutely identical in sound, is the same as the Ancient Greek pronunciation, may seem incredible to any English scholar; yet this system, for Ancient Greek, is actually upheld as correct by many Greeks and some Englishmen, so that it may not be superfluous to note one or two arguments on the other side. First, as to euphony—let any one pronounce after the Modern Greek fashion ' οἱ υἱοὶ ἔχοιεν τὴν ὑγίειαν (which may be transliterated ee ee-eé éhee-en teen eeyeé-ee-an), and then assert, if he can, that Greek in this form is a language likely to be tolerated by a people with a keen appreciation for beauty ; then, as to ambiguity, is it probable that there was no distinction in pronunciation between the first and second person plural of the pronoun, that ' we ' and ' you ' were identical ? Yet according to the modern pronunciation ἡμεῖς and ὑμεῖς are both eemeéss. But the unanswerable argument is this : if there were no distinctions in pronunciation, how did distinctions in spelling arise, and how were they preserved ? Any student of early inscriptions knows that the Greeks, by a gradual and tentative process, adopted the Phoenician symbols to express their speech, not according to philological rules of derivation, but according to the sound ; and each dialect adapted the characters to express the sound it used ; e.g. some dialects denoted ου by O, others by OY, according to the breadth of their pronunciation. Yet there is not a shadow of epigraphical evidence for any general confusion, during the classical period, between the different symbols used to denote the sounds which in Modern Greek have become identical. So soon as the confusion began in speech, it penetrated also into writing, as was inevitable ; thus καί is often written KE after the third century A.D., and locally a little earlier. That this confusion did take place at this period, and not before, in writing may be taken as an unanswerable proof that it did not exist before in speech. Yet, strange to say, this very fact is quoted by some to prove that in classical times the pronunciation was confused. Which is the true inference may fairly be left to the decision of any unprejudiced reader. On the other hand ει and ι, which must always have been similar sounds, are confused in writing in Boeotia and sometimes even in Attica as early as the fourth century B.C. That a similar confusion does not occur in other sounds that have since become identical, except in a few late or dialectical inscriptions in which the beginning of this tendency can be seen, is a sufficient proof that in the common Greek of the best period no such confusion existed.

We English are at a disadvantage in discussing this matter, because the system now used in our schools and universities is obviously incorrect, in substituting our thin English vowel scale of a e i for the broader sounds almost universal among other languages (it would be a simple change to pronounce a always as in father, and so on). But even in spite of this drawback, we do at least preserve the distinction between the different vowels, and keep their relative values approximately correct; and therefore our pronunciation, even without reform, is superior to one which sinks all the vowels to e; while a slight reform would bring our system very near to correctness by restoring the true Erasmian pronunciation.

When we approach the question of pronunciation by accent, we are on more delicate ground; for here the practice of many foreign scholars is with the modern Greeks against us. And we must at once acknowledge that it is our English practice to ignore the accents altogether in speech, so that they become purely conventional signs, and a vexation of spirit to the learner and even sometimes to the advanced student of Ancient Greek. That a familiarity with Modern Greek pronunciation would be a great help in this respect cannot be denied; but whether this pronunciation affords a true indication of classical usage is quite another question. Whether the accent in Ancient Greek was a pitch accent, or of some other nature not easy for modern ears to detect and follow, is a difficult and complicated question which cannot here be discussed. But there are very clear indications that it was not in classical times a stress accent, such as that now used in Modern Greek and Modern English. Where there is a fixed system of stress accents, the long and short quantity of vowels must at once disappear, as in Modern Greek, where o and ω for instance are indistinguishable in pronunciation. The evidence of poetry seems conclusive on this matter. If pronounced by stress accent, any Ancient Greek verse is indistinguishable from prose ; and in reading Ancient Greek poetry the order of the words may be and is often inverted by a Modern Greek without any discomfort either to reader or to hearer. The fact is, that as soon as a stress accent becomes predominant in pronunciation, all scansion of verse must be by that and that alone, as it is in English and in Modern Greek ; and as it came to be in Greek when this change had taken place. And therefore, in Byzantine writers, as in Modern Greek, accent alone rules the verse ; pronounced by accent, Sophocles'

$$\text{ἔχεις τι κεἰσήκουσας ἤ σε λανθάνει}$$

is pure prose, and only such a line as Tzetzes'

$$\text{Ἀγορακρίτῳ χάριτας ποιῶν τῷ ἐρωμένῳ}$$

can be scanned as verse. That all classical poetry was scanned by an arbitrary system, which had no relation to the actual pronunciation of the language, is surely a paradox which is not worth discussing. And this certainly would have been the case, if the pronunciation of the accented syllable in Ancient Greek was similar to that heard in Modern Greek speech.

Thus much has been said upon some points of controversy, because they are usually raised by the advocates of the advantage of learning Modern Greek ; and by putting this study upon a false footing, they either attract students for mistaken reasons, or repel them by assertions which a classical scholar will resent. Now apart from these erroneous considerations, Modern Greek is of the greatest utility and interest ; and in its present developed stage it may well attract many to study the living language. On the other hand, to have remained 2000 years without change

or development in grammar or pronunciation, as some imagine
to be the case with Modern Greek, would be a proof of death
rather than of vitality in a language.

Nothing could be more arbitrary than the distinction made by
some of the purists in Greece, who apparently define development
or improvement as 'a change which took place in the classical
age or in the present century,' and corruption as 'a change
which took place during mediaeval times.'

It may not be superfluous to add a few words, from a practical
point of view, as to the utility of a knowledge of Ancient Greek
in learning the Modern language. It is obvious that such
knowledge must be a very great help, and is indeed indispensable
for a thorough and scientific study of the Romaic tongue. Yet,
paradoxical as it may seem, I have known several instances in
which those who started without any knowledge of Ancient
Greek made even more rapid progress at first than others who
enjoyed the same facilities for learning, and a knowledge of
the Ancient language as well. Nor do I believe this result to
have been due entirely to accident. Often, while the classical
student is ransacking his memory for the ancient word or idiom
which seems to him most simple or most likely to survive, or
while he is trying to fit the sounds he hears into the spelling of
some ancient form, his apparently less well-equipped companion
will have learnt or recognised the word commonly used by the
people he is among. To make quick progress in first beginning
Modern Greek two things are necessary—first, to learn it by ear
and not by eye ; otherwise the confusing spelling and the variety
of symbols that may denote one sound will make it almost
impossible to recognise at first any spoken word ; and secondly,
to forget, until the most familiar words and idioms are mastered,
that any such language as classical Greek exists. In a short
time, of course, those who are familiar with classical Greek will
find their knowledge invaluable for enlarging their vocabulary

and for explaining usages—not to speak of reading books and newspapers. But it must be borne in mind that all dialects now in use for any purpose vary between the two extremes of classical Greek and the Romaic of popular speech ; and that anybody who knows both will find he can by the help of his knowledge understand any compromise or mixture that he may come across ; while if he learns only what is itself a compromise, he is always liable to meet some new dialect constructed on different lines or compounded in different proportions.

It is impossible to find any Modern Greek which can be set up as a universally recognised standard ; but the classical scholar who has learnt the true spoken tongue need never be unable to explain any of the phenomena he may meet, or to understand and make himself understood in any written or spoken dialect which he may have occasion to use.

ERNEST GARDNER.

ATHENS, Nov. 1891.

REMARKS.

THE following rules must be borne in mind by any foreigner trying to pronounce Modern Greek, especially if he be already familiar with ancient Greek.

(1) All words are pronounced entirely by accent, quantity being completely ignored; the accent is a stress accent in Modern Greek, and practically to a foreign ear lengthens the vowel on which it falls.

(2) There is consequently apart from accent no distinction between short and long vowels, whether so by nature or position; thus of the two forms o, ω, one is superfluous; ε and η, as will be seen, differ in kind, not merely in length.

(3) In pronunciation, there is absolutely no distinction between αι and ε, nor between ει, η, ι, οι, υ, υι : the diphthongs proper have all sunk to simple vowels. Thus the only vowel sounds in the language are the five simple vowels α, ε, ι, o, and oυ; all others being merely different manners of writing the same sounds.

(4) There is no distinction in pronunciation between the rough breathing (‘) and the smooth (’).

CONTENTS.

A SHORT AND EASY MODERN GREEK GRAMMAR.

THE ALPHABET.

Capitals.	Small letters.	Names.	Pronunciation.
A	α	Ἄλφα	alpha.
B	β	Βῆτα	veeta.
Γ	γ	Γάμμα	ghamma.
Δ	δ	Δέλτα	dhelta.
E	ε	Ἔψιλον	aípsilon.
Z	ζ	Ζῆτα	zeeta.
H	η	Ἦτα	eeta.
Θ	θ	Θῆτα	theeta.
I	ι	Ἰῶτα	eeóta.
K	κ	Κάππα	kappa.
Λ	λ	Λάμβδα	lamvdha.
M	μ	Μῦ	mee.
N	ν	Νῦ	nee.
Ξ	ξ	Ξῖ	xee.
O	ο	Ὄμικρον	ómicron.
Π	π	Πῖ	pee.
P	ρ	Ῥῶ	rho.
Σ	σ, ς	Σίγμα	sigma.
T	τ	Ταῦ	taf.
Υ	υ	Ὕψιλον	eépsilon.
Φ	φ	Φῖ	fee.
X	χ	Χῖ	khee.
Ψ	ψ	Ψῖ	psee.
Ω	ω	Ὤμεγα	ómegha.

VOWELS.

N.B.—The following table is put in a definite way for the sake of clearness; though the vowel-sounds vary irregularly between the two extreme sounds given in each case.

The vowels are seven in number.

They are pronounced as follows, each vowel varying in sound according to accent and circumstances :—

α { accented,   like *a* in father,   *e.g.* γάλα, milk ; *pron.* ghála.
{ unaccented,   „ *a* „ Fr. malle,   „ καλός, good ;   „ kalóss.

ε { accented,   like *a* in name, *e.g.* χέρι, hand ;   *pron.* haíri.
{ unaccented,   „ *e* „ met,   „ δώδεκα, twelve :   „ dhódheka.

η ⎫
⎪ all ⎧ accented, like *ee* in meet,   ἥρως, hero ; *pron.* eéros.
ι ⎬   ⎪   μύτη, nose ;   „   meéti.
⎪   ⎪   *e.g.*   γίδα, goat ;   „   yeédha.
⎪   ⎪   μάτι, eye ;   „   máti.
υ ⎭   ⎩   βρύσι, fountain ; *pron.* vreéssi.
         unaccented, like *i* in hit,   γλυκύς, sweet ;   „   ghlikeéss.

ω ⎫   ⎧ accented, like *au* in autumn ⎫   ⎧ νὰ ἰδῶ, let me see,
⎬ both ⎨   ⎬ *e.g.* ⎨   *pron.* na idhaú.
ο ⎭   ⎩ unaccented, like *o* in on   ⎭   ⎩ ὅλος, all, *pron.*
                                                             aúlos.

DIPHTHONGS.

The simple vowel-sounds are often represented in writing by two vowels.

αι is pronounced like *ai* in aim, and ⎫ *e.g.* μαχαίρι, knife, *pron.*
   is therefore equivalent to ε   ⎭   makhaíri.

ει ⎫   ⎧ ἐκεῖνο, that ; *pron.* ekeéno.
οι ⎬ = *ee* or *i*,   *e.g.* ⎨ μοῖρα, fate ;   „   meéra.
υι[1] ⎭   ⎩ μυῖα, fly ;   „   meéa.

ει, ου, υι are therefore equivalent to η, ι, υ.

---

[1] υι is not common.

αυ

ευ

ηυ

In these the first vowel has its usual sound, the second sounds like *v* before vowels and the consonants β, γ, δ, ζ, μ, ν, ρ, and like *f* before the other consonants.

e.g.

αὐγά, eggs ;
pron. avghá.
αὐτά, these ;
pron. aftá.
εὐαγγέλιον, gospel ;
pron. evanghélion.
εὐλογιά, small-pox ;
pron. evloghiá.
εὔκολος, easy ;
pron. éfkolos.
ηὗρα, I found ;
pron. eévra.

ὀυ is pronounced like *oo* in moon, *e.g.* κουνῶ, I shake, *pron.* koonaú.

When the second of two vowels has a diæresis over it, each vowel is pronounced as it would be if alone, *e.g.* καϋμένος, poor fellow, *pron.* kaïmaínos.[1]

Any *i*-sound followed by an accented vowel is pronounced as the semi-vowel *y*, and is written ι, ει, &c.

CONSONANTS.

The consonants are pronounced as follows :—

Letters.	Pronunciation.	Examples.	Pronunciation.
β =	*v.*	βάλλω, I throw.	vállo.
γ =	*gh* or rather half-way between *g* and *y.*	γάτα, cat.	ghátα.
	y before ι or ε sounds.	γυναῖκα, woman. γέρος,	yinaíka. yaíros.
	ng before ξ, χ, γ.	ἄγγελος, angel.	ánghelos.
δ =	*th* in though, flat *th.*	δέκα, ten.	dhéka.
ζ =	*z.*	ζητῶ, I desire.	zitaú.
θ =	*th* in think, sharp *th.*	θυγατέρα, daughter.	thighataíra.
κ =	*k.*	καλός, good.	kalóss.
	kh before ε and ι sounds.	κυρία, lady.	khireéa.
	g after ν and γ.	τὸν κύριον, master (acc.).	ton gírion.
λ =	*l.*	λιόνω, I melt.	liaúno.

[1] This is a true diphthong. Another example may be seen in such words as ὁρολόγιο, when the *g*, which is not heard in pronunciation, still serves to keep the vowels *o*, *ι* from coalescing into οι.

B 2

μ =	m.	μάλαμμα, gold.	málama.
	n.	ναί, yes.	nay.
ν =	m in the article before a word beginning with π.	τὸν πόλεμο, the war.	tom baúlemo.
ξ =	x.	ὄξω, get out !	óxo.
π =	p.	παπᾶς, priest.	papáhss.
	b after μ and ν.	ἔμπορος, merchant.	émboros.
ρ =	trilled r.	ῥάφτης, tailor.	ráhftis.
σ =	ss (hard s).	σαράντα, forty.	saránda.
		ὡς, as.	auss.
	z (soft s), before β, δ, λ, μ, ν, ρ.	Σμύρνη, Smyrna.	Zmírnee.
τ =	t.	τώρα, now.	tóra.
	d after ν.	πέντε, five.	pénde.
	d at the beginning of a word preceded by the ν of the article or by δέν.	δὲν ταιριάζει, it doesn't fit.	dhen deriähzi.
χ =	ch in loch, or kh.	χάνω, I lose.	kháno.
	softer, like a guttural h before ε and ι sounds.	χέρι, hand.	haíri.
φ =	f.	φέρω, I bring.	féro.
ψ =	ps.	ψωμί, bread.	psomeé.

Though double consonants are written in modern Greek, e.g. βάλλω, this doubling has no effect on the pronunciation, except in the case of γγ.

Iota Subscript.

η (and ω in literary forms) is sometimes written with an iota subscript, which is not pronounced. νὰ γράφῃς, that you may write, pron. na gráfis.

Rough and Smooth Breathings.

In Modern Greek the ancient marks continue to exist in writing, according to the ancient usage, but are ignored in speaking.

E.g.   ἅγιος, holy, pron. áh-yos.
      εἴδετε, you saw, pron. eédhete.
      ῥάφτης, tailor, pron. ráhftis.
      ἀνοησία, thoughtlessness, pron. anoïsseéa.

ELISION AND CRASIS: APOSTROPHE.

When two vowels come together in different words, it is customary in speech and also sometimes in writing that either elision or crasis should take place; in either case an apostrophe (or breathing) is inserted in writing.

E.g.   τοῦ 'λεγε for τοῦ ἔλεγε

σοῦ τοὖπα for σοῦ τὸ εἶπα

τῶνα for τὸ ἕνα.

ACCENTUATION.

The accent of a Modern Greek word cannot be placed further from the end of the word than the antepenultimate syllable, or the penultimate when the last vowel is originally long by nature.

An apparent exception to this rule is found in such forms as ἐβράδειασε, evening came on. But in such words εια is pronounced as one syllable, *e.g.* evrádhyassay. To indicate this the mark ‿ is often placed under the letters: ἐβράδειασε.

There are three accents: the acute (´), the grave (`), the circumflex (ˆ).

The *acute* may stand on any of the three last syllables.

E.g.   ἄνθρωπος, man, ῥίχνω, I throw, καλός, good.

The *grave* may only be placed on the last syllable.

It is used instead of the acute when a word with an acute accent is followed by other words in the same sentence.

E.g. τὸ μικρὸ πιάτο, the little plate,—instead of τό μικρό πιάτο.

The *circumflex* may only be placed on the last and penultimate syllables; on the last only when it is long, and on the penultimate only when it is long and the last short.[1]

E.g.   συγχωρῶ, I forgive. χῶμα, earth.

---

[1] All rules as to the circumflex accent are purely literary, since it cannot be distinguished from the acute in pronunciation.

For the purposes of accentuation η, ω, and the diphthongs count as long syllables ; ε and ο short ; while α, ι, and υ may be either long or short.

N.B.   This distinction of long and short syllables is a survival from ancient Greek, in which it was made in pronunciation.   In Modern Greek it exists only in writing, and its use in deciding the accentuation is therefore arbitrary. The rules of accentuation are, as might be expected under the circumstances, frequently violated in popular spoken Greek, especially when a word changes its accent from rule in declension.

Proclitics and Enclitics.

The few words without accent falling into the class of *proclitics* are, for the purposes of accentuation, considered as part of the word following them.

They are the article ὁ, ἡ, οἱ, ἡ (αἱ), and the preposition εἰς.

The enclitics throw their accents back on the preceding word, unless they begin a sentence.

The genitive and accusative cases of the personal pronoun are examples of enclitics.

Rules.—1. If the preceding word has a circumflex accent on the last syllable, or an acute accent on either of the last two syllables, the enclitic loses its accent.

τὸ κρασί μου instead of τὸ κρασὶ μοῦ, my wine.
τοῦ παιδιοῦ του   „   „ τοῦ παιδιοῦ τοῦ, of his child.
τὸ σπίτι σας   „   „ τὸ σπίτι σᾶς, your house.

2. If the preceding word has a circumflex on the penultimate syllable, or an acute accent on the antepenultimate, the enclitic transfers its accent to the last syllable of the preceding word, and that accent becomes acute.

E.g. τὸ γράψιμόν του instead of τὸ γράψιμον τοῦ, his hand-writing.

PUNCTUATION.

The semicolon (;) is used as the mark of interrogation ; and for the semicolon a dot placed above the line is used (·).

The other marks of punctuation are used as in English.

EXERCISE IN READING.

N.B.—The following transliteration must be regarded as merely approximate, as the sounds in English and Modern Greek differ so widely :—

Ξαπλομένος	ταῖς	πρὸ	ἄλλαις	εἰς	τῆς	Λιάκουρας	τοὺς
Xaplomaínos	taiss	pro	álless	eess	teess	Lyákoorass	tooss

λόφους
laúfooss

μὲ τὴν πλῶσκα μου 's τὸ χέρι,
may teem blaúska mooss to háiri,

ἐφαντάσθηκα	πῶς	ἤμουν	μὲ	τοὺς	γέρους	μου
efandásthika	pauss	eémoon	may	tooss	yaírooss	moo

συντρόφους
sindraúfouss

καθὼς πρῶτα 's τὸ ληιμέρι.
kathaúss praúta sto limaíri ;

ἐλαφρὰ τὸν νοῦν μου εἶχε τὸ γλυκὸ κρασὶ σηκώσει
elafrá ton noon moo eéhay to glikó krasseé sikaússi

ἐνθυμούμουν τὰ παληά μας κ' ἔψαλλα 's τὴν κάθε   δόσι
enthimoómoon ta palyá mas kaípsala steen káthe dhaússi

ὢ τί ἔγειναν ποῦ εἶναι
au tee aí-yinan poo éenay

αἱ ἡμέραι μας ἐκεῖναι.
ay eemaíray mass ekeénay.

ἐμπροστά μου τὸ Βαλτέτσι μὲ ταῖς δάφναις τοῦ ἐφάνη,
embrostá moo to Valtétsi may taiss dháfness too efáhni,

καὶ ὁ Μάρκος ὅταν ἐπῆρε τῶν μαρτύρων τὸ στεφάνι,
kay o Márcos aútan epeéray taun marteéron to stefáhni,

καὶ τῆς Ἀμπλανῆς αἱ μαύραις ἀπὸ Τούρκους πεδιάδαις,
kay teess Amblaneéss ay mávress apo Toórkooss paidhiádhess,

καὶ τῆς Κλείσοβας αἱ δέκα τῶν Ἀράβων χιλιάδαις,
kay teess Kleéssovass ay dhéka taun Arávaun hilyádhess,

καὶ ὁ Καραΐσκος ὅταν 's τὴν Ἀράχοβαν νικοῦσε,
kay o Karaïskos aútan steen Arákhovau nikoóssay,

καὶ τὸν κάμπον ἐρωτοῦσα, καὶ ὁ κάμπος μ' ἐρωτοῦσε
kay taun gambon airotoóssa, kay o cambos m' airotoóssay

ὦ τί ἔγειναν ποῦ εἶναι
au tee aí-yinan poo eénay

αἱ ἡμέραι μας ἐκεῖναι.
ay eemaíray mass ekeénay.

Ὦ σημαία τῆς Ἑλλάδος! παλαιὰ καὶ δοξασμένη
Au seemáya teess Elládhos! palayá kay dhoxazmaínee

's τὴν καλύβα μου ὡς πότε θέ να στέκης σκονισμένη;
steeng galeéva moo auss paútay thay na staíkeess skonizmaínee ?

μαῦρε μου ἀνδρειωμένε, εἰς τὸν σταῦλο μου γερνᾶς
mávray moo andhreeaumaínay, eess ton stávlo moo yernáhss

κὴ ἄρχισες τοῦ τουφεκιοῦ μου τὴν βροντὴν νὰ λησμονᾶς,
kyarkheéssess too toofekyóo moo teen vronteén na leesmonáhss,

'ξέχασες πῶς καβαλλάριν εἰς τὴν ῥάχι σου με εἶχες
xaíkhassess pauss kavalláreen eess teen rákhee soo may eéklees

καὶ σὰν ἄνεμος πετοῦσες μὲ ἀγριωμέναις
kay sahn áhnemauss petoossess may aghreeaumainess

τρίχαις.
treékhess.

ὦ τί ἔγειναν ποῦ εἶναι

au tee ái-yinan poo eénay

αἱ ἡμέραι μας ἐκεῖναι.

ay eemaíray mass ekeénay.

THE "ARTICLE" AND THE "NOUN."

Gender.—There are three genders, masculine, feminine, neuter.

Number.—There are two numbers, singular and plural.

Case.—There are four cases, nominative, accusative, vocative, genitive.

The dative is wanting, and is replaced by the genitive or accusative, or the accusative with a preposition.

THE "ARTICLE."

There is a definite and an indefinite article.

The definite article is declined as follows :—

	Singular.				*Plural.*		
	Masc.	*Fem.*	*Neut.*		*Masc.*	*Fem.*	*Neut.*
Nom.	ὁ	ἡ	τό		οἱ	αἱ, ἡ	τά
Acc.	τό(ν)	τή(ν)	τό		τούς	ταίς, τῆς	τά
Gen.	τοῦ	τῆς	τοῦ		τῶ(ν)	τῶ(ν)	τῶ(ν)

N.B.—The final *v* of the article is only retained before vowels, and the consonants κ, ξ, π, τ, ψ, but even then it is often dropped.

The indefinite article is declined as follows :—

	Masc.	*Fem.*	*Neut.*
Nom.	ἕνας	μιά	ἕνα
Acc.	ἕνα(ν)	μιά(ν)	ἕνα
Gen.	ἑνοῦς, ἑνός, ἕνα	μιᾶς	ἑνοῦς, ἑνός, ἕνα

THE "NOUN."

We may divide nouns into five declensions.

The following table shows the chief distinctions:—

1.	2.	3.	4.	5.
Masc. nouns in âs, ῆς, ές, οῦς.	Masc. nouns in ης.	Masc. nouns in ας.	Masc. words in ος.	Neuter words in α, ος, ιμον.
Fem. nouns in έ, οῦ.	Fem. nouns in α, η.	Fem. nouns in α.	Neut. words in ο and ι.	
Acc. adds ν to the stem.	Acc. same as 1.	Acc. α.	Acc. { Masc. ο(ν). Neuter same as Nom.	Acc. same as Nom.
Gen. { masc. drops s. fem. adds s.	Gen. same as 1.	Gen. same as 1.	Gen. ον or ιοῦ.	Gen. ατος, ους, or ιματος.
Plural Gen. δ ω ν.	Plural Gen. ῶν, always accented.	Plural Gen. ω ν, for the most part unaccented.	Plural Gen. ω ν or ιῶν.	Plural Gen. άτων, ῶν, ιμάτων.

FIRST DECLENSION.

The first declension contains masculine nouns ending in âs, ŷs és, oûs, and feminine nouns in é and oû.

Skeleton Declension of a Noun of First Declension.

	Sing.		*Plur.*
	Masc. Nouns.	*Fem. Nouns.*	*Both*
Nom.	— s	—	— δαις
Acc.	— (ν)	— (ν)	— δαις
Voc.	—	—	— δαις
Gen.	—	— s	— δων

The dash stands for the stem of the word.   The final ν follows the same rule as in the article.

It is thus visible that the masc. nouns form the Genitive singular by dropping s from Nom., the feminine by adding s to the Nom.; both masc. and fem. add ν to the stem for the Acc.; the Vocative in both masc. and fem. is simply the stem of the word.   The plural is formed in both in the same way ; by adding δαις to the stem for the Nom. Voc. and Acc. cases ; and δων for the Genitive.

Examples.

ὁ παπᾶς, the priest.

Sing.			*Plur.*	
Nom.	ὁ παπᾶς,	the priest.	οἱ παπάδαις,	the priests.
Acc.	τὸν παπᾶ(ν),	the priest.	τοὺς παπάδαις,	the priests.
Voc.	παπᾶ,	priest.	παπάδαις,	priests.
Gen.	τοῦ παπᾶ,	of the priest.	τῶν παπάδων,	of the priests.

ἡ ἀλεποῦ, the fox.

Nom.	ἡ ἀλεποῦ,	the fox.	αἱ ἀλεπούδαις
Acc.	τὴ(ν) ἀλεποῦ(ν),	the fox.	ταῖς ἀλεπούδαις
Voc.	ἀλεποῦ,	fox.	ἀλεπούδαις
Gen.	τῆς ἀλεποῦς,	of the fox.	τῶν ἀλεπούδων ·

Compound words like νοικοκύρης, 'master of the house,' are similarly declined ; the only difference being in the accent, which is not on the last syllable. .

SECOND DECLENSION.

The second declension contains masculine nouns ending in ης, and feminine words ending in a, η.

Skeleton Declension.

	Singular.		Plural.
	Masc.	*Fem.*	*Both.*
Nom.	— ς	—	— αις
Acc.	— (ν)	— (ν)	— αις
Voc.	—	—	— αις
Gen.	—	-— ς	— ων accented.

From this it is visible that for the Genitive the masculine nouns drop their Nom. final *s*, while the feminine nouns add a final *s* to the Nom. ; both masc. and fem. add ν to the stem for the Accusative, and have simply the stem for the Vocative ; to form the plural both masc. and fem. nouns take *ais* for Nom., Voc., Acc., and ῶν always accented for the Gen.

Examples.

ὁ κλέφτης, the thief.

	Sing.	Plur.
Nom.	κλέφτης	κλέφταις
Acc.	κλέφτην	,,
Voc.	κλέφτη	,,
Gen.	κλέφτη	κλεφτῶν

ἡ θάλασσα, the sea.

	Sing.	Plur.
Nom.	θάλασσα	θάλασσαις
Acc.	θάλασσα(ν)	,,
Voc.	θάλασσα	,,
Gen.	θάλασσας	θαλασσῶν

ἡ καρδιά, the heart.

	Sing.	Plur.
Nom.	καρδιά	καρδιαίς
Acc.	καρδιά(ν)	,,
Voc.	καρδιά	,,
Gen.	καρδιᾶς	καρδιῶν

ἡ μύτη, the nose.

	Sing.	Plur.
Nom.	μύτη	μύταις (μύτες)
Acc.	μύτη(ν)	,,
Voc.	μύτη	,,
Gen.	μύτης	μυτῶν

Words ending in ι are declined similarly; they differ only in spelling, not in pronunciation. They have no genitive plural.

NOTE.—Feminine words ending in ι are often written ις by educated Greeks, e.g. κυβέρνησις, government, and declined according to classical usage.

ή βρύσι, the spring (fountain).

	Sing.	Plur.
Nom.	βρύσι	βρύσαις
Acc.	βρύσι(ν)	,,
Voc.	βρύσι	,,
Gen.	βρύσις	—

THIRD DECLENSION.

The third declension contains masculine words in ας and feminine words in α.

The words belonging to this declension differ from those in the second by having no ν in the Acc. Sing., and having the ων of the Gen. Plur. accented in only a few instances.

Skeleton Declension.

	Sing.		Plur.
	Masc.	Fem.	Both.
Nom.	— ς	—	— αις
Acc.	—	—	— ʼ
Voc.	—	---	---
Gen.	—	ς	ων mostly unaccented.

From this it is seen that the masc. words form the sing. Acc., Voc., Gen., by cutting off the ς; the fem. take ς in the gen.; while the plural endings are αις for Nom., Acc., Voc., and ων (unaccented mostly) for the Gen.

Examples.

ἡ ἐλπίδα, hope.   ἡ νύχτα.

	Sing.	Plur.		Sing.	Plur.
Nom.	ἐλπίδα	ἐλπίδαις	Nom.	νύχτα	νύχταις
Acc.	,,	,,	Acc.	,,	,,
Voc.	,,	,,	Voc.	,,	..
Gen.	ἐλπίδας	ἐλπίδων	Gen.	νύχτας	νυχτῶν

ὁ πατέρας, the father.   ὁ μῆνας, the month.

	Sing.	Plur.		Sing.	Plur.
Nom.	πατέρας	πατέραις	Nom.	μῆνας	μῆναις
Acc.	πατέρα	,,	Acc.	μῆνα	.,
Voc.	,,	,,	Voc.	,,	,,
Gen.	,,	πατέρων	Gen.	,,	μηνῶν

FOURTH DECLENSION.

The fourth declension contains masc. words in ος, and neuter words in ο and ι.

This declension contains the greatest number of words.

Skeleton Declensions.

Masc. words in ος.   Neuter words in ο.

	Sing.	Plur.		Sing.	Plur.
Nom.	— ος	— οι	Nom.	— ο(ν)	— α
Acc.	— ο(ν)	— ους	Acc.	— ο(ν)	— α
Voc.	— ε	— οι	Voc.	— ο(ν)	— α
Gen.	— ου	— ων, ῶνε	Gen.	— ου	— ων

Neuter words in ι.

	Sing.	Plur.
Nom.	— ι	— ια
Acc.	— ι	— ια
Voc.	— ι	— ια
Gen.	— ιοῦ	— ιῶν

Neuter words in ί.

	Sing.	Plur.
Nom.	— ί	— ιά
Acc.	— ί	— ιά
Voc.	— ί	— ιά
Gen.	— ιοῦ	— ιῶν

Examples.

ὁ ἄνθρωπος (ἄθρωπος), the man.

	Sing.	Plur.
Nom.	ἄνθρωπος	ἄνθρωποι
Acc.	ἄνθρωπο(ν)	ἀνθρώπους
Voc.	ἄνθρωπε	ἄνθρωποι
Gen.	ἀνθρώπου	ἀνθρώπων

τὸ βιβλίο(ν).

	Sing.	Plur.
Nom.	βιβλίο(ν)	βιβλία
Acc.	,,	,,
Voc.	,,	,,
Gen.	βιβλίου	βιβλίων

τὸ χέρι, the hand.

	Sing.	Plur.
Nom.	χέρι	χέρια
Acc.	,,	,,
Voc.	,,	,,
Gen.	χεριοῦ	χεριῶν

τὸ πουλί, the bird (fowl).

	Sing.	Plur.
Nom.	πουλί	πουλιά
Acc.	,,	,,
Voc.	,,	,,
Gen.	πουλιοῦ	πουλιῶν

FIFTH DECLENSION.

The fifth declension includes neuter nouns in α, ος, ιμον.

Skeleton Declensions.

Words in α.

	Sing.	Plur.
Nom.	— α	— ατα
Acc.	— α	— ατα
Voc.	— α	— ατα
Gen.	— ατος	— άτω(ν)

Words in ος.

	Sing.	Plur.
Nom.	— ος	— η
Acc.	— ος	— η
Voc.	— ος	— η
Gen.	— ους	— ῶν

Words in ιμον.

	Sing.	Plur.
Nom.	— ιμον	— ίματα
Acc.	— ιμον	— ίματα
Voc.	— ιμον	— ίματα
Gen.	— ίματος, ίματου	— ιμάτων

Examples.

τὸ πρᾶγμα (πρᾶμμα).

	Sing.	Plur.
Nom.	πρᾶγμα	πράγματα
Acc.	„	„
Voc.	„	„
Gen.	{ πράγματος / πράγματου	πραγμάτω(ν)

τὸ ἔτος, the year.

	Sing.	Plur.
Nom.	ἔτος	ἔτη
Acc.	„	„
Voc.	„	„
Gen.	ἔτους	ἐτῶν

τὸ γράψιμον, the writing.

	Sing.	Plur.
Nom. Voc. Acc.	γράψιμον	γραψίματα
Gen.	γραψίματος	γραψιμάτω(ν)

WORDS FOR EXERCISE IN THE DECLENSIONS.

1st.

ὁ ψωμᾶς, the baker.
ὁ παπουτζῆς, the shoemaker.
ὁ καφές, the coffee.

ὁ κοσκινᾶς, the sievemaker.
ὁ τενεκές, the tin.
ἡ μαϊμοῦ, the ape.

2nd.

ἡ σειρά, the row.
ἡ μέλισσα, the bee.
ἡ γλῶσσα, the tongue.

ἡ σκάλα, the stair.
ἡ στιγμή, the moment.
ἡ πόλι (πόλις), the town.

3rd.

ἡ γυναῖκα (gen. ῶν), the woman.
ἡ λαμπάδα, the torch.

ὁ ἀέρας, the air, wind.
ἡ φροντίδα, the care.

4th.

ὁ ἀδελφός, the brother.
ὁ φίλος, the friend.
ὁ ποταμός, the river.
τὸ φύλλο(ν), the leaf.

τὸ ξύλον, the wood.
τὸ κλειδί, the key.
τὸ μάτι, the eye.
τὸ λουλοῦδι, the flower.

5th.

τὸ δῶμα, the terrace.
τὸ κρέας, the meat.[1]
τὸ ἄνθος, the flower.

τὸ δάσος, the thicket.
τὸ βγάλσιμον, the dislocation.
τὸ φέρσιμον, the freight, behaviour.

NOTES ON THE DECLENSIONS.

Several words are of different genders in the singular and plural, e.g.

ὁ πλοῦτος, wealth ; τὰ πλούτη, riches.
ὁ χρόνος the year ; τὰ χρόνια, the years.

Other words have two plural forms, e.g. ἡ νύφη, the bride : αἱ νύφαις and αἱ νυφάδαις. Others again have two forms in some of the cases : τοῦ μηνός and τοῦ μήνα, two Genitive forms of ὁ μῆνας.

Plural Nom. οἱ μῆνοι and οἱ μῆναις.
„ Acc. τοὺς μήνους and τοὺς μῆναις.

ὁ γέρος (occasionally ὁ γέροντας), the old man.
Gen. τοῦ γέρου, τοῦ γέροντα, τοῦ γερόντου.

ὁ μάστορας, the craftsman.
Gen. τοῦ μάστορα, and μαστόρου.

DIMINUTIVES.

Modern Greek has several endings like our English *kin* in lambkin, *ling* in darling &c., but they are more commonly used, and may in fact be added to almost any words. Diminutives are often used as terms of endearment.

---

[1] Genitive κρέατος.

C

The most important are:

(1) to form masc. words—ά κ η ς, ο ύ λ η ς, e.g. Πέτρος, Πετ-ράκης, Peter, Peterkin ; άντρας, ἀντρούλης, man, mannikin.

(2) to form fem. words—ο ῦ λ α, ί τ ζ a, e.g. ἀδελφή, ἀδελφούλα, sister, little sister ; πέτρα, πετρίτζα, stone, pebble.

(3) to form neuter words —άκι, άρι (this is the most common), e.g. πιάτο, πιατάκι, plate, little plate ; παιδί, παιδάρι, child, little child.

AMPLIATIVES.

There are also several endings for amplifying words :

(1) to form masc. words, ο ς. or a ρ ο ς, added to words of fem. or neuter gender, e.g. μύτος, or μύταρος, big nose, from μύτη. nose.

(2) a, a ρ a, ο ῦ κ λ a to form feminine words, e.g. χέρα. χερούκλα, from χέρι, hand.

PATRONYMICS.

Patronymics commonly end in ό π ο υ λ ο ς, ά δ η ς, ε ί δ η ς, ί δ η ς.

e.g. Ἀργυρόπουλος, Ἀναστασιάδης, Ἡρακλείδης, Κωνσταντινίδης.

FORMATION OF THE FEMININE.

The common endings for the formation of corresponding femi-nine words are ι σ σ a and ρ a.

e.g. δάσκαλος, teacher ; fem. δασκάλισσα.
πλύστης, washerman ; fem. πλύστρα.

THE ADJECTIVE.

The adjective has different endings for each of the three genders : we divide adjectives into three declensions.

FIRST DECLENSION.

The adjectives of this declension end in ος, η (α), ο(ν).

The feminine form ends in α when the termination is preceded by a vowel or liquid, but sometimes even in this case the ending is η.

Examples.

καλός, good.

	Singular.			Plural.		
	Masc.	*Fem.*	*Neut.*	*Masc.*	*Fem.*	*Neut.*
Nom.	καλός	καλή	καλό(ν)	καλοί	καλαίς	καλά
Acc.	καλόν	καλή(ν)	καλό(ν)	καλούς	καλαίς	καλά
Voc.	καλέ	καλή	καλό(ν)	καλοί	καλαίς	καλά
Gen.	καλοῦ	καλῆς	καλοῦ	καλῶν	καλῶν	καλῶν

ἅγιος, holy.

	Singular.			Plural.		
	Masc.	*Fem.*	*Neut.*	*Masc.*	*Fem.*	*Neut.*
Nom.	ἅγιος	ἅγια	ἅγιον	ἅγιοι	ἅγιαις	ἅγια
Acc.	ἅγιον	ἅγια(ν)	ἅγιον	ἅγιους	ἅγιαις	ἅγια
Voc.	ἅγιε	ἅγια	ἅγιον	ἅγιοι	ἅγιαις	ἅγια
Gen.	ἅγιου	ἅγιας	ἅγιου	ἅγιων	ἅγιων	ἅγιαν

The following are similarly declined : -

μικρός, little.   μαῦρος, black.   γνωστός, known.
κακός, bad.   μεγάλος, great.   κόκκινος, red.

SECOND DECLENSION OF ADJECTIVES.

The second declension contains adjectives ending in ης, α, ικο(ν) and in ης, ισσα (ίδισσα), ικο(ν).

Ex. ζηλιάρης, jealous.

	Singular			Plural		
Masc.	*Fem.*	*Neut.*	*Masc.*	*Fem.*	*Neut.*
N. ζηλιάρης	ζηλιάρα	ζηλιάρικο(ν)	ζηλιάριις	ζηλιάραις	ζηλιάρικα
A. ζηλιάρη(ν)	ζηλιάρα(ν)	,,	,,	,,	,,
V. ζηλιάρη	ζηλιάρα	,,	,,	,,	,,
G. ζηλιάρη	ζηλιάρας	ζηλιαρικοῦ	ζηλιαρῶν	ζηλιαρῶν	ζηλιαρικῶν

αὐθάδης, headstrong, αὐθάδιτσα, αὐθάδικον, is similarly declined.

THIRD DECLENSION.

The third declension contains adjectives ending in ύς, ειά, ύ.

Ex. γλυκύς, sweet.

	Singular			Plural		
	Masc.	*Fem.*	*Neut.*	*Masc.*	*Fem.*	*Neut.*
Nom.	γλυκύς	γλυκειά	γλυκύ	γλυκεῖς	γλυκειαίς	γλυκά
Acc.	γλυκύ(ν)	γλυκειά(ν)	,,	,,	,,	,,
Voc.	γλυκύ	γλυκειώ	,,	,,	,,	,,
Gen.	γλυκύ	γλυκειάς	,,	γλυκειῶν	γλυκειῶν	γλυκειῶν

The following are similarly declined :—

βαρύς, heavy.   φαρδύς, broad.

παχύς, fat.   μακρύς, long.

The adjectives in ύς have also a collateral form in ός,

e.g. γλυκός, γλυκή, γλυκό.

The adjective πολύς has πολλή for the fem. It is declined as follows :—

	Masc.	Fem.	Neut.	Masc.	Fem.	Neut.
	Singular.			*Plural.*		
Nom.	πολύς	πολλή	πολύ	πολλοί	πολλαίς	πολλά·
Acc.	πολύ(ν)	πολλή(ν)	,,	πολλούς	,,	,,
Voc.	πολύ	πολλή	,,	πολλοί	,,	,,
Gen.	πολλοῦ	πολλῆς	πολλοῦ	πολλῶν	πολλῶν	πελλἕν

Exercise 1.—A.

Τὰ λουλούδια εἶνε ὥμορφα. Τὸ σπῆτι τοῦ παπουτζῆ εἶνε παληό. Δόσε τοῦ κοριτζιοῦ ἕνα καλὸ βιβλίο. Ὁ φίλος τοῦ πατέρα εἶνε ἄρρωστος. Τὰ ὡραῖα περιβόλια τοῦ ἐμπόρου. Ἥτανε πολλοὶ ἄνθρωποι ἐκεῖ. Πόσα χρόνια ἐκάθισες 's τὴν Αἴγυπτο ; Φέρε δύο καφέδαις γλυκεῖς. Αἱ θυγατέραις τοῦ νοικοκύρη ἔχουν ἀκριβὰ φορέματα. Αὐταὶ αἱ γυναῖκαις εἶνε φιληνάδαις τῆς Ἑλένης.

τὸ λουλοῦδι, the flower.	ἐκεῖ, there.
εἶνε, is, are.	πόσα, how much.
ὥμορφος, pretty.	ἐκάθισες, thou hast dwelt.
τὸ σπῆτι, the house.	ἡ Αἴγυπτος, Egypt.
παληός, old.	φέρε, bring.
δόσε, give.	δύο, two.
τὸ κορίτζι, the girl.	ἡ θυγατέρα, the daughter.
τὸ βιβλίο, the book.	ἔχουν, have.
ὁ φίλος, the friend.	ἀκριβός, dear.
ἄρρωστος, ill.	φόρεμα, dress.
ὡραῖος, beautiful.	αὐταί αἱ, these.
τὸ περιβόλι, the garden.	ἡ φιληνάδα, the friend (f.).
ὁ ἔμπορος, the merchant.	Ἑλένη, Helen.
ἥτανε, were.	

NOTE.—Proper names often have the definite article placed before them.

Exercise 1.—B.

The merchants have beautiful houses. Give the little girl a pretty flower. Are you not afraid of thieves? (use the sing. pron. and verb). Have you lived long in Constantinople?

Ladies' clothes are dear.   Ink is black.   His handwriting is not good.   She is not ill.   The weather is very bad to-day.   On the first day of the year.

are you not afraid of, δὲν φοβᾶσαι ἀπό with Acc.

long—say, much time (time = καιρός).

in Constantinople, trans. by εἰς with Acc.   The Greeks usually call Constantinople, ἡ πόλις.

the ink, τὸ μελάνι.

black, μαῦρος.

she is not, δὲν εἶνε.

the weather, ὁ καιρός.

to-day, σήμερα.

on, trans. simply by Acc.

first, πρῶτος.

day, ἡ ἡμέρα (ἡ μέρα).

DIMINUTIVES.

The most common diminutive endings for adjectives are οὔτζικος, ο 'τζικη, οὔτζικο, and ούλης, οῦλα, οῦλι.

Ex. καλούτζικος, καλούτζικη, καλούτζικο, rather good. ἀσπρούλης, ἀσπροῦλα, ἀσπροῦλι, whitish.

COMPARISON.

The ancient comparative suffix τερος, τερη, τερο(ν), still exists, and is occasionally used ; but has for the most part given way to the word πλιό (πιώ), more, placed before the adjective.

e.g. πιὸ ὤμορφο, prettier.   μικρότερος, smaller.

The suffix form is preferred by literary dialect ; ω or o is then written before the suffix according to the ancient rule.

The following adjectives form their comparatives irregularly :

μεγάλος, great ; μεγαλήτερος, greater (μεγαλείτερος).
καλός, good ; καλήτερος (καλλίτερος).
κακός, bad ; χειρότερος [κακώτερος].
πολύς, much ; περισσότερος.

The English *than* after the comparative is usually translated by ἀπὸ with the Acc. or sometimes by παρά with the Nom. :—

εἶνε μεγαλείτερος ἀπὸ τὸν Κάρολο, he is bigger than Charles.

The superlative is expressed by placing the definite article before the comparative : ὁ καλλίτερος, or ὁ πιὸ καλός, the best.

PRONOUNS.

PERSONAL PRONOUNS.

1st.

	Singular.		Plural.	
	Emphatic.	Unemphatic.	Emphatic.	Unemphatic.
Nom.	ἐγώ	—.	ἐμεῖς	— -
Acc.	(ἐ)μένα(νε)	μέ	ἐμᾶς	μᾶς
Gen.	ἐμοῦ, ἐμενοῦ	μοῖ	ἐμᾶς	μᾶς

2nd.

Nom.	σύ, ἐσύ	—	(ἐ)σεῖς	—
Acc.	ἐσέ, ἐσένα(νε)	σέ	ἐσᾶς	σᾶς
Gen.	ἐσενοῦ.	σοῦ	ἐσᾶς	σᾶς

3rd. Emphatic Form.

Singular.

	Masc.	Fem.	Neut.
Nom.	αὐτός	αὐτή	αὐτό
Acc.	αὐτόν(ε)	αὐτήν(ε)	αὐτό(νο)
Gen.	αὐτοῦ, αὐτουνοῦ,	αὐτῆς	αὐτοῦ, αὐτουνοῦ
	(αὐτηνοῦ)	αὐτηνῆς	

Plural.

	Masc.	Fem.	Neut.
Nom.	αὐτοί (αὐτηνοί)	αὐταίς (αὐτηναίς)	αὐτά, αὐτάνα
Acc.	αὐτούς, αὐτουνούς	αὐταίς (αὐτηναίς)	αὐτά, αὐτάνα
	(αὐτηνούς)		
Gen.	αὐτῶν(ε), αὐτωνῶν	αὐτῶν, αὐτωνῶν	αὐτῶν, αὐτωνῶν
	(αὐτηνῶν)	(αὐτηνῶν)	(αὐτηνῶν)

3rd.   Unemphatic Form.

| | *Singular.* | | | *Plural.* | | |
	Masc.	*Fem.*	*Neut.*	*Masc.*	*Fem.*	*Neut.*
Nom.	—	—	---	—	—	—
Acc.	τόν(ε)	τήν(ε)	τό	τούς	ταίς (τῆς)	τά
Gen.	τοῦ	τῆς	τοῦ	τῶν (τούς)	τῶν (τούς)	τῶν (τούς)

1 If the subject of the verb is a personal pronoun, it is usually not expressed; as it is made clear by the verbal termination which person is meant.

e.g. λέγω, I say ; λέγεις, thou sayest ; λέγει, he says.

The pronoun must be inserted if the subject is to be emphasized.

e.g. ἐγὼ λέγω, I say ; ἐσὺ λέγεις, thou sayest.

2. In order to further emphasize the pronoun, the emphatic and the enclitic forms are often used together in the oblique cases.

e.g. ἐμένα με ξέρεις ; do you know *me ?*

3. When the pronoun to be emphasized is the indirect object of the verb, it is often used with the preposition εἰς.

e.g. εἰς ἐσᾶς τῶπα (τὸ εἶπα), I said it to you (it was to you I said it).

4. The oblique cases of the enclitic pronoun stand immediately before the governing verb, except when the verb is in the imperative mood, in which case they follow it.

e.g. τόνε ξέρω, I know him ; τοὺς εἶδα, I saw them ; δέν το βλέπω, I do not see it ; πάρ' το, take it ; ἅς τονε, let him be.

5. In the compound tenses of a verb the oblique cases of the pronoun stand either between the auxiliary and the participle, or before the auxiliary.

e.g. τὸν εἶχα εἰπεῖ or εἶχα τὸν εἰπεῖ, I had told him.

6. When a verb has both a direct and an indirect object, the indirect always comes first.

e.g. τοῦ τῶπα (τοῦ τὸ εἶπα), I told it to him.
τούς το ἔδωσα, I gave it to them.

DEMONSTRATIVE PRONOUNS.

τοῦτος, τούτη, τοῦτο, this.
αὐτός, αὐτή, αὐτό, this.
ἐκεῖνος, ἐκείνη, ἐκεῖνο, that.

τοῦτος is declined regularly. ἐκεῖνος is declined like the emphatic pronoun αὐτός.

The demonstrative pronouns have the definite article after them.

e.g. αὐτὸς ὁ καθρέφτης, this looking-glass; ἐκείνη ἡ γυναῖκα, that woman.

POSSESSIVE PRONOUNS.

Singular.					*Plural.*				
ὁ,	ἡ,	τὸ	......	μου, my.	οἱ,	αἱ (ἡ),	τὰ	......	μου, my.
,,	,,	,,	......	σου, thy.	,,	,,	,,	,,	...... σου, thy.
,,	,:	,,	......	του, his.	,,	,,	,,	,,	του, his.
,,	,,	,,	......	της, her.	,,	,,	,,	,,	...... της, her.
,,	,,	,,	......	του, its.	,,	,,	,,	,,	του, its.
,,	,,	,,		μας, our.	,,	,,	,,	,,	...... μας, our.
,,	,,	,,	......	σας, your.	,,	,,	,,	,,	...... σας, your.
,,	,,	,,	......	των, their.	,,	,,	,,	,,	...... των, their.

(1) The possessive adjectives are thus expressed by the genitive of the personal pronoun.

e.g. ὁ πατέρας μου, my father; ἡ μητέρα των, their mother; τὸ ὡρολόγι σου, thy watch.

(2) When the possessive adjective is emphatic, the adjective δικός (ἐδικός, εἰδικός, ἰδικός, own) is used together with the genitive of the pers. pron.

This form is always used when in English the possessive pronoun stands alone.

e.g. τὸ δικό μου τὸ καπέλο εἶνε πιὸ ὤμορφο ἀπὸ τὸ δικό σου.

My hat is prettier than yours.

NOTE.—The repetition of the article, as above, is not absolutely necessary.

RELATIVE PRONOUNS.

ποῦ, who, which (indeclinable).

ὁ ὁποῖος, ἡ ὁποία, τὸ ὁποῖο, which (in written language only).

INTERROGATIVE PRONOUNS.

ποιός, ποιά, ποιό; who? which?
τί; what?

ποιός is declined regularly. The genitive has the collateral forms ποιανοῦ, ποιανῆς, ποιανῶν. τί is indeclinable; when it occurs alone it means what? e.g. τί κάνεις; what are you doing? In conjunction with another word, it means also what kind of, e.g. τί βιβλίο εἶνε αὐτό; what kind of book is that, or what book is that?

ποιός is used both alone and with a substantive.

REFLEXIVE PRONOUNS.

1. The reflexive pronoun ἑαυτόν is used in the compound expression τὸν ἑαυτό(ν) μου, myself; τὸν ἑαυτόν σου, thyself; τὸν ἑαυτὸν του, himself, itself, τὸν ἑαυτόν της, herself. This form may be intensified by adding ἴδιος.

e.g. ἐντρέπουμαι ἀπὸ τὸν ἴδιο τὸν ἑαυτό μου. I am ashamed of myself.

2. The reflexive pronoun is only expressed when it is to be emphasized, otherwise it is understood in the verb.

e.g. πλύνομαι, I wash myself.

INDEFINITE PRONOUNS AND PRONOMINAL ADJECTIVES.

1. ὅποιος, ὅποια, ὅποιο; he or she who, whoever, whatever.

e.g. ὅποιος σὲ ἴδη θὰ γελάσῃ, whoever sees you will laugh.

ὅποιος sometimes has καὶ ἄν used together with it.

e.g. ὅποιος καὶ ἄν ἔλθῃ, whoever may come.

2. κάθε, every (indeclinable), is always used as an adjective, *e.g.* κάθε πρᾶγμα, everything ; κάθε 'μέρα, every day ; κάθε τι, everything ; κάθε τι τὸν ἐρεθίζει, everything annoys him.

καθένας, every one, (compound of κάθε and ἕν a ς, one).

e.g. καθένας τὸ ξέρει, every one knows it.

κάθε is also used with other numbers to denote recurrence.

e.g. κάθε πέντε 'μέραις every five days.

ὅλος, ὅλη, ὅλο, all, has the article following as in English.

e.g. ὅλα τὰ πράγματα, all the things.

ὅλοι οἱ μαθητάδαις, all the students.

3. κάπειος, κάποια, κάποιο, some one, a certain.

κάμποσος, κάμποση, κάμποσο, a certain number, a good many.

e.g. Ἦτανε κάμποσος κόσμος εἰς τὸ θέατρον.   There were a good many people in the theatre.   (κόσμος = French 'monde.')

τέτοιος, τέτοια, τέτοιο, such a.

{ ὅσος, ὅση, ὅσο, how much, how many, how great.
{ τόσος, τόση, τόσο, so much, so many, so great.

κἄτι, some, is used in the singular with neuter words only, in the plural with words of all three genders.

e.g. κἄτι σπουδαῖον πρέπει νὰ εἶνε, it must be something important.

κἄτι στρατιώταις, some soldiers.   κἄτι τι, something.

θά σου εἴπω κἄτι τι, I will tell you something.

ὁ δεῖνα(ς), ἡ δεῖνα, τὸ δεῖνα }
ὁ τάδε(ς), ἡ τάδε, τὸ τάδε } , so and so, such an one.

ὁ δεῖνα καὶ ὁ τάδε, such an one and such another.

μερικοί, μερικαίς, μερικά, some.

4. κανένας or κανείς, καμμιά, κανένα, any one (no-one) is used in negative and interrogative sentences like the French *aucun*.

e.g. ηὕρες κανένα εἰς τὸ σπῆτι ; did you find any one in the house (at home)?

δὲν ηὗρα κανένα or κανένα δὲν ηὗρα, I found no-one, or (by ellipsis) κανένα, no-one.

τίποτε (τίποτα, τίποτες), anything, nothing, used like κανένας.

e.g. εἶπες τίποτε; did you say anything ? δὲν εἶπα τίποτε, I said nothing, or τίποτε, nothing.

5. ὁ ἴδιος, ἡ ἴδια, τὸ ἴδιο, the same.
αὐτὸς ὁ ἴδιος τὸ εἶπε, he said it himself.

μόνος, μόνη, μόνο, or μόναχος, μονάχη, μόναχο, alone, is used with the genitive of the personal pronoun; it means *by myself*, *yourself*, &c.

e.g. μόνος του τὸ ἔκαμε, he did it by himself.

ἄλλος, ἄλλη, ἄλλο, other.

Mode of Address.

The second person singular is usually used in addressing a person. In consequence of foreign influence those who wish to be very polite frequently use the 2nd. pers. plur. The true Modern Greek form of polite address is to use τοῦ λόγου σου to define the person spoken to, *e.g.* ποῦ γεννήθηκες, τοῦ λόγου σου? where were you born?

The forms τοῦ λόγου του, &c. are also used.

e.g. τοῦ λόγου του εἶνε ἰατρός, he is a doctor (this gentleman is a doctor).

τοῦ λόγου της εἶνε γειτόνισσά μας, she (or this lady) is our neighbour.

After the prepositions εἰς (σέ) *into*, διά, *for*, and ἀπό, *from*, the article is omitted in the form mentioned above, *e.g.* διὰ λόγου του γράφω, I am writing for him.

τοῦ λόγου μου is also used as a reflexive form.
αἰσθάνομαι τοῦ λόγου μου καλλίτερα, I feel better.

Exercise 2.—A.

Μοῦ λένε πῶς ἀπέθανε. Δέν με ξέρει. Ἐσεῖς θὰ πᾶτε, ἐμεῖς δὲν θὰ πᾶμε. Θά τους στείλω εἰς τὴν Σμύρνην. Θὰ πάω μαζύ σας. Θά τοῦ το εἰπῶ. Πές το! Γράψετέ το! Ἂς τηνε νὰ φύγῃ. Ἐσένα πῶς σου φαίνεται; Τοῦ λόγου σου δέν τόνε ξέρεις. Αὐτὸς γράφει καὶ ἐκείνη διαβάζει. Τί σοῦπε (= σοῦ εἶπε). Ἦλθε κανείς; Ὄχι, κανείς. Ἐδιάβασες τὸ γράμμα ποῦ 'πῆρα προχτές; Ναὶ, τὸ ἐδιάβασα. Θά τους δώσῃς τὰ βιβλία; Μάλιστα, θά τούς τα δώσω. Αὐτὸς ὁ κύριος εἶνε γνωστός μου.

λένε, (they) say.	ξέρεις, you know.
πῶς, that, how.	γράφει, (he, she) writes.
ἀπέθανε, (he, she) is dead.	διαβάζει, (he, she) reads.
δέν, not.	εἶπε, (he, she) said.
ξέρει, (he, she) knows.	ἦλθε, (he, she) came.
θὰ πᾶτε, (you) will go.	ὄχι, no.
θὰ πᾶμε, we shall go.	ἐδιάβασες, (you) read.
θὰ στείλω, (I) shall send.	(the interrogative is indicated by the
εἰς, into, to.	tone.)
ἡ Σμύρνη, Smyrna.	τὸ γράμμα, the letter.
θὰ πάω, I shall go.	'πῆρα, I received.
μαζύ and μαζὺ μέ, with.	προχτές, the day before yesterday.
θὰ εἴπω, I shall say.	ναί, yes.
πές, say.	ἐδιάβασα, I have read.
γράψετε, write.	θὰ δώσῃς, you will give.
Ἄς, let.	μάλιστα, certainly.
νὰ φύγῃ, that she may go away.	θά δώσω, I shall give.
πῶς; how?	κύριος, gentleman (sir).
φαίνεται, it appears, seems.	γνωστός μου, an acquaintance of mine.

Exercise 3.—A.

Τὸ κρασί μας εἶνε καλλίτερον ἀπὸ τὸ δικό σας. Αὐτὸς εἶνε μεγαλείτερος ἀπὸ τὴν ἀδερφή του. Ξέρετε κάποιον Ἀντώνιον Ἀναστασιάδην ποῦ μένει εἰς τὴν Σμύρνην; Ἄλλα βιβλία δὲν ἔχετε; Τοῦ λόγου σου δὲν εἶσαι Γερμανός; Ὄχι, εἶμαι Ἄγγλος. Ἦτανε πολὺς κόσμος 's τὸ κοντζέρτο. Τί ὥρα εἶνε; Ποιός σᾶς το εἶπε; Ποιοί εἶνε ἐκεῖνοι οἱ νέοι; Τοῦ ἔδωσες τίποτε; Ὄχι, τίποτε. Δέν μου εἶπε τίποτε διὰ ἐσᾶς. Καθένας ἔχει τὴν γνώμην του. Ποιανοῦ το εἶπε; Δέν το εἶπε κανενός. Κάθε τόπος ἔχει τὰ ἔθιμά του.

τὸ κρασί, the wine.	ὥρα, hour.
ἡ ἀδερφή (ἀδελφή), the sister.	τί ὥρα εἶνε; what o'clock is it?
ξέρετε, you know.	εἶπε, (he, she, it) said.
μένει, (he, she) remains.	ὁ νέος, the young man.
ἔχετε, you have.	ἔδωσες, you gave.
εἶσαι, you are.	διά, for.
ὄχι, no.	ἔχει, (he, she, it) has.
εἶμαι, I am.	ἡ γνώμη, the opinion.
ὁ Ἄγγλος, the Englishman.	ὁ τόπος, the place.
ἦτανε, (he, she, it) was.	τὸ ἔθιμον, the custom.
τὸ κοντζέρτο, the concert.	

Exercise 2.—B.

Tell it to me. To whom have you given the wine? Are you
not from Constantinople? Do you know this gentleman? Who
read the letter to you? He himself. I shall give you nothing.
I have no other books. Did you find any one at home? No one.
These pens are worse than mine. We will go with you. I will
tell you something. Ask him what o'clock it is.

from, ἀπό with Acc.   at home, 's τὸ σπῆτι.
read, διάβασε.   the pen, ἡ πέννα.
ἔχω, (I) have.   ask, ρώτησε, (ρώτηξε).
you found, ηὕρετε.

Exercise 3.—B.

He who has money is not always happy. We will give both
the letters to you. No one has seen us. I love only you. We
know it, but you do not know it. We go to Mytilene every three
weeks. Have you any acquaintances there? The lady there is
my cousin. He does not feel well. He is as stupid as he is
rich.

money, παράδαις.   (we) go, πηγαίνομε(ν).
always, πάντοτε.   there, ἐκεῖ.
happy, εὐτυχής.   the lady, ἡ κυρία.
we shall give, θὰ δώσομε(ν).   the cousin, ἡ ἐξαδέρφη.
both, καὶ τὰ δύο.   she is my cousin, εἶνε ἐξαδέρφη μου.
(he &c.) saw, εἶδε.   (the article is not used in cases like
I love, ἀγαπῶ.   this.)
only, μόνον.   (he, she) does not feel, δὲν αἰσθάνεται.
(we) know, ξέρομε(ν).   (say, in Greek, ' feel himself well.')
three, τρεῖς.   well, καλά.
week, ἑβδομάδα.   stupid, κουτός.
to, εἰς with Acc.   rich, πλούσιος.

THE VERB.

Voices.—The verb has two voices :

The active,   *e.g.* γράφω,   I write.

The passive, ,, γράφεται, it is written.

Moods.—There are three moods :

Indicative,   *e.g.* γράφω,   I write.

Subjunctive, ,, νὰ γράφῃ, that he may write.

Imperative,   ,, γράφε,   write.

There is no infinitive proper.   It is expressed by means of the particle νά with the subjunctive : *e.g.* δὲν 'μπορῶ νὰ γράψω, I cannot write.   Two abbreviated infinitives are in use as participles ; these will be discussed under the formation of the compound tenses.

Tenses.—There are three simple tenses :

Present,   *e.g.* γράφω,   I write.

Imperfect, ,, ἔγραφα, I was writing.

Aorist,   ,, ἔγραψα, I wrote.

There are four compound tenses :

Perfect,   *e.g.* ἔχω γράψει,   I have written.

Pluperfect,   ,, εἶχα γράψει, I had written.

Future,┬   ,, θὰ γράψω,   I shall write.

Future Perfect, ,, θὰ ἔχω γράψει, I shall have written.

There are two participles :

Present Active, *e.g.* γράφοντας, writing.

Perfect Passive, ,, γραμμένος, written.

Classification.—There are two kinds of verbs : (1) simple, and (2) contracted.

In contracted verbs the a or ε preceding the termination coalesces with the vowel of the termination, *e.g.* ὁμιλῶ for ὁμιλάω, I speak.

The letter immediately preceding the termination is called the characteristic letter.

Personal Endings of the Verb.

Present Indicative.		Present Subjunctive.	
Sing.	*Plur.*	*Sing.*	*Plur.*
— ω	— ομε (ουμε)	— ω	— ωμε
— εις	— ετε	— ης	— ετε
— ει	— ουν (ουνε)	— η	— ουν (ουνε)

N.B.—There is no difference in pronunciation between Indic. Pres. and Subj. Pres.

Imperfect Indicative.		Future Indicative.
Sing.	*Plur.*	
— α	— αμε	θά is placed before the Subjunctive
— ες	— ετε (ατε)	to express the Future.
— ε	— αν(ε)	

Conditional.

ἤθελα with infinitive ending in ει.

Note.—The English conditional may also be translated by the particle θά with Imperfect or Pluperfect: *e.g.* θὰ εἶχα, I should have.

θά comes from θέ (a shortened form of θέλει) and νά. It is also used in this form : *e.g.* θὲ νὰ βλέπω, I shall see.

Imperative, 2nd pers. sing. —ε, plur. —ετε. Instead of these forms, and for the other persons, νά or ἅς with the subjunctive is used.

Present Participle.

— οντας (indeclin.).

The Auxiliaries ἔχω and εἶμαι.

Before proceeding to the conjugation of the regular verb, it is necessary to give the irregular auxiliaries. These possess only the present, imperfect and future tenses.

Ἔχω, I have.

Present Indicative.			Present Subjunctive.		
Sing.	*Plur.*		*Sing.*		*Plur.*
ἔχω, I have.	ἔχομε(ν)	(νὰ) ἔχω, that I may have.		(νὰ) ἔχωμε(ν)	
ἔχεις	ἔχετε	,, ἔχῃς		,, ἔχετε	
ἔχει	ἔχουν(ε)	,, ἔχῃ		,, ἔχουν(ε)	

Imperfect Indicative.		Future Indicative.		
Sing.	*Plur.*	*Sing.*		*Plur.*
εἶχα, I had.	εἴχαμε	θὰ ἔχω, I shall have.		θὰ ἔχωμε
εἶχες	εἴχετε	,, ἔχῃς		,, ἔχετε
εἶχε	εἴχαν(ε)	,, ἔχῃ		,, ἔχουν(ε)

Conditional.

Sing.	*Plur.*
ἤθελα ἔχει, I should have.	ἠθέλαμε ἔχει
ἤθελες ,,	ἠθέλατε ,,
ἤθελε ,,	ἤθελαν ,,

Imperative.

νὰ or ἂς with Subjunctive.

Present Participle.

ἔχοντας, having.

NOTE.—The perfect of ἔχω is sometimes rendered by another verb ἔλαβα, I have *got*. The third pers. of ἔχω is used impersonally to mean *there is;* it takes the Acc. *c.g.* ἔχει κανένα ιατρὸν ἐδῶ; is there no doctor here ?

Note also τὶ ἔχεις; what is the matter with you ?

D

Exercise 4.—A.

Ἔχω τὸ βιβλίο. Ἔχεις πατέρα καὶ μητέρα; Ἔχει πολλοὺς φίλους. Ἔχομεν ὀλίγους παράδαις. Δὲν ἔχετε ἕνα ὡραῖο σκυλάκι. Τί ἔχουνε οἱ φίλοι σας; Δὲν εἶχα χαρτί. Εἶχες τὴν ἄδειά του. Εἶχε ἕνα πιάτο καὶ ἕνα πηροῦνι. Μιὰ φορὰ εἴχαμε ἕνα γατάκι καὶ ἕνα σκυλάκι. Δὲν εἴχατε καιρὸν νὰ πᾶτε; Τί εἴχανε οἱ ἀδελφοί σας; Σήμερα δὲν ἔχω καιρὸ, ἀλλ᾽ αὔριο θὰ ἔχω. Θὰ ἔχωμε γράμματα; Νὰ ἔχετε ὑπομονή. Εἶχε πολὺν κόσμον ἐκεῖ; Δὲν ἔχει καλλίτερο φαγὶ ἀπ᾽ αὐτό. Ἂν εἶχα χρήματα θὰ εἶχα καὶ φίλους. Ἂν εἶχες θάρρος θὰ εἶχες παράδαις. Τοῦ λόγου σου δὲν ἔχεις ἕνα θεῖο 'ς τὴ Βιέννη; Τὸ ἔχετε; Δὲν τὸ ἔχομεν. Ἔχουνε τὰ βιβλία; Δὲν τἄχουνε (= τὰ ἔχουνε).

τὸ βιβλίο, the book.	σήμερα, to-day.
ἡ μητέρα, the mother.	αὔριο, to-morrow.
ὁ φίλος, the friend.	τὸ γράμμα, the letter.
ὡραῖος, beautiful.	ὑπομονή, patience.
τὸ σκυλάκι, the little dog.	δὲν, not.
τὸ χαρτί, the paper.	πολὺς κόσμος, many people.
ἡ ἄδεια, the permission.	ἐκεῖ, there.
τὸ πιάτο, the plate.	τὸ φαγί, the food.
τὸ πηροῦνι, the fork.	τὰ χρήματα, the money.
μιὰ φορά, once (one time).	τὸ θάρρος, the courage.
τὸ γατάκι, the little cat.	καὶ, and.
ὁ καιρός, the time.	ὁ θεῖος, the uncle.
νὰ πᾶτε, to go.	ἡ Βιέννη, Vienna.
ὁ ἀδελφός, the brother.	

Exercise 4.—B.

Who has the best knife? He has no patience. Had they much to do? Will you have time to-morrow? When shall we have the letter? If I had more time, I should have more money. Have you courage? Were there many people in the theatre? She will have paper and ink to-morrow. Have you not time now? This evening I shall not have much to do. If they had friends, they would have greater hopes. Good luck to him (trans. may he have good luck). Had you (τοῦ λόγου σου) not a house? Yes, I have it still. Have you the ticket? Yes, I have it in my pocket. Had he it? No, he had not. There is not a better book than yours.

the knife. τὸ μαχαῖρι.
much to do, say *much work*.
work, ἡ δουλειά.
time, ὁ καιρός.
the theatre, τὸ θέατρο(ν).
the ink, τὸ μελάνι.

this evening, ἀπόψε.
hope, ἡ ἐλπίδα.
good luck, ἡ τύχη.
yet, ἀκόμη.
the ticket, τὸ μπιλλιέτο.
yes, ναί or μάλιστα.

εἶμαι, I am.

Present Indicative.

Sing.	Plur.
εἶμαι, I am.	εἶμαστε
εἶσαι	εἶστε
εἶνε	εἶνε

Present Subjunctive.

Sing.	Plur.
(νὰ) ἦμαι, I may be.	(νὰ) ἤμαστε
,, ἦσαι	,, ἦστε
,, ἦνε	,, ἦνε

Imperfect Indicative.

Sing.	Plur.
ἤμουν (ἤμουνα), I was.	ἤμαστε
ἤσουν, ἤσουνα	ἤσαστε
ἦταν, ἤτανε, ἤτονε	ἦταν, ἤτανε

Future Indicative.

Sing.	Plur.
θὰ ἦμαι, I shall be.	θὰ ἤμαστε
θὰ ἦσαι	,, ἦστε
,, ἦνε	,, ἦνε

Conditional.

θὰ ἤμουνα, I should be.

Imperative.

Singular.	Plural.
	νὰ ἤμαστε, let us be.
νὰ ἦσαι, be,	νὰ ἦστε, be ye.
νὰ ἦνε, let him be.	νὰ ἦνε, let them be.

or   ἂς ἦσαι, &c.

Participle.

ὄντας, being.

D 2

The missing tenses of εἶμαι are sometimes supplied from the
Aorist of στέκομαι, to stand.   (See under the irregular verbs.)

> ἐστάθηκα, I was.
> ἔχω σταθῆ, I have been.
> εἶχα σταθῆ, I had been.
> θὰ ἔχω σταθῆ. I shall have been.

Exercise 5.—A.

Εἶνε 'ς τὸ σπῆτι; Ποιὰ εἶνε αὐτὴ ἡ κυρία; Εἶνε φίλη μου. Ποιὰ
εἶνε αὐτὰ τὰ παιδιά; Ποῦσαι, παιδί; Ποῦ ἤσουνα 'ψές ('χθές);
Σὲ τρεῖς μῆναις ποῦ θὰ εἶσαι; Αὐτὸς ἤτανε μεγαλείτερος ἀπὸ σένανε.
(·)ὰ εἶνε 'ς τὸ σπῆτι αὔριο; Ἂν εἶχα τὰς γνώσεις ποὔχει αὐτὸς θὰ
ἤμουνα εὐτυχής. Σὰν ἤτανε νέα, τὰ μαλλιά της ἤτανε μαῦρα· τώρα
εἶνε ἄσπρα. Τοῦ λόγου σου δὲν ἤσουνα μιὰ φορὰ 'ς τοῦ Μιχάλη τὸ
σπῆτι; Ἤμουνα γραμματικὸς εἰς ἕνα βιβλιοπωλεῖο. Ὅλοι ἤμαστε
ἄρρωστοι. Αὔριον 'ς ταῖς ἕξι ὥραις θὰ ἦμαι ἐδῶ. Νὰ ἦσαι ἥσυχος.
Ἂς ἦνε ἐλεύθερος. Ἄμποτε νὰ ἤμουνα γερός! Πάντοτε νὰ ἦσαι
καλά.

'ς τὸ σπῆτι, at home.	νέα, young girl.
ἡ κυρία, the lady.	τὰ μαλλιά, the hair.
φίλη μου, my friend, a friend of mine.	μαῦρος, black.
τὸ παιδί, the child, young fellow, waiter, &c.	ἄσπρος, white.
	ὁ γραμματικός, the secretary, clerk.
ποῦσαι = ποῦ εἶσαι, usual way to call a waiter.	τὸ βιβλιοπωλεῖον, the bookshop.
	ἄρρωστος, ill.
'ψές, yesterday.	's ταῖς ἕξι ὥραις, at six o'clock.
σέ, in (here = after).	ἥσυχος, quiet.
τρεῖς, three.	ἐλεύθερος, free.
μεγαλείτερος, bigger, older.	ἄμποτε, if only.
ἡ γνῶσι, the acquaintance.	γερός, strong.
εὐτυχής, fortunate, lucky.	πάντοτε, always.
σάν, when.	καλά, well.

Exercise 5.—B.

He was not at home yesterday.   Why is she not here now?
Where do you come from?   I come from Germany.   I was very
ill.   At such a time they will not be at their shop.   Was he not
a relative of Mr. Argyropoulos?   No, he was the son of Michael,

the baker.   Athens was a village sixty-five years ago, now it is a large and beautiful city.   May you always be well and happy ! If he were not so uneducated he would now have a place.   Where is the gentleman who was in your house yesterday ?   He is from London.   I shall be at the shop at five o'clock.   We were at the theatre with them.

why ? διατί ; γιατί ;

from where ? ἀπὸ ποῦ ;

Germany, ἡ Γερμανία.

very, πολύ.

at such a time, τέτοια ὥρα.

the shop, τὸ μαγαζί.

the relative, ὁ συγγενής.

the gentleman, ὁ κύριος.

no, ὄχι.

the son, ὁ υἱός (γιός).

Athens, αἱ 'Αθῆναι (ἡ 'Ατῆνα).

sixty-five years ago, ἀπ' ἐδῶ καὶ ἐξῆντα πέντε ἔτη.

the village, τὸ χωριό.

the city, ἡ πόλι.

uneducated, ἀγράμματος.

now, τώρα.

the place, ἡ θέσι.

at five o'clock, 's τὰς πέντε ὥραις.

the baker, ὁ ψωμᾶς.

* Note the following idioms : Ἔχετε πολὺν καιρὸν ἐδῶ ; (Have you much time here ?) Have you been here long ?   Πόσον καιρὸν ἔχετε ἐδῶ ; How long have you been here ?   Ἦλθε 's τὸ σπῆτι μου, (He came into my house) He has been in my house.   Δὲν ἦλθε κανείς, No one has been here.   'Επῆγα εἰς τὸ σπῆτι του, I have been in his house.   'Επῆγατε 's τὴν Ρώμην ; Have you been in Rome ?

THE REGULAR VERB.

γράφω, I write.

Active Voice.

Indicative Mood.

Present Tense.

Sing.	*Plur.*
γράφω, I write.	γράφομε(ν), γράφουμε
γράφεις	γράφετε
γράφει	γράφουν(ε)

Imperfect Tense.

ἔγραφα, I was writing.	(ἐ)γράφαμε(ν)
ἔγραφες	(ἐ)γράφατε, ἐγράφετε
ἔγραφε	ἔγραφαν, (ἐ)γράφανε

Aorist.

ἔγραψα, I wrote.	(ἐ)γράψαμε(ν)
ἔγραψες	(ἐ)γράψετε, (ἐ)γράψατε
ἔγραψε	ἔγραψαν

Perfect.	Pluperfect.
ἔχω γράψει, I have written.	εἶχα γράψει, I had written.

Future.

θὰ γράφω, or ⎫ θὰ γράψω, ⎬ I shall write.	θὰ γράφωμε, γράψωμε
θὰ γράφῃς, γράψῃς	θὰ γράφητε, γράψετε
θὰ γράφῃ, γράψῃ	θὰ γράφουν(ε), γράψουν(ε)

Future Perfect.

θὰ ἔχω γράψει, I shall have written.

Conditional.

θὰ ἔγραφα, I should write.	θὰ ἐγράφομε (γράφουμε)
., ἔγραφες	,, ἐγράφετε
.. ἔγραφε	,, ἐγράφουν(ε)

or

ἤθελα γράφει	ἠθέλομεν γράφει
ἤθελες ,,	ἠθέλατε ,,
ἤθελε ,,	ἤθελαν (ἠθέλανε) γράφει

Past Conditional.

ἤθελα γράψει, I should have written.	ἠθέλαμε γράψει
ἤθελες ,,	ἠθέλατε ,,
ἤθελε ,,	ἤθελαν (ἠθέλανε) γράψει

or   θὰ εἶχα γράψει, I should have written.

Subjunctive Mood.

Present.

(νὰ) γράφω, that I may write	(νὰ) γράφωμε (γράφουμε)
., γράφῃς	,, γράφετε
,, γράφῃ	,, γράφουν(ε)

Aorist.

(νὰ) γράψω, that I may write.   (νὰ) γράψωμε, γράψουμε
 „ γράψῃς   „ γράψετε
 „ γράψῃ   „ γράψουν(ε)

Imperative.

Present.

γράφε, write.   γράφετε, write (ye).
ἃς γράφῃ, let him write.   ἃς γράφοινε, let them write.

Aorist.

γράψε, write.   γράψετε, γράψτε.
ἃς γράψῃ, let him write.   ἃς γράψουν(ε).

Infinitive (used only in the compound tenses).

Present. γράψει.   Aorist. γράψει.

Present Participle.   γράφοντας, writing.

Passive Voice.

Present.

Sing.	Plur.
γράφομαι, γράφουμαι, I am written, &c.	γραφούμαστε (γραφόμεθα)
γράφεσαι	γράφεστε (γράφεσθε)
γράφεται	γράφουνται (γράφονται)

Imperfect.

(ἐ)γράφομουν(α), I was written.	(ἐ)γραφούμαστε, (ἐ)γραφόμαστε
(ἐ)γράφουσουν, (ἐ)γραφόσοινα	(ἐ)γραφούσαστε, (ἐ)γραφόσαστε
(ἐ)γράφουνταν, (ἐ)γραφόταιε	(ἐ)γράφουνταν, (ἐ)γραφόντουσαι

Aorist.

(ἐ)γράφθηκα (γράφτηκα), I was written.	(ἐ)γραφθήκαμε
(ἐ)γράφθηκας	(ἐ)γραφθήκατε, (ἐ)γραφθήκετε
(ἐ)γράφθηκε	(ἐ)γράφθηκαν, (ἐ)γραφθήκανε

Perfect.   ἔχω γραφθῆ, I have been written.
Pluperfect. εἶχα γραφθῆ, I had been written.

Future.

θὰ γράφωμαι, or γραφθῶ,   θὰ γραφώμαστε, γραφθοῦμε
  I shall be written.

,, γράφεσαι, γραφθῆς   ,, γράφεστε, γραφθῆτε

,, γράφεται, γραφθῇ   ,, γράφωνται, γραφθοῦνε

Future Perfect. θὰ ἔχω γραφθῆ, I shall have been written.

Conditional.
Sing.   *Plur.*

θὰ ἐγραφόμουν, I should be written.   θὰ (ἐ)γραφούμαστε

.. ἐγραφήσουν   ,, (ἐ)γραφούσαστε

,, ἐγράφουνταν   ,, (ἐ)γραφόντουσαν

    or ἤθελα γραφθῆ, I should be written.

Past Conditional. θὰ εἶχα γραφθῆ, I should have been written.

Subjunctive.
Present.

(νὰ) γράφωμαι, that I may be written. (νὰ) γραφώμαστε, γραφούμαστε

,, γράφεσαι   ,, γράφεστε

,, γράφεται   ,, γράφουνται

Aorist.

(νὰ) γραφθῶ, that I may be written.   (νὰ) γραφθοῦμε(ν)

,, γραφθῆς   ,, γραφθῆτε

,, γραφθῇ   ,, γραφθοῦνε

Imperative.

γράφου, be written.   γράφεστε

ἂς γράφεται, let him be written.   ἂς γράφουνται (γράφωνται)

Aorist Infinitive.   ### Perfect Participle.

    γραφθῆ   γραμμένος, written

Contracted Verbs.

Most contracted verbs end in ἀω; there are also some in ἑω, but the people usually conjugate them like verbs in ἀω.

ἀ π α τ ά ω, to deceive.

Active Voice.

Present Indicative.

ἀπατάω, ἀπατῶ, I deceive.	ἀπατάομε, ἀπατοῦμε
ἀπατάεις, ἀπατᾷς	ἀπατάετε, ἀπατᾶτε
ἀπατάει, ἀπατᾷ	ἀπατάουν(ε), ἀπατοῦν(ε)

Imperfect.

ἀπατοῦσα, I was deceiving.	ἀπατούσαμε
ἀπατοῦσες	ἀπατούσατε
ἀπατοῦσε	ἀπατοῦσαν

Aorist.

ἀπάτησα, I deceived.	ἀπατήσαμε
ἀπάτησες	ἀπατήσατε
ἀπάτησε	ἀπάτησαν

Perfect.	Pluperfect.
ἔχω ἀπατήσει, I have deceived.	εἶχα ἀπατήσει, I had deceived.

Future.	Future Perfect.
θὰ ἀπατῶ θὰ ἀπατήσω } I shall deceive.	θὰ ἔχω ἀπατήσει { I shall have deceived.

Conditional.	Past Conditional.
θὰ ἀπατοῦσα or ἤθελα ἀπατήσει	θὰ εἶχα ἀπατήσει

Subjunctive.

Present.	Aorist.
(νὰ) ἀπατῶ	(νὰ) ἀπατήσω

Imperative.

Present.   Aorist.

ἀπάταε, ἀπάτα   ἀπατᾶτε   ἀπάτησε   ἀπατήσετε, ἀπατῆστε
ᾶς ἀπατάῃ, ᾶς ἀπατᾷ   ᾶς ἀπατοῦν(ε)   ᾶς ἀπατήσῃ   ᾶς ἀπατήσουν(ε)

Aorist Infinitive.   ἀπατήσει   Pres. Participle.   ἀπατῶντας.

Passive Voice.

Present Indicative.

ἀπατοῦμαι, I am deceived.   ἀπατούμαστε
ἀπατᾶσαι   ἀπατᾶστε
ἀπατᾶται   ἀπατοῦνται

Imperfect.

ἀπατούμουν(α), I was being deceived.   ἀπατούμαστε
ἀπατούσουν(α)   ἀπατούσαστε
ἀπατούνταν   ἀπατοῦνταν

Some verbs have the following endings for the Pres. Indic. :—

ιοῦμαι, —ιέμαι,   --ιούμαστε, --ιόμαστε
—ιέσαι   ιοῦστε,   — ιέστε
---ιέται   —ιοῦνται

e.g. βαριοῦμαι, to be weary.

Present Indicative.

βαριοῦμαι, βαριέμαι, I am weary.   βαριούμαστε, βαριόμαστε
βαριέσαι   βαριοῦστε, βαριέστε
βαριέται   βαριοῦνται

Imperfect.

(ἐ)βαριούμουν(α), I was weary.   (ἐ)βαριούμαστε
(ἐ)βαριούσουν(α)   (ἐ)βαριούσαστε
(ἐ)βαριούνταν(ε)   (ἐ)βαριοῦνταν(ε)

Aorist.	Perfect.	Pluperfect.
ἀπατήθηκα	ἔχω ἀπατηθῆ	εἶχα ἀπατηθῆ

Future.	Future Perfect.
θὰ ἀπατῶμαι ⎫ θὰ ἀπατηθῶ ⎭	θὰ ἔχω ἀπατηθῆ

Conditional.	Past Conditional.
θὰ ἀπατούμουν or ἤθελα ἀπατηθῆ	θὰ εἶχα ἀπατηθῆ

Subjunctive.

Present. νὰ ἀπατοῦμαι   Aorist. νὰ ἀπατηθῶ.

Imperative.

Present.		Aorist.	
ἀπατάου	ἀπατᾶστε	ἀπατήσου	ἀπατηθῆτε
ἂς ἀπατᾶται	ἂς ἀπατοῦντα	ἂς ἀπατηθῆ	ἂς ἀπατηθοῦν

Aorist Infinitive. ἀπατηθῆ   Perfect Participle. ἀπατημένος

VERBS IN έω.

θαρρῶ, I believe.

Active Voice.

θαρρῶ	θαρροῦμεν
θαρρεῖς	θαρρεῖτε
θαρρεῖ	θαρροῦν

Passive Voice.

This usually has the forms in ιέμαι, &c., cited above. Occasionally the following endings occur :—

— οῦμαι	— ούμαστε (— ούμεθα)
— εῖσαι	— εῖστε
— εῖται	— οῦνται

The remaining forms follow the άω conjugation.

EXERCISES IN CONJUGATION.

On the Present Tense (Active).

Endings for uncontracted forms :—

— ω	— ομε (— ουμε)
— εις	— ετε
— ει	— ουν(ε)

The Active Present of the following verbs is conjugated as above (like γράφω) :—

διαβάζω, I read.	τρέχω, I run.
ρίχνω, I throw.	σέρνω, I pull.

Endings for contracted forms : —

for the forms in έω we have

for	άω	we have	ῶ	ῶ
,,	άεις	,,	ᾷς	εῖς
.,	άει	.,	ᾷ	εῖ
.,	άουμε	.,	οῦμε(ν)	οῦμε(ν)
,,	άετε	,,	ᾶτε	εῖτε
.,	άουνε	,,	οῦν(ε)	οῦν(ε)

Both the forms in άω and ῶ are often used indifferently in the singular; verbs in έω are only used in the contracted forms.

Conjugate the following verbs like ἀπατάω :—

(ἐ)ρωτάω, I ask ; γελάω, I laugh ; ἀγαπάω, χαιρετάω, I salute ; (ὁ)μιλάω, I speak ; φιλάω, I kiss. (The two last are more often conjugated like θαρρῶ.)

ζάω, I live, is conjugated as follows : ζῶ, ζῆς, ζῇ, ζοῦμε, ζῆτε. ζοῦν(ε).

The Subjunctive is the same as the Indicative, except that for ει, whenever it occurs in the termination, η is written.

Exercise 6.—A.

Ποιὸ βιβλίο εἶνε αὐτὸ ποῦ διαβάζεις ; Γιατὶ τρέχεις ; ἔχομε καιρό· δὲν εἶνε ἀργὰ ἀκόμη. Τὸ ξέρει αὐτὸς ; Γιατὶ δέν το ρίχνεις κάτω ; Σᾶς πειράζει αὐτό ; Ὄχι, δέν με πειράζει καθόλου. Γράφομε κάθε 'μέρα 's τὸν πατέρα μας. 'Μιλᾶς ρωμαϊκά ; Ξέρω ὀλίγα. Δέν τα ὁμιλῶ καλά. Γιατὶ δέν τον ἐρωτᾶς ; Ἀγαπᾶτε αὐτοὺς τοὺς νέους ; Μάλιστα, τοὺς ἀγαποῦμε πολύ. Ἡ μητέρα μοῦ σε χαιρετάει. Τί κάμνει ; εἶνε καλά ; Καλὰ εἶνε, σε εὐχαριστῶ. Τὰ κορίτζια γελοῦνε. Ποῦ τρέχετε ; Διαβάζουν ἕνα γράμμα. Τί σας γράφει ὁ πατέρας σας ; Τί βαστᾶς 's τὸ χέρι ; Τί κάμνεις ; εἶσαι καλά ; Καλά, εὐχαριστῶ. Τί κάμνετε ; εἶστε καλά ; Καλά, σᾶς εὐχαριστοῦμε.

δέν ἀκόμη, not yet.
ἀργά, late.
ξέρω, I know.
ρίχνω, I throw.
κάτω, below, down.
πειράζει (impersonal), it matters.
δὲν καθόλου, not at all.
κάθε 'μέρα, every day.
ρωμαϊκά, modern Greek.
(ὀ)λίγος, little.

καλά, well.
(ἐ)ρωτῶ, I ask.
ὁ νέος, the young man.
μάλιστα, certainly ; yes, indeed.
κάμνω, I do. τι κάμνεις, τί κάνεις ; how do you do ?
εὐχαριστῶ, thank you.
τὸ κορίτζι, the girl.
βαστῶ, I hold, carry.

Exercise 6.—B.

Who is that young man who is laughing ? He is my cousin. Do you like music ? How do you know that ? Never mind (It does not matter). How is your brother ? Is he well ? There he is just passing. To whom are you writing ? I am writing a letter to Malvina. What do you want, madam ? We pass his shop every day. Do you speak Modern Greek ? Yes, but I cannot speak the fine language they have in the newspapers in Athens. I speak very little. Do you like wine ? Who is knocking at the door ? Beer spoils my appetite. Will you change me a Turkish pound ? What do they ask you for ? He loves you. What are you whispering ? When do you shut your shop ? The girl kisses her mother.

the cousin, ὁ ἐξάδελφος.
the music, ἡ μουσική.
how ? πῶς.
to pass, περνάω.

there he is just passing, νὰ ποῦ περνάει (νά = there he is).
the lady, ἡ κυρία.
very, πολύ.

the language, ἡ γλῶσσα.
fine, ὡραῖος.
the newspaper, ἡ ἐφημερίδα.
the wine, τὸ κρασί.
the door, ἡ πόρτα.
to spoil, χαλνῶ.
the beer, ἡ μπίρα.

the appetite, ἡ ὄρεξι.
to change, χαλνῶ.
a Turkish pound, μιὰ λίρα τουρκική.
to whisper, κρυφομιλάω.
to shut, σφαλνῶ.
to kiss, φιλῶ.

On the Imperfect.

To form the imperfect, the augment ε is usually placed before the verb; and the proper terminations, given below, are affixed. *e.g.* γράφω, ἔγραφα.

Exceptions :—

1.   Contracted verbs usually neglect the augment.   βαστοῦσα, I kept ; for ἐβαστοῦσα.

2.   Of the uncontracted verbs, those of more than two syllables usually do not take the augment.   καταλαβαίνω, I understand ; καταλάβαινα.

3.   Verbs beginning with vowels commonly neglect the augment ; but the rule, when observed, is that the initial vowel lengthens from a and ε to η, and from o to ω ; while αι always remains unchanged.   Examples :—

Pres.	Imp.
ἀκούω, I hear.	ἄκουα or ἤκουα.
ἐγγίζω, I touch.	ἔγγιζα or ἤγγιζα.
ὁμιλῶ, I speak.	ὁμιλοῦσα or ὡμιλοῦσα.
εὑρίσκω, I find.	εὑρίσκα or ηὑρίσκα.

From this list of exceptions, it is obvious that the only verbs which usually take the augment are those which are dissyllabic, and also begin with a consonant ; but most of the verbs in ordinary use belong to this class.   λέγω, ἔλεγα.

The augment η is used in the verb θέλω (originally ἐθέλω), and also in many other cases from false analogy.   *e.g.* ἤλεγα, ἤγραφα.

NOTE.—In the case of verbs compounded with prepositions, the augment, if used, is affixed before the preposition ; not after, as in ancient Greek.

ENDINGS OF THE IMPERFECT.

For uncontracted verbs.				For contracted verbs.		
Pers.	*Sing.*	*Plur.*		*Pers.*	*Sing.*	*Plur.*
1	- α	— αμε		1	— οῦσα	— οὖσαμε
2	- ες	—- ατε or ετε		2	— οῦσες	— οὖσετε
3	--- ε	--- αν		3	— οῦσε	--- οῦσαν

Examples.

Imperfect like γράφω.

νομίζω, I think.
πίνω, I drink.
διαβάζω, I read.
γυρίζω, I turn.

Imperfect like ἀπατῶ.

γελῶ, I laugh.
προτιμῶ, I prefer.
περπατῶ, I walk.
λησμονῶ, I forget.
φορῶ, I wear.
κρατῶ, I hold.

The Imperfect is used like the French Imperfect to denote an action or state in past time which is repeated or lasts a certain time.

e.g. περπατοῦσα
{
I used to walk.
I often walked.
I was walking for some time.
I was walking at the time when something else [happened.
}

ἔγραφα, I used to write &c.

Exercise 7.—A.

Τὸ πρωΐ 'περιπατοῦσαν δύο ὥραις, τὸ μεσημέρι ἔγραφαν γράμματα. Ὡμιλούσατε καὶ 'γελούσατε. Ἀπὸ κεῖνο'τὸν καιρὸ μαῦρα φορέματα φορούσε. Κάθε πρωΐ ἐπερνούσε ἀπὸ τὸ μαγαζί μας. Τὴν ὥρα ποῦ αὐτὴ ἐδιάβαζε τὰ γράμματα, ἐγὼ ἐδιάβαζα τὴν ἐφημερίδα.

τὸ πρωΐ, in the morning.	μαῦρος, black.
ἡ ὥρα, the hour.	φόρεμα, dress.
δύο, two.	περνῶ ἀπὸ, I call (in) at.
τὸ μεσημέρι, at mid-day.	τὴν ὥρα ποῦ, while.
ἀπὸ, since.	

Exercise 7.--B.

Every morning we used to read the newspaper, then we drank coffee. At eight o'clock we went for a walk in the garden and spoke of various things. Was he not wearing a white hat? We called at their house every day. While you were laughing and talking I was reading and writing. When I was returning from the village, I used to smoke a cigar.

then, ἔπειτα.
the coffee, ὁ καφές.
at eight o'clock, 's ταὶς ὀχτὼ ὥραις.
the garden, τὸ περιβόλι.
different, διάφορος.
the thing, τὸ πρᾶγμα.
I speak of, ὁμιλῶ γιά.

white, ἄσπρο.
the hat, τὸ καπέλο.
when I was returning, the pres. part. of
 γυρίζω.
I smoke, φουμάρω.
the cigar, τὸ πούρου.

On the Aorist.

The rules for the augment are the same as in the Imperfect.

Aorist endings.

Pers.	Sing.	Plur.
1	— σα	— σαμε
2	— σες	— σατε
3	— σε	— σαν

The characteristic letter of the verb undergoes a change when brought into conjunction with the σ of the Aorist ending :—

1. β, π, φ combine with the σ to form ψ :

e.g. κρύβω, I hide ; ἔκρυψα.
 βάφω, I dye ; ἔβαψα.

Note.—The verbs in εύω having υ (in pronunciation = φ before r) as characteristic letter also form their aorist in ψ :

e.g. πιστεύω, I believe ; ἐπίστεψα.
 γυρεύω, I seek ; ἐγύρεψα.

2. γ, κ, χ combine with the σ to form ξ :

> *e.g.* φυλάγω, I guard ;   ἐφύλαξα.
> πλέκω, I plait, knit ; ἔπλεξα.

3. ζ occasionally changes to ξ :

> *e.g.* φωνάζω, I call ;   ἐφώναξα.
> νυστάζω, I am sleepy ; ἐνύσταξα.
> παίζω, I play ;   ἔπαιξα.

4. Verbs in ζω, θω, and those that have a vowel as character-istic letter, have the Aorist endings added directly after the vowel :

> *e.g.* σχίζω, I tear ; ἔσχισα.
> γνέθω, I spin ; ἔγνεσα.
> ἀκούω, I hear ; ἄκουσα.

NOTE.—(*a*) The ending σα changes the characteristic α and ε of contracted verbs into η :

> *e.g.* ἀπατάω   ἀπάτησα.
> φιλέω   ἐφίλησα.

Exceptions to the above rule :—

> πεινάω, I am hungry ;   ἐπείνασα.
> διψάω, I am thirsty ;   ἐδίψασα.
> φορέω, φορῶ, I wear (clothes, &c.) ; ἐφόρεσα.
> γελάω, I laugh ;   ἐγέλασα.
> (ἐ)μπορῶ, I can ;   ἐμπόρεσα.
> προσκαλῶ, I invite ;   ἐπροσκάλεσα.

(β) A few contracted verbs have ξ in their Aorist (as if formed from a Present in ζ) :

> *e.g.* φυσάω, I blow ; ἐφύσηξα.
> τραβάω, I pull ; ἐτράβηξα.

5. (*a*) Verbs whose characteristic letter in the Present is ν preceded by ε, α, or ο, lose the ν before the Aorist termination σα, and ο is written ω in the Aorist :

> *e.g.* δένω, I bind ;   ἔδεσα.
> μαλλόνω, I scold ; ἐμάλλωσα.
> δαγκάνω, I bite ; ἐδάγκασα.

(*b*) Verbs whose characteristic letter in the Present is τ preceded by φ, or ν preceded by χ, lose the τ or ν, and the φ or χ
combines with the σ of the Aorist termination to form ψ or ξ :

> *e.g.* κόφτω, I cut ;   ἔκοψα.
> δείχνω, I show ;   ἔδειξα.

6. Verbs in λλω, μω, ρω, and some in νω, have no σ in the
Aorist ; the characteristic letter remains the same as in the
Present, but if ε is the letter preceding it is generally changed
to ει :

> *e.g.* στέλλω, I send ; ἔστειλα.
> φέρω, I bring ; ἔφερα.
> μένω, I remain ; ἔμεινα.

NOTE.—Verbs in λω and ρω have a popular form for the
Present in νω :

> *e.g.* στέλνω for στέλλω.
> φέρνω ,,   φέρω.
> σέρνω ,,   σύρω, I drag ; Aorist ἔσυρα.

7. Verbs in αίνω have ανα in the Aorist :

> ζεσταίνω, I warm ; ἐξέστανα.

8. Many verbs in ίζω, and some others, have a collateral form
for the Present in νάω ; but the Aorist always comes from the
first form :

> *e.g.* γυρίζω, γυρνάω, I turn ;   (ἐ)γύρισα.
> σφαλίζω, σφαλνάω, I shut ; (ἐ)σφάλισα ((ἐ)σφάληξα).
> ξεχάνω, ξεχνάω, I forget ;   ξέχασα.

Some other verbs, again, having only the form νάω in the
Present, form their Aorist as from a Present in αίνω or άνω :

> *e.g.* κιρνάω, I serve wine ; ἐκέρασα.
> κρεμνῶ, I hang up ;   ἐκρέμασα.

USE OF THE AORIST.

The Aorist indicates indefinite past action : *e.g.* ἔστειλα, I sent. It is distinguished on the one hand from the Imperfect, which denotes repetition or continuance, and on the other from the Perfect, which denotes action completed at the present time.   It occupies therefore the same position as the French *passé indéfini*, and is often used where the English idiom prefers the Perfect : *e.g.* ἔστειλα τὸ γράμμα, I have sent the letter.

In verbs whose Present expresses a state or condition, the Aorist expresses the beginning of that state as past :

πεινῶ, I am hungry ;   ἐπείνασα, I have got hungry, I am hungry. νυστάζω, I am sleepy ; ἐνύσταξα.

In particularly vivid speech the Aorist is used to express future action ; the action is represented as so near and certain as to be practically past :

e.g. φύγε ἤ σε σκότωσα, go away, or I'll kill you (or you're a dead man).

NOTE.—It will be observed that the above rules are merely practical ; and the philologist may take exception to the lack of explanation of the forms given ; but such explanations would necessitate a knowledge of ancient Greek only possessed by those to whom the explanations would be superfluous.   In many cases the ancient Greek rule, based on philological reasons, is violated from the influence of analogy :

e.g. ἔπαιξα, ἐφύσηξα.

Exercise 8.—A.

Ἔσκυψε καὶ ἐσήκωσε τὸ βιβλίο. Ἄναψαν τὰ κηριά. Γιατὶ δὲν ἤναψες (ἄναψες) τὴ λάμπα ; Ἔκοψες τὸ χέρι σου ; Ἐρράψαμε τὰ φορέματά σας πολλαὶς φοραίς: γιατί τα σχιζετε ; Εἶσαι ἄρρωστος· σὲ ἔβλαψαν τὰ βαρειὰ φαγιά. Τὸν ἐγύρεψα παντοῦ. Με γύρεψε κανείς ; Ὄχι, δέν σας ἐγύρεψε κανείς. Δέν το ἐπίστεψα. Ψὲς (χθὲς) ἐχορέψαμε ὅλη τῇ νύχτα. Πόσαις ʼμέραις ἔλειψε ;

σκύφτω, I bend, stoop.
σηκόνω, I lift.
ἀνάφτω, I light.
τὸ κηρί, the candle.
ἡ λάμπα, the lamp.
κόφτω, I cut.
τὸ χέρι, the hand.
ῥάφτω, I sew.
τὸ φόρεμα, the dress.
σχίζω, I tear.

βλάφτω, I injure.
ἄρρωστος, ill.
βαρύς, heavy.
γυρεύω, I look for, ask for.
παντοῦ, everywhere.
χορεύω, I dance.
ἡ νύχτα, the night.
ὅλος, all.
λείπω, I am absent.

Exercise 8.—B.

She lighted the lamp. Why have you not written the letter?
I have cut my finger. Have you sewn the dress? The heavy
wine has done you harm. I bent down and lifted up the ticket.
Some one asked for you. How long did you dance? Have you
heard the story? He did not believe it. They were a year
away.

the finger, ὁ δάχτυλος.   the year, ὁ χρόνος.
the story, ἡ ἱστορία.

Exercise 9.—A.

Ἐπάστρεψε ἡ δοῦλα τὰ πιάτα;   Μοῦ ἔδειξε τὸ σπῆτι του.
Ἐπαίξατε χαρτιά;   Μᾶς ἔκλεψαν ἕνα ὡρολόγι. Ἔρριξε τὸ μπαστοῦνι
ὄξω ἀπὸ τὸ παραθύρι. Δὲν ἐφυλάξατε τὸ μυστικό. Ποιὸς μὲ φώναξε;
Δὲν ἔσιαξες τὴν κάμαρα ἀκόμη;   Γρήγορα ἐνύσταξες· δὲν εἶνε ὀχτὼ
ἀκόμη. Ἔσφιξε τὸ χέρι μου. Ἄλλαξε πολὺ ἡ ὄψι σου. Ἄνοιξαν
τὸ μπαούλι; Δὲν ἄνοιξε τὰ μάτια του. Ποῦ ἔτρεξαν τὰ παιδιά;
Διατὶ ἔσπρωξες τὸ σκυλί; Δὲν μ᾿ἐκύτταξε καθόλου. Τὸν ἐκύτταξα
καλὰ καλά. Γιατὶ ἐτρόμαξε!

παστρεύω, I clean, make clean.
ἡ δοῦλα, the maidservant.
τὸ χαρτί, the card, the paper.
κλέφτω, I steal.
τὸ ὡρολόγι, the watch, clock.
τὸ μπαστοῦνι, the stick.
τὸ παραθύρι (ἡ παράθυρα), the window.
ὄξω ἀπό, out of.
φυλάγω, to keep, to guard.
τὸ μυστικό, the secret.
σιάζω, to put to rights, to tidy up.
ἡ κάμερα, the room.
γρήγορα, quickly, soon.

ὀχτώ, eight.
σφίγγω, I press, squeeze.
ἀλλάζω, to change.
ἡ ὄψι, the appearance.
ἀνοίγω, I open.
τὸ μπαούλι, the box.
τὸ μάτι, the eye.
σπρώχνω, I push.
τὸ σκυλί, the dog.
κυττάζω, I see.
καλὰ καλά, very well, thoroughly.
τρομάζω, I am afraid.

Exercise 9.—B.

We opened all the doors and windows. They called him. I shall change my clothes. Have we not kept the secret? I am sleepy (use the Aorist). She threw the book on the ground. The children ran home. The smoke suffocated her. She sighed and squeezed my hand. We have not seen her at all. The maid-servant heard the noise and was afraid.

on the ground, χάμου.	I suffocate, πνίγω.
home, εἰς τὸ σπίτι τῶν.	I sigh, στενάζω. Aor. ἐστέναξα.
the smoke, ὁ καπνός.	the noise, ὁ κρότος.

Exercise 10.—A.

'Εδιάβασε τὸ γράμμα καὶ τό 'σχισε (τὸ ἔσχισε). Ἄκουσες τὴ βροντή; 'Αδειάσαμε τὸ ποτῆρι. Ἔδεσε τὸ ἄλογο σὲ μιὰ ἐξώπορτα. Ποιὸς ἔδεσε αὐτὰ τὰ βιβλία; Γιατὶ φωνάζει τὸ παιδί; Τὸ δάγκασε ἕνα σκυλί. Ἔπιασε τὸ σκυλὶ ἀπὸ τὸ αὐτί. Τί ὥρα ἐγύρισε 'ς τὸ σπῆτι; Τί γυρεύεις; ἔχασα τὸ πορτοφόλι μου. Ἄρχισαν τὰ μαθήματα. 'Εσφάληξε τὴν πόρτα καὶ ἔχασε τὸ κλειδί. Πότε ἔφθασε τὸ βαπόρι;

ἡ βροντή, the thunder.	τὸ αὐτί, the ear.
ἀδειάζω, I empty.	τί ὥρα, what o'clock.
τὸ ποτῆρι, the glass.	τὸ πορτοφόλι, the portfolio.
δένω, I bind.	ἀρχίζω, I begin.
τὸ ἄλογο, the horse.	τὸ μάθημα, the lesson.
σέ (εἰς, 's), to.	τὸ κλειδί, the key.
ἡ ἐξώπορτα, the door, the gate.	τὸ βαπόρι, the steamboat.
πιάνω, I seize.	φθάνω, I arrive.
ἀπό, (here) on.	

Exercise 10.—B.

He turned the leaf. Did you ever hear or read anything like that? We emptied the glasses and filled them again. He came back from the market at eleven o'clock. The glass is broken. We have lost the ring. They have forgotten it. The play has not begun yet. When did you shut the shop? Where did you buy these cigars? His father arrived yesterday. Have you put out the light? Have you forgotten the name? He has left his handkerchief here.

I turn, γυρίζω.
the leaf, τὸ φύλλο.
I fill, γεμίζω.
I refill, ξαναγεμίζω.
at eleven o'clock, 's ταῖς ἕνδεκα (ὥραις).
the market, ἡ ἀγορά.
I break, σπάνω (is broken, ἔσπασε).
the ring, τὸ δαχτυλίδι.
the play (say the representation),
  ἡ παράστασι.

I buy, ἀγοράζω.
cigar, τὸ ποῦρο.
the light, τὸ φῶς.
I put out, σβύνω.
the name, τὸ ὄνομα.
the handkerchief, τὸ μανδύλι.
I leave, ἀφήνω.
here, ἐδῶ.

Exercise 11.—A.

Δέν σου 'μίλησε κανείς. Ἤργησες πολὺ σήμερα. Ἡ μητέρα 'φίλησε τὸ παιδί της. Μὲ 'ρώτησαν ἂν ἤμουνα ἀπὸ τὴν Σμύρνην. Ἠγαπήσαμε τὸν νέον. Τὸν ἐξυπνήσαμε 's ταῖς τέσσεραις. Διώρθωσες τὸ θέμα; Βούλωσα ἕνα δόντι. Δὲν ἐσαρώσαμε τὴν κάμερα. Ἔχω σινάχι, ἐκρύωσα δυνατά. Ποιὸς ἐκούνησε τὸ τραπέζι; Πόσα 'πληρώσατε διὰ τὸ μπιλιέτο; Ἔστειλες τὰ γράμματα ποὔγραψα; Ἔσυρε τὸ σάκκο 'πίσω του. Οἱ στρατιῶταις (σολδάταις) ἐδείρανε τὸν λῃστήν. Ὁ παπουτζῆς ἔφερε τὰ παπούτζια μου.

ἀργέω, ἀργῶ, to be late.
σήμερα, to-day.
ἀγαπῶ, I love. Aorist, I have got fond of.
ὁ νέος, the young man.
ξυπνῶ (ξυπνάω), I waken.
διορθόνω, I correct.
τὸ θέμα, the exercise.
βουλόνω, I seal, stop ; ἐβούλωσα, I have had (a tooth) stopped.
τὸ δόντι, the tooth.
σαρύνω, I sweep.
τὸ συνάχι, the cold in the head.
κρυόνω, I catch cold.

δυνατά, badly (lit. strongly).
κουνῶ, I move.
τὸ τραπέζι, the table.
πληρόνω, I pay.
διά, γιά, for.
στέλνω, I send.
ὁ σάκκος, the sack.
ὀπίσω, 'πίσω, behind.
ὁ στρατιώτης (σολδάτος), the soldier.
δέρνω, I strike, beat.
ὁ λῃστής, the robber.
τὸ παποῦτζι, the boot, shoe.
ὁ παπουτζῆς, the shoe-maker.

Exercise 11.—B.

We asked the gentleman if he was a German. When did you wake this morning? They stayed out late yesterday. He had a tooth stopped. He caught cold. He pulled my hair. We have kept this book for him. We paid twenty-five drachmas. Mr. Stilianopoulos has sold his house. I have not sent the letters yet. Have they brought the newspaper? They quarrelled.

if, ἄν.
the German, ὁ Γερμανός.
when ? πότε;
at what o'clock ? τί ὥρα;
this morning, τὸ πρωΐ.
the hair, τὰ μαλλιά.

I keep, κρατέω.
twenty-five, εἰκοσιπέντε.
the drachma, ἡ δραχμή.
I sell, πουλῶ.
I quarrel, μαλλόνω.

SUBJUNCTIVE, IMPERATIVE, CONDITIONAL.

*On the compound tenses, and the conjunctions which introduce
them.*

Both the present and the Aorist Subjunctive have the same
endings as the Present Indicative, but it is usual to write η, ω in
the Subjunctive instead of the ει, ο, of the Indicative. The
Aorist Subjunctive has the same characteristic letter as the Indicative.

The particle νά is usually followed by the Subjunctive, and
may be translated into English in the following various ways.

1.   By the Infinitive, with or without *to* preceding it.

δεν 'ξέρω νὰ διαβάζω τουρκικά.   I cannot read Turkish.
θέλω νὰ φύγω.   I wish to go away.

2.   By the Imperative.

νὰ τόνε κυττάξῃς καλὰ καλά! Watch him well.
νά το γράφῃ αὐτός! Let him write it.

NOTE.—In this case and the following νὰ seems to be used after
some verb understood like πρεπει (il faut).

3.   By some equivalent of the verb ought.

νά το γράφω; am I to write it?
νὰ τόνε προσκαλέσω; Ought I to invite him?
νά σου διαβάσῃ τὸ γράμμα; Is he to read the letter to you?

4.   By some equivalent of the verb to wish.

νά τον πάρῃ ὁ λύκος! The deuce take him (ὁ λύκος = wolf).

A wish may also be expressed with νά omitted.

ὁ θεὸς φυλάξῃ.   God forbid.

νὰ occurs in oaths.

νὰ χαρῶ τὰ μάτια μου !   Bless my eyes.

The particle θά with the Subjunctive is used for the Future.

δὲν θά τον ξεχάσω ποτέ μου.   I shall never forget him.

The Subjunctive is also used after a large number of particles :

e.g. γιὰ νά in order that, so that.
γιὰ να μή, lest.
'σὰν, if.

and after the indefinite pronoun and adverb,

ὅποιος, who-ever.
ὅπου, wherever.

and after ἴσως, perhaps, instead of the future.

e.g. σοῦ το λέγω γιὰ νὰ μὴ νομίζῃς πῶς εἶνε κακὸς ἄνθρωπος.
I tell you, lest you should think that he is a bad man.
ἴσως ἔλθῃ ἀπόψε, he will perhaps come this evening.
ὅποιον ἴδῃς πές του πῶς—, whoever you see, tell him that—.

The compound tenses (perfect, pluperfect, future perfect) are formed from the tenses of ἔχω and the Aorist Infinitive. The ending for the present and Aorist infinitive is ει.

The Conditional is expressed by the particle θά or (Pres. Cond. only) by the imperfect of the verb θέλω, I wish (Imperfect ἤθελα, Aorist ἠθέλησα) and the Imperfect or Pluperfect of the verb. Occasionally the third person of the Imperfect of θέλω is used instead of the particle θὰ.

e.g. θὰ ἤμαστε εὐτυχεῖς }
ἤθελε ,,   ,,   } we should he happy.

The Imperfect Conditional of a dependent clause in English is translated by the Greek Imperfect Indicative.

If I were. ἂν ἤμουν.

In dependent clauses containing either a perf. cond. or pluperf. conditional verb, the verb is always translated into Greek by the Imperf. Conditional.

e.g. ἄν το ἤξερα θά το ἔλεγον may mean either if I knew it I should say it or—if I had known it, I should have said it.

The Imperative 2nd person (Pres. and Aorist endings ε, ετε) may only be used in affirmative sentences, in negative sentences μή (μήν) with the Subjunctive is used.

e.g. γράφε, γράψε, write ! $\left\{ \begin{array}{l} μὴ\ γράψῃs! \\ μὴ\ γράφῃs! \end{array} \right\}$ do not write !

The particle ἄς with the Subjunctive is the usual rendering of the Imperative for the first and third persons ; but it is not used for the second.

ἂς εἰσέλθῃ, let him come in.
ἂς γράψωμε, let us write.
ἂς γράψῃ, let him write.

Must is translated by πρέπει with νὰ following ; like the French il faut que.

e.g. πρέπει νὰ τόνε πληρώσῃs, you must pay him.

Exercise 12.—A.

Ποῦ εἶνε ὁ Κάρολος ; Τὸν γυρεύει ὁ ἰατρός· Θέλει νὰ ὁμιλήσῃ διὰ τὴν πούλησι τοῦ σπητιοῦ. Τί νὰ γράψω τοῦ ἀδελφοῦ μου ; Γράψε τοῦ ὅτι ἔφθασε ὁ πατέρας μου καὶ χαιρέτησέ τον ἀπὸ μέρος μου. Σὲ παρακαλῶ νὰ μὴ τὸ ξεχάσῃς. Τί θέλετε νά ἀγοράζητε ; Ξέρει γερμανικά ; Πότε θὰ φθάσῃ τὸ βαπόρι ; Θέλετε νὰ πουλήσητε τὰ ἄλογά σας ; Διάβασε τοῦτο τὸ γράμμα. Μὴν ἀκούσῃς ὅτι λέγουν αὐτοί. Ἄκουσε ὅτι διαβάζομεν, ἀλλὰ μὴ 'μιλᾶς. Σήμερα μᾶς ἔστειλαν ἕνα ὡραῖο κρασὶ ἀπὸ τὴν Σάμον. Θέλεις νά το δοκιμάσῃς ; Ἄν 'μπορέσω θά σου στείλω παράδες· Ἐλεύθερος θέλω νὰ ζῶ. Δὲν 'μποροῦν νὰ ξεχάσουν αὐτὴν τὴν ἰστορία. Μὴν τρέχῃς· ἔχομε καιρόν. Τρεξε ! Τρεξε ! ἄλλως θὰ ἀργήσῃς. Ἄς ἀκούσωμε ἕνα ἀπὸ τὰ τραγούδια ποῦ ξέρεις. Πρέπει νά τον γυρέψωμε.

ὁ ἰατρός, the doctor.
ἡ πούλησι, the sale.
ἀπὸ μέρος μου, for me.
παρακαλέω } I beg, request,
παρακαλῶ } (form for *please*).

γερμανικά, German.
δοκιμάζω, I try, taste.
ἐλεύθερος, free.
τὸ τραγοῦδι, the song.
ἄλλως, otherwise.

Exercise 12.—B.

May I bring you a glass of wine (trans. by νὰ and Subj.)?
Do you wish (θά and Subj.) to read the book that I have bought?
When will he send you the money? Do not forget (νὰ) to invite
him. Take care; the dog will bite you. If he does not pay me
I shall have no money to-morrow. As soon as you have read it
you will believe it. (As soon as = ἀφοῦ, use Aor. Subj.). Can he
swim? Have you not cut your hand? Run quickly, so as not
to come too late. We will not sell the horse so cheap. He has
forgotten to fix the hour. Ask him whether he is a Persian or a
Turk. We cannot believe such a thing. He must take the
letters to the post. May she open the window? Shut the
window. Go (περιπατῶ) quickly. Don't cut the paper. Don't
laugh. He will be angry if (ὅταν and Subj.) he hears it. When
will the lectures begin? I shall speak to him (Gen.) about (γιά)
them. Call your brother. Do not conceal it. When am I to
expect them to-morrow? You must take care not to take cold.
Let us go quicker. What can I offer you?

I take care, προσέχω.
I swim, κολυμπάω.
to come too late, ἀργέω.
cheap, φτηνά.
the Persian, ὁ Πέρσης.
such a thing, τέτοιο πρᾶγμα
the post, ἡ πόστα.

I cut, κόφτω.
I am angry, θυμόνω.
I conceal, κρύβω.
I expect, προσμένω. Αορ. ἐπρόσμενα.
  „   καρτερῶ. Αορ. (ἐ)καρτέρησα.
I offer, προσφέρω.

Passive Form.

The Passive proper seldom has its original meaning. Many
verbs occur only in this form, and then have mostly an active
meaning, *e.g.* ἔρχομαι, I come.

Some verbs occur in both active and passive form. Some of
these have the ordinary active and passive signification of the
verb; but the majority have—

1. A reflexive force : χτενίζω, I comb ; χτενίζουμαι, I comb my hair.

2. A reciprocal force : ἀνταμόμεστα, we met each other.

Present.

Endings :

Pers.	Sing.	Plur.
1	— ομαι (ουμαι)	— όμεστα (ούμεστα), (ομεθα)
2	— εσαι	— εστε (εσθε)
3	— εται	— ονται (— ουνται)

Endings for contracted verbs in άω :

Pers.	Sing.	Plur.
1	— οῦμαι	— ούμαστε
2	— ᾶσαι	— ᾶστε
3	— ᾶται	— οῦνται

For contracted verbs in έω and many in άω :

Pers.	Sing.	Plur.
1	— ιοῦμαι (— ιέμαι)	— ιόμεστα (— ιούμεστα)
2	— ιέσαι	— ιέστε (ιοῦστε)
3	— ιέται	— ιοῦνται

Imperfect.

Pers.	Sing.	Plur.
1	— όμουν	— ούμαστε (— ωμαστε)
2	— ουσουν (— όσουν[α])	— ούσαστε (— όσαστε)
3	— ουνταν (— όταν[ε])	— ουνταν (— όντουσαν)

For contracted verbs in άω :

Pers.	Sing.	Plur.
1	— ούμουν	— ούμαστε
2	— ούσουν(α)	— ούσαστε
3	— ούνταν(ε)	— οῦνταν(ε)

For some contracted verbs in έω and άω the same as above with ι prefixed, e.g. —ιούμουν, ιούσουν, &c.

Conjugate the Present and Imperfect Passive of the following verbs :—

πλένομαι, I wash myself (πλένω, I wash).
χάνομαι, I am lost, I perish (χάνω, I lose).
κοιμοῦμαι, I sleep.
στενοχωροῦμαι (στενοχωρέω, I am straitened, compel).
κάθομαι, I sit down.

Aorist.

Endings (Indicative) :

Pers.	Sing.	Plur.
1	— θηκα	— θήκαμε
2	— θηκες	— θήκετε (θήκατε)
3	— θηκε	— θηκαν (θήκανε)

The Aorist Passive is formed from the stem of the Aorist Active, the above Passive terminations being substituted for the σα, σας, &c., of the Active, and affecting the preceding consonant differently from the Active Aorist σ. The following table shows these differences :—

Present.	Aorist Act.	Aorist Pass.
ζ	ξ	χθ
e.g. πειράζω	ἐπείραξα	(ἐ)πειράχθηκα, to annoy.
φ	ψ	φθ
e.g. γράφω	ἔγραψα	ἐγράφθηκα, to write.
ζ, θ	σ	σθ
e.g. σχίζω	ἔσχισα	(ἐ)σχίσθηκε, to tear.
vowel or ν*	σ	θ
e.g. χάνω	ἔχασα	(ἐ)χάθηκα, to lose.
ἀγαπῶ	ἀγάπησα	ἀγαπήθηκα, to love.
αίν	αν	άθ
e.g. ζεσταίνω	ἐζέστανα	(ἐ)ζεστάθηκα, to warm.
λ and ρ	λ and ρ	λθ and ρθ
e.g. φέρω	ἔφερα	ἐφέρθηκα, to carry.

* Note.—Exceptions occur, such as ἀκούω, ἄκουσα, ἀκούσθηκα, to listen.

Subjunctive.

The Present has the same endings as the Indicative in pronunciation ; but in writing it is customary to substitute ω for ο in the first person singular, according to the ancient rule.
The Aorist has the following :—

Sing.	*Plur.*
— ῶ	— οῦμε
— ῇς	— ῆτε
— ῇ	— οῦνε

These endings are affixed to the verb, after the Indicative ending ηκα has been taken away, *e.g.* Indicative, ἀκούσθηκα, I was heard ; Subj. νὰ ἀκουσθῶ.

The Passive Subjunctive is used and the Future formed in the same way as in the Active, *e.g.* θὰ ἀκουσθῶ, I shall be heard.

Imperative.

Present endings :   — οῦ

                      — ᾶστε

Aorist : The second person singular of the Passive Aorist Imperative has the same characteristic letter as the Active, when that letter is σ, ψ, or ξ.

Present.	Act. Aorist.	Imperat. Aor. Pass.
e.g. γράφω	ἔγραψα	γράψου

Verbs which have no active take ς, ψ, or ξ in the Pass. Aor. Pass. in the same way, if the Aorist Active would have taken one of these letters.

Pres.	Act. Aor. (not used).	Imperat. Aor. Pass.
e.g. κοιμοῦμαι	ἐκοίμασα	κοιμάσου

Verbs in λ, ρ take σ :

Pres.	Act. Aorist.	Imperat. Aor. Pass.
e.g. φέρω	ἔφερα	φέρσου

The second person plural is the same as the Passive Aorist Subjunctive.

N.B.—It will be observed that this Imperative is derived from the ancient Middle Aorist, and not from the Passive.

Infinitive.

The Aorist is used in the formation of compound tenses, and is the same as the third person of Aorist Subjunctive in pronunciation, the η of the Subjunctive becoming η in the Infinitive.

Pres.	Pass. Aorist.	Aorist Infinitive.
e.g. δανείζομαι	(ἐ)δανείσθηκα	δανεισθῆ, to borrow.

Compound Tenses.

The formation of these and the Conditional is obvious, and may be seen in the table.

Perfect Participle.

The ending is μένος (μένη, μένο). The Perfect Participle is formed from the Passive Aorist in the following manner :—

1. σθ in the Passive Aorist becomes σμένος in the Perfect Participle :

Pres.	Act. Aor.	Pass. Aor.	Perf. Pass. Part.
e.g. σχίζω, I tear.	ἔσχισα	(ἐ)σχίσθηκα	σχισμένος

2. χθ becomes γμένος :

e.g. πειράζω, I annoy.	ἐπείραξα	(ἐ)πειράχθηκα	πειραγμένος

3. φθ becomes μμένος :

e.g. γράφω, I write.	ἔγραψα	ἐγράφθηκα	γραμμένος

4. θ usually becomes μένος :

e.g. τυπόνω, I press.	ἐτύπωσα	(ἐ)τυπώθηκε	τυπωμένος

Some verbs in ἀω have σμένος :

διψάω, I thirst.   —   —   διψασμένος
πεινάω, I hunger.   —   —   πεινασμένος

The Perfect Passive Participle is often used instead of the
Aorist Infinitive in active or passive compound tenses. Instead
of εἶχα γράψει, we have εἶχα γραμμένο, I had written ; and instead
of εἶχε γραφθῆ, we more commonly have ἦτανε γραμμένον, it had
been written.

Intransitive verbs may have a Perfect Passive Participle
(cf. διψάω and πεινάω above). περνάω, I pass, has περασμένος.

Examples of some verbs in the Passive Voice (where the
Active is not given there is none) :—

Pres.	Aorist.	Aor. Imp.	Perf. Part.	Active.
χάνομαι	(ἐ)χάθηκα	χάσου	χαμένος	χάνω, I lose.
τραβιοῦμαι	(ἐ)τραβήχθηκα	τραβήξου	τραβηγμένος	τραβῶ, I draw.
συλλογίζομαι (συλλογιοῦμαι), I consider.	(ἐ)συλλογίσθηκα	συλλογίσου	συλλογισμένος, (thoughtful, pensive).	
φοβοῦμαι (I am afraid)	(ἐ)φοβήθηκα	φοβήσου	—	(φοβίζω), (I make afraid)
κοιμοῦμαι, I sleep.	(ἐ)κοιμήθηκα	κοιμήσου	—	—
ῥίχνομαι	(ἐρ)ρίχτηκα*	ρίξου	ριγμένος	ῥίχνω, I throw.
κουράζομαι	(ἐ)κουράστηκα	—	κουρασμένος	κουράζω, I tire.

* The ending θηκα is often pronounced τηκα, especially
after χ, φ, σ.

σιχαίνομαι (I dislike)	(ἐ)σιχάθηκα	σιχάσου	σιχαμένος (loathsome)	—
λερνόμαι	(ἐ)λερώθηκα	λερώσου	λερομένος (dirty)	λερόνω, I soil.
ξουρίζομαι	(ἐ)ξουρίσθηκα	ξουρίσου	ξουρισμένος	ξουρίζω, I shave.
θυμοῦμαι (I remember)	(ἐ)θυμήθηκα	θυμήσου	—	(θυμίζω)
χρειάζομαι (I need)	(ἐ)χρειάσθηκα	—	—	—
ξαπλόνομαι (I go to bed)	(ἐ)ξαπλώθηκα	ξαπλώσου	ξαπλομένος	ξαπλόνω, I stretch.

Exercise 13.—A.

Τόνε φοβᾶσαι; ὄχι, δὲν τόνε φοβοῦμαι καθόλου. Τὸν καιρὸ ὅπου ἤμουνα 'ς τὴ Σύρο δὲν τον ἐφοβούμουν, ἀλλὰ ἐδῶ τον ἐφοβήθηκα. Μή τον φοβᾶσαι! εἶνε καλὸς ἄνθρωπος· δὲν θά σε πειράξῃ. "Οτι καὶ ἄν ἴδω δὲν θὰ φοβοῦμαι. Κοιμᾶται ὁ ἀδελφός σου; "Οχι, δὲν ἐκοιμήθηκε ἀκόμη. 'Αφοῦ εἶσαι κουρασμένος νὰ κοιμηθῇς. Κοιμήσου. Κύτταξε μὴ λερωθῇς· εἶνε λάσπαις 'ς τὸν δρόμο. Τὸ μανδύλι σου εἶνε λερωμένο. Τὸ σκυλί μας 'χάθηκε. Νὰ χαθῇς, μασκαρᾶ! Μὴν ἀφήσῃς τὰ γράμματα 'ς τὸ τραπέζι, γιατὶ θὰ χαθοῦν. 'Τραβήχθηκε 'ς τὴν κάμαρά μου. Τί συλλογιέσαι; Συλλογίζομαι τὸν φίλο μου. Δὲν πίνω πλιὸ κρασί· τὸ 'σιχάθηκα. ὁ κλέφτης ρίχθηκε 'πάνω του καί τον ἐσκότωσε. Τί ὥρα θὰ κοιμηθῇς; Θυμᾶσαι τὸν νέον ἐκεῖνον ποῦ 'μιλοῦσε τὰ 'Αρμενικά; Ποῦ κοιμᾶστε; 'Εκεῖνο τὸν καιρὸν ἐβρισκότανε 'ς τὴ Βιέννη.

ὄχι, no.
τὸν καιρὸν ὅπου, when.
ἡ Σύρος, Syros.
ἀλλά, but.
ὅτι καὶ ἄν, whenever.
κυττάζω, I look.
ἡ λάσπη, the mud.
ὁ δρόμος, the way, road.
τὸ μανδύλι, the handkerchief.

νὰ χαθῇς, a curse (may you be lost).
ὁ μασκαρᾶς, masker—fool, zany.
δὲν—πλιό, no more.
ὁ κλέφτης, the thief, robber.
σκοτόνω, I kill.
τὰ 'Αρμενικά, Armenian.
'Βρίσκομαι, (εὑρίσκομαι) I am (Je me trouve).
ἡ Βιέννη, Vienna.

Exercise 13.—B.

I am afraid of him (Acc.) (use Aorist of verb). Now I am thinking of your friend (use Aor. of συλλογίζομαι or θυμοῦμαι). You ought to consider that. The letters are all lost. I have been reading and writing the whole day; now I am tired. I was in Nauplia last week (say the past week). He was dressed in black. Dress yourself. He is not dressed yet. I could not go to sleep. He will get shaved. He stretched himself on the ground (χάμου) and fell asleep. Do you want (σοῦ χρειάζεται) the knife still? Lie down on the sofa. They met one another.

Nauplia, τὰ Ναύπλια.
I dress, 'ντύνω (ἐνδύνω).
I dress myself, 'ντύνομαι. Aorist, 'ντύθηκα. Imperat. Aor. 'ντύσου. Participle Perf. Pass. 'ντυμένος.

the sofa, ὁ καναπές.
to meet one another, πιάνομαι (from πιάνω, I take). Aorist, 'πιάσθηκα. Perf. Pass. Part., πιασμένος.

Verbs with Contracted Present (Indicative and Subjunctive) and Aorist Subjunctive.

In speaking some verbs are contracted in the tenses above referred to. The contractions are as follows :—

Present Indic.	Contracted form.	Present Indic.	Contracted form.
λέγω, I say.	λέω	πάγω, I go.	πάω
λέγεις	λές	πάγεις	πᾶς
λέγει	λέει	πάγει	πάει
λέγομε	λέμε	πάγομε	πᾶμε
λέγετε	λέτε	πάγετε	πᾶτε
λέγουνε	λένε	πάγουν(ε)	πᾶνε

Note.—The shortened forms are also used for the Aorist Subjunctive, e.g. ποῦ νὰ πάω; where shall I go?

F

Present Indic.	Contracted form.	Aorist Subj.	Contracted form.
τρώγω, I eat. (τρώνω)	—	(νὰ) φάγω	φάω, used as Aor. Subj. of τρώγω.
τρώγεις	τρῶς	φάγεις	φᾶς
τρώγει	τρώει	φάγει	φάει
τρώγομε	τρῶμε	φάγαμε	φᾶμε
τρώγετε	τρῶτε	φάγετε	φᾶτε
τρώγουν(ε)	τρῶνε	φάγουνε	φᾶνε

Present Indic.	Contracted form.	Aorist Subj.	Contracted form.
θέλω, I wish.	—	κλαίω (κλαίγω)	I weep.
θέλεις	θές	κλαίεις	κλαῖς
θέλει	θέ	κλαίει	κλαῖ
θέλομε	θέμε	κλαίομε	κλαῖμε
θέλετε	θέτε	κλαίετε	κλαῖτε
θέλουν(ε)	θένε	κλαίουνε	κλαῖνε

φταίω, I am wrong, is contracted like κλαίω.

Exercise 14.—A.

Ποῦ θὰ πᾷς ἀπόψε; Θὰ πάω ʼς τὸ θέατρο; Σὲ ποιὸ θέατρο; ʼΣ τὸ θέατρο τῆς ᾽Αλάμβρας. ᾽Επείνασα· πᾶμε νὰ φᾶμε. Τί θὰ φᾶνε σήμερα; Αὐτοὶ δὲν τρῶνε ποτὲ φροῦτα. Διατί; φοβοῦνται μή τους βλάψῃ. Τί θές; θέλω νὰ πλύσω τὰ χέρια μου. Τί κλαῖς, κορίτζι; Μὲ ἐδάγκασε τὸ σκυλί. Σὺ φταῖς, δὲν ἔπρεπε νὰ το σπρώξῃς. Ποιὸς λέει ὅτι ἔφθασε ὁ ὑπουργός; ᾽Εμεῖς το λέμε.

τὰ φροῦτα, the fruit.
πλύνω (πλένω), I wash.
δαγκάνω, I bite.

σπρώχνω, I push.
ὁ ὑπουργός, the (cabinet) minister.

Exercise 14.— B.

Let us go and dine (say eat). Where is he going? He is going to get shaved. What are you eating? I am eating fruit. What would you like (τί θές) to eat? Shall I go home now? What are you crying for? We have lost our money. You dine very late. What do you say? I say that you are wrong. No, your brothers are wrong.

IRREGULAR VERBS.

Present Indic.		Aorist.	Aorist Subj.	Aorist Imperative.		Perf. Pass. Part.
				Sing.	Plur.	
ἀναιβαίνω (ἀναβαίνω) (ἀνηβαίνω)	}I go up	ἀνέβηκα	ἀναιβῶ	ἀναίβα	{ ἀναιβῆτε ἀναιβᾶτε	—
ἀποθαίνω (παιθαίνω)	}I die	{ ἀπόθανα πέθανα	}πεθάνω	—	—	ἀποθαμμένος
ἀρέσω, I please		ἄρεσα	ἀρέσω			
ἀφήνω, I leave		ἄφησα ἀφῆκα	ἀφήσω ἀφήκω	ἄφησε ἄφες ἄς	ἀφῆστε ἀφῆτε	ἀφημένος
βάζω (βάλλω) (βάνω)	}I put, lay	ἔβαλα	βάλω	βάλε	—	βαλμένος
	Pass.	(ἐ)βάλθηκα				
βαριοῦμαι (βαριέμαι)	}I am weary	(ἐ)βαρέθηκα				
βγάζω (βγάλλω) (βγάνω)	}I pull out	ἔβγαλα	βγάλω	βγάλε	βγάλτε	βγαλμένος βγαμένος
	Pass.	(ἐ)βγάλθηκα				
βγαίνω, I go out		(ἐ)βγῆκα ἤβγα	ἔβγω βγῶ			
βλέπω, I see		εἶδα	ἰδῶ διῶ	ἰδές	—	ἰδωμένος
βρέχω, I wet		ἔβρεξα	βρέξω	βρέξε	—	βρεγμένος
	Pass.	βρεχθῶ βραχῶ	—	—		βρεμμένος
βρίσκω (εὑρίσκω)	}I find	{ ηὗρα βρῆκα (εὑρῆκα)	βρῶ εὕρω	βρέ εὑρέ	βρῆτε εὑρῆτε	
	Pass.	βρέθηκα				

NOTE.—'βγάλλω is derived by metathesis from ἐκβάλλω, and similarly 'βγαίνω from ἐκβαίνω.

Exercise 15.—A.

Ποιὸς εἶνε κάτω; Εἶνε ὁ κὺρ Μιχάλης. Ἃς ἀνεβῇ μιὰ στιγμή.
Δὲν 'μπορῶ νὰ ἀναιβῶ, γιατὶ πονεῖ τὸ ποδάρι μου. Σοῦ ἄρεσε ὁ
περίπατος; Μάλιστα, μοῦ ἄρεσε πολύ. Τὸ καπέλο μου 'χάθηκε· δέν
το βλέπω πουθενά. Μήπως τὸ ἄφησες 'ς τὴν καμαρά μου; Γύρεψέ
το νὰ τόβρῃς (τὸ βρῆς). Δέν το ηὗρα καὶ δὲν πιστεύω ὅτι θὰ τόβρω.
Νά το· ἡ δοῦλα το εἶχε βάλει 'ς τὸ ἁρμάρι. Θὰ πᾷς 'ς τὸ μαγαζί
τώρα; βαριοῦμαι νὰ πάω· εἶνε μακρειά. Βαρέθηκα τὴ ζωή. Μπορεῖς
νὰ βγάλῃς αὐτὸ τὸ καρφί; Βγαίνει κάθε βράδυ 'ς ταῖς ὀχτὼ ὥραις.
Ἔβγα ἀπ' ἐκεῖ νὰ σὲ ἰδῶ. Εἶδες τὸν ἀδελφόν μου. Ὄχι, δέν τον εἶδα
οὔτε χτὲς οὔτε σήμερα. Τὸ μανδύλι μου εἶνε βρέμμενο· στέγνωσέ το.
Πῶς 'βρέθηκες ἐδῶ; (How is it you are here?) Ὁ πατέρας σου ζῇ
ἀκόμη; Ὄχι, ἀπόθανε ἀπ' ἐδῶ καὶ δύο χρόνια.

κάτω, downstairs.	τὸ ἀρμάρι, the cupboard.
κὺρ, abbreviation of κύριος.	μακρειά, far.
ἡ στιγμή, the moment.	ἡ ζωή, the life.
πονῶ, I hurt.	τὸ καρφί, the nail.
τὸ ποδάρι, the foot.	τὸ βράδυ, the evening.
ὁ περίπατος, the walk.	στεγνόνω, I dry.
δὲν—πουθενά, nowhere.	ἀπ' ἐδῶ καὶ δύο χρόνια, two years ago.
μήπως, perhaps.	

Exercise 15.—B.

Have you found my ring? What ring? I never saw you
with (a) ring. Yes, I forgot that I had not shown it to you; I
bought it yesterday evening. I have left it (lying) about somewhere (πουθενά), but I don't remember where. Did he find the
way alone? The flowers pleased me very much. I shall have a
tooth pulled out (use Active). We saw him yesterday with his
father. That is impossible, his father is not here; it must have
been his brother (θὰ ἦτο, &c.). When will you go out to-morrow
evening? I shall not go out; I have too much to do (translate
much work). Do you see this scarf-pin? is it not pretty? I am
thoroughly tired of that sort of thing.

never, δὲν—ποτέ.	the tooth, τὸ δόντι.
yesterday evening, ψές τὸ βράδυ.	the work, ἡ δουλειά.
the flower, τὸ λουλοῦδι.	scarf-pin, ἡ καρφίτζα.

IRREGULAR VERBS—(continued).

Present Indic.	Aorist.	Aorist Subj.	Aorist Imperative. Sing.	Plur.	Perf. Pass. Part.
γίνομαι { I happen, become }	ἔγινα (ἐ)γείνηκα	γίνω γενῶ	γεῖνε γείνου	—	γινωμένος
δίνω } I give (δίδω) }	{ ἔδωσα { ἔδωκα	δώσω δώκω	δός —	δόσετε —	δομένος δοσμένος
ἔρχομαι, I come	ἦλθα ἦρθα	ἔλθω ἔρθω	ἔλα	ἐλᾶτε	ἐρχωμένος
κάθομαι } I sit, live κάθουμαι }	{ ἐκάθησα { ἔκατσα	καθήσω κάτσω	κάθισε κάτσε	καθήστε	καθισμένος
καίω }-I burn καύω }	{ ἔκαψα { Pass. (ἐ)κάηκα	κάψω Pass. καῶ	κάψε	κάψτε	καμμένος
κάμνω } do, make κάνω }	ἔκαμα	κάμω	κάμε	κάμετε	καμωμένος
καταλαβαίνω } I under- καταλάβω } stand }	(ἐ)κατάλαβα				
καταβαίνω, I go down, like ἀναβαίνω					
κλαίω, I weep	ἔκλαψα	κλάψω	κλάψε	κλάψτε	κλαμμένος
λαμβάνω } I receive λαβαίνω }	ἔλαβα				
λέγω, I say	εἶπα	εἴπω 'πῶ	πές εἰπές	πῆτε π+τε εἰπῆτε εἰπέτε	εἰπωμένος
μαθαίνω { I learn, μανθάνω { experience }	ἔμαθα	μάθω	μάθε	μάθετε	μαθημένος
μαζόνω } I collect μαζεύω }	{ ἐμάζωξα { ἐμάζεψα	μαζώξω μαζέψω	μάζωξε μάζεψε	μαζώξετε μαζέψτε	μαζεμμίνος
μεθῶ, I get drunk	(ἐ)μέθυσα	μεθύσω	μέθυσε	μεθύστε	μεθυσμένος
μπαίνω } I go in (ἐμβαίνω) }	{ ἐμβῆκα { ἐμπῆκα	ἔμπω	ἔμπα	ἐμπᾶτε	
ντρέπομαι { I feel shy, (ἐντρέπομαι) { I am { ashamed }	ἐντράπηκα	'ντραπῶ			

Exercise 16.—A.

Πότε ἔγινε αὐτό; Τὰ πορτογάλλια δὲν εἶνε ἀκόμη γινωμένα (ripe). Θὰ σε δείρω ἄν το πῆς σὲ κανένα ἄλλον. Δόσε μου ἕνα ἀπ' αὐτὰ τὰ ὡραῖα τριαντάφυλλα. Θά σου δώσω ὅλα. Σὲ εὐχαριστῶ. Σὲ πιρακαλῶ νὰ μου δώσῃς τὸ μπιλιέττο. Ἀπὸ ποῦ ἔρχεσαι; Ἔρχομαι ἀπὸ τὸ σπῆτι καὶ πάω 's τὸ σχολειό. Δὲν ἦλθαν ἀκόμη οἱ φίλοι σας; Ὄχι, δὲν ἦλθαν. Πότε θἄρθῃς νὰ με ἰδῇς; Ἐλᾶτε 'δῶ, θὰ σε πῶ κάτι τι. Ποῦ κάθεσαι τώρα; Κάθομαι 's τὸν Φραγκομαχαλλᾶ. Κάτζε (ὀ)λίγο νὰ σου διαβάσω ἕνα ποίημα. Πόσον καιρὸν ἐκάθισες 's τὴν Γερμανίαν;

Κάψε αὐτὸ τὸ γράμμα γιὰ νὰ μή το βρῇ κανεὶς καί το διαβάσῃ. Τὸ σπῆτι (ἐ)κάηκε. Τί θὰ κάμῃς ἀπόψε; Θὰ μείνω ’ς τὸ σπῆτι. Δὲν ξέρω ποῦ νὰ πάω. Κατάλαβες τί σοῦπα (= σοῦ εἶπα); Μάλιστα, καταλαβαίνω ὅλα, ἀλλὰ δὲν μπορῶ νά σε ἀπαντήσω. Θά το ’πῇς τοῦ δασκάλου; Μάλιστα, θά τού το ’πῶ. Ποῦ ἔμαθες τὰ ρωμάϊκα; Τἄμαθα (τὰ ἔμαθα) ’ς τὴν πολι καὶ ’ς τὰς ᾿Αθήνας. Εἶνε ἄρρωστος αὐτὸς ὁ ἄνθρωπος; Ὄχι, εἶνε μόνον μεθυσμένος· κάθε ἑβδομάδα δύο φοραὶς μεθᾷ. Ἔμπα μέσα! Ὄχι, ντρέπομαι νάμπω. Γιατὶ νάντραπῇς;

τὸ πορτογάλλι, the orange.	ὁ Φραγκομαχαλλᾶς, the Frankish quarter.
τὸ τριαντάφυλλο, the rose.	τὸ ποίημα, the poem.
εὐχαριπτῶ, I thank.	ἀπαντῶ, I answer.
τὸ σχολειό, the school.	
	ἡ ἑβδομάδα, the week.

Exercise 16.—P.

You have come (too) late; I have no time now to speak to (with μέ) you. Come to me (say to my house) at ten o'clock to-morrow, but do not forget the hour. Can you tell me where Mr. Zamacopoulos lives? Come with me and I will show you the house. Tell him not to come to-morrow (use subj.) Pick up all the letters that are (lying) on the ground and burn them. Give me the key. Haven't I given it to you? Shall I say anything else (ἄλλο τίποτε) to your brother? Yes, give him this bottle of wine, and ask him to try it. We did not understand what he said. He speaks so quickly that (ὅπου) no one can understand him (κανείς—δὲν). I learnt to-day, that the church was burnt (down). Do not go in : the dog will bite you. Tell me, are the ladies of Smyrna beautiful? Indeed (εἶνε ἀλήθεια ὅτι) I have never seen prettier women anywhere. About a hundred people were gathered together on the spot where the murder took place. We have lived four years in this house. Sit down for a little ! Thank you, I won't sit down, I I haven't time. Come down out of that tree (say from), you young rascal, or I will give you the stick. Please give (νὰ and subj.) me ink and paper; I want to write to my brother. Do not leave the wine on the table ; I know quite well (σιγοῦρα) that he will get drunk if he finds it.

at ten o'clock, ’s ταὶς δέκα ὥραις.	the murder, ὁ φόνος.
the hour, ἡ ὥρα.	four, τέσσαρα.
I try, δοκιμάζω.	the tree, τὸ δένδρο (δέντρο).
about a hundred, καμμιὰ ἑκατοσταριά.	I give the stick, σαπίζω ἀπὸ ξύλον.
the spot, τὸ μέρος.	

Irregular Verbs—(continued).

Pres. Indic.	Aorist Indic.	Aorist Subj.	Aorist Imperative. Sing.	Plur.	Perf. Pass. Part.
παθαίνω, I suffer	ἔπαθα	πάθω	πάθε	πάθετε	
παίρνω, I take	(ἐ)πῆρα	πάρω	πάρε	πάρτε	παρμένος
	Passive (ἐ)πάρθηκα	Passive παρθῶ			
πετῶ { I fly away, I throw away }	(ἐ)πέταξα	πετάξω	πέταξε	πετάξτε	πεταγμένος
πηγαίνω, I go	ἐπῆγα	πάω Pres. Subj.	πήγαινε	—	πηγαιμένος
		πάω	(νὰ) πᾶς ἄμε	πᾶτε ἄμετε	
πίνω, I drink	ἔπια ἤπια	πιῶ	πίε	πίετε	πιωμένος, drunken
πέφτω, I fall	ἔπεσα	πέσω	πέσε	πέστε	πεσμένος
πλέω, I sail	ἔπλευσα	πλεύσω	πλεῦσε	πλεύσετε	
πνέω, I breathe	ἔπνευσα	πνεύσω	πνεῦσε	πνεύσετε	
πρήσκομαι { I swell up }	(ἐ)πρήσθηκα	πρησθῶ	—	—	πρησμένος
σηκόνω, I lift up Passive.	ἐσήκωσα	σηκώσω	σήκωσε	σηκῶστε	σηκωμένος
σηκόνομαι, I stand up	(ἐ)σηκώθηκα	σηκωθῶ	σηκώσου σήκου σήκω	σηκωθῆτε	
σταίνω { I erect, set up } (στήνω)	ἔστησα	στήσω	στῆσε	στήσετε	στημένος
στέκω { I stand, stand still } στέκομαι	(ἐ)στάθηκα	σταθῶ	στάσου Pres. Imper. στέκα	σταθῆτε	
τρέφω, I nourish	ἔθρεψα	θρέψω	θρέψε	θρέψετε	θρεμμένος
τρέχω, I run	ἔτρεξα	τρέξω	τρέξε Pres. Imperative. τρέχα	τρέξετε τρεχᾶτε	
τρώγω, I eat	ἔφαγα Pass. (ἐ)φαγώθηκα	φάγω φάω	φάγε φᾶ	φάγετε φᾶτε	φαγομένος
τυχαίνω, I happen	ἔτυχα	τύχω			
ὑπόσχομαι, I promise	ὑποσχέθηκα	ὑποσχεθῶ	ὑπόσχου	ὑπόσχεσθε	ὑποσχεμένος
φαίνομαι, I appear	(ἐ)φάνηκα	φανῶ	φανοῦ	φανῆτε	
φεύγω, I go away	ἔφυγα	φύγω	φύγε Pres. Imperative. φεῦγα	φύγετε φευγᾶτε	
χαίρομαι χαίρω } I rejoice	(ἐ)χάρηκα	χαρῶ	χαροῦ	χαρῆτε	
χορταίνω { I am satisfied }	(ἐ)χόρτασα	χορτάσω	χόρτασε	χορτάστε	χορτασμένος

Exercise 17.—A.

Ἔπεσα κάτω καὶ ἐχτύπησα τὸ κεφάλι μου. Τί ἔπαθες; (What has happened to you?) Ποιὸς 'πῆρε τὰ σιγάρα μου; Δέν τα 'πῆρε κανείς. Μὴ πάρῃς τὸ ψαλίδι, γιατί τὸ χρειάζομαι. Πόσα κονδύλια μου ἔχεις παρμένα ὥς τώρα; πρέπει νὰ εἶνε καμμιὰ δεκαριά. Πήγαινε γρήγορα! Δὲν ἔχομε καιρὸν νὰ χάσωμε (to lose). Μὲ 'κέντησε μιὰ μέλισσα καὶ 'πρήστηκε τὸ χέρι μου. Τὸ βελόνι ἔπεσε κάτω· σήκωσέ το. Σήκου! σήκου! δέκα ὧραις (ἐ)κοιμήθηκες. Σάν τον εἶδα ἀπὸ μακρειὰ ἐστάθηκα νὰ κρυφθῶ. Στάσου, μὴν φύγῃς ἀπὸ 'δῶ. Τί στέκεσαι καί με κυττάζεις; Τρέχα γρήγορα! φέρε μου τὸ φαγί! Ἔτυχε μιὰ μέρα νὰ ἤμαστε μαζύ. Τοῦ ὑποσχέθηκα νά τον πληρώσω αὔριον. Μοῦ ἐφάνηκε κάπως παράξενος. Ἐχάρηκα πολὺ ποὺ (when) ἄκουσα πῶς ὁ πατέρας σου ἔγινε καλά. Σήμερα ἔφαγα πολὺ καὶ μ' ὅλο τοῦτο δὲν ἐχόρτασα.

χτυπῶ, I strike.	τὸ βελόνι, the needle.
τὸ κεφάλι, the head.	σάν, when.
τὸ σιγάρο, the cigarette.	κρύβω, I hide.
τὸ ψαλίδι, the scissors.	μαζύ, together.
τὸ κονδύλι, the pen.	κάπως, somewhat.
καμμιὰ δεκαριά, about ten.	παράξενος, wonderful.
κεντάω, I sting.	μ' ὅλο τοῦτο, in spite of that.
ἡ μέλισσα, the bee.	

Exercise 17.—B.

Take the knife; I do not want it any longer. Take care that you don't fall. There is no lamp on the stairs. Your hand is swollen. What has happened to you? A bee stung me. Why is he not up yet? It is past seven o'clock (εἶνε αἱ ἑφτὰ περασμέναις). He must get up every morning at six o'clock. Stop! (στάσου). Where are you going? No one is allowed to go in there. Do not run so quickly, or you will fall. You promised me to come. Why did you not keep your word? Make no promises (promise nothing) that you cannot keep. I beg of you not to go away. He appears to be an Englishman. How (τί) do you do? I am very well, thank you. I am glad, (to hear it). That seems wonderful to me.

the stairs, ἡ σκάλα.	I keep, κρατῶ, κρατέω.
seven o'clock, ἑφτὰ ὧραις.	the Englishman, ὁ Ἄγγλος, Ὁ Ἰγγλέζος.
no one is permitted, δὲν ἐπιτρέπεται σὲ κανένα.	well, καλά.

IMPERSONAL VERBS.

Pres. Indic.	Aorist.	Aorist Subj.
ἀστράφτει, it lightens.	ἄστραψε	ἀστράψῃ
βραδειάζει, it grows late.	(ἐ)βράδειασε	βραδειάσῃ
βρέχει, it rains.	ἔβρεξε	βρέξῃ
νυχτόνει, night comes on.	(ἐ)νύχτωσε	νυχτώσῃ
βροντᾷ, it thunders.	(ἐ)βρόντησε	βροντήσῃ
χιονίζει, it snows.	(ἐ)χιόνισε	χιονίσῃ
ψηχαλίζει, it drizzles.	(ἐ)ψηχάλισε	ψηχαλίσῃ

Imperfect.

πρέπει, it is necessary. (ἔπρεπε, no Aorist).

μέλει, it concerns. ἔμελε ,, ,,

νοιάζει, it concerns (τί σε νοιάζει; What does it matter to you?)

Aorist.

κακοφαίνεται, it displeases. κακοφάνηκε κακοφανῇ

Exercise 18.—A.

Διατί δὲν βγαίνεις; Μοῦ φαίνεται πῶς θὰ βρέξῃ. 'Σ τὴ Σμύρνη δὲν χιονίζει συχνά. Ἐβράδειασε, πρέπει νὰ φύγωμε. Ὄχι, κάτσε ἀκόμη ὀλίγο· ἴσα μὲ (till) ταῖς ἔνδεκα ἔχετε καιρόν. Νὰ ποὺ πέφτει βροχή (There is rain falling already). Βροντᾷ καὶ ἀστράφτει. Δὲν μου μέλει δι' αὐτό (That does not matter to me).

συχνά, often.

Exercise 18.—B.

I am sorry (it displeases me) that I cannot give you an umbrella; it is raining hard. It has been thundering and lightening. You must get off, before night comes on, so that you may not lose your way. It does not matter so much to me for (διά) the money, as for the friend I have lost.

the umbrella, ἡ ὀμπρέλλα.   hard, τρομερά.

NUMERALS.

Cardinals.	Ordinals.
1. ἕνας, μιά, ἕνα	πρῶτος, πρώτη, πρῶτο(ν), first
2. δύο (δυό)	δεύτερος, η, ο(ν)
3. τρεῖς, τρία	τρίτος, η, ο(ν)
4. τέσσεροι (τέσσερις), τέσσαραις, τέσσερα	τέταρτος, η, ο(ν)
5. πέντε	πέφτος, η, ο(ν)
6. ἕξι	ἕκτος
7. ἐφτά	ἕβδομος
8. ὀχτώ	ὄγδοος
9. ἐννιά	ἔννατος
10. δέκα	δέκατος
11. ἕντεκα (ἕνδεκα)	ἐνδέκατος
12. δώδεκα	δωδέκατος
13. δεκατρεῖς, δεκατρία	δέκατος τρίτος
14. δεκατέσσεροι (δεκατέσσερις), δεκατέσσερες, δεκατέσσαρα	„ τέταρτος
15. δεκαπέντε	
16. δεκάξι, δεκαέξι	
17. δεκαφτά	
18. δεκοχτώ	
19. δεκαννιά	
20. εἴκοσι	εἰκοστός
21. εἴκοσι ἕνας, εἴκοσι μιά, εἴκοσι ἕνα	εἰκοστὸς πρῶτος
22. εἴκοσι δυό	„ δεύτερος
23. εἴκοσι τρεῖς, εἴκοσι τρία	
24. εἴκοσι τέσσαροι (τέσσαρις, τέσσαραις, τέσσαρα)	
25. εἴκοσι πέντε	
26. „ ἕξι	
27. „ ἐφτά	
28. „ ὀχτώ	
29. „ ἐννιά	
30. τριάντα	τριακοστός
40. σαράντα	τεσσαρακοστός
50. πενῆντα	πεντηκοστός
60. ἑξῆντα	ἑξηκοστός
70. ἑβδομῆντα	ἑβδομηκοστός

Cardinals.	Ordinals.
80. ὀγδῶντα (ὀγδοῆντα)	ὀγδοηκοστός
90. ἐνενῆντα	ἐνενηκοστός
100. ἑκατό	ἑκατοστός
101. „ μιά	
102. „ δύο	
110. „ δέκα	
120. „ εἴκοσι	
200. διακόσιοι, διακόσιαις, διακόσια	διακοσιοστός
300. τρακόσιοι, &c.	τριακοσιοστός
400. τετρακόσιοι	τετρακοσιοστός
500. πεντακόσιοι	πεντακοσιοστός
600. ἑξακόσιοι	ἑξακοσιοστός
700. ἑφτακόσιοι	ἑπτακοσιοστός
800. ὀχτακόσιοι	ὀκτακοσιοστός
900. ἐννεακόσιοι	ἐνεακοσιοστός
1,000. χίλιοι	χιλιοστός
2,000. δύο χιλιάδαις	δὶς χιλιοστός
3,000. τρεῖς „	τρὶς „
4,000. τέσσαραις χιλιάδαις	
10,000. δέκα „	μυριοστός
100,000. ἑκατὸ „	ἑκατοντάκις μυριοστός
1,000,000. ἕνα μιλιοῦνι	μιλιουνιοστός
ἕνα ἑκατομμύριο.	

The Cardinals 1—4 are declined, and also from 200 upwards. ἕνας has already been declined as the indefinite article.

Δύο has a genitive δυονῶν. τρεῖς, τέσσαρες are declined as follows :—

	Masc.	Fem.	Neut.
Nom. and Acc.	τρεῖς	τρεῖς	τρία
Gen.	τριῶν	τριῶν	τριῶν

	Masc.	Fem.	Neut.
Nom.	τέσσαροι (τέσσαρις)	τέσσαραις	τέσσαρα
Acc.	τέσσαρους (τέσσαρις)	„	„
Gen.	τεσσάρων	τεσσάρων	τεσσάρων

The numbers above 200 are declined regularly.

The ordinals above 30 are most commonly expressed by means of the cardinals.

Numeral nouns may be formed by adding one of the suffixes -αριά, -άρα, -άρι, -άρης.

δωδεκαριά, a dozen.
σαρανταριά, number of forty—two score.
πεντάρα or πεντάρι (a piece of money of five lepta), a halfpenny.
δεκάρι (ten lepta), a penny.
τριαντάρης, a person thirty years old.
πενηντάρης, a person fifty years old.

DISTRIBUTIVE AND FRACTIONAL NUMERALS.

Distributives are expressed by means of the cardinals with the preposition ἀπὸ prefixed, e.g. ἀπὸ δυό, two apiece, ἀπὸ εἴκοσι, twenty apiece.

Fractions are expressed as follows :—

μίσος, half (adj.), τὸ μισό, the half (noun) ; τὸ τρίτο, the third ; τὸ τέταρτο, the quarter (also τὸ κάρτο) ; τὸ πέφτο(ν) the fifth ; &c.

The Days of the Week.

ἡ Κυριακή, Sunday.
ἡ Δευτέρα, Monday.
ἡ Τρίτη, Tuesday.
ἡ Τετάρτη (Τετράδη), Wednesday.
ἡ Πέφτη (Πέμπτη), Thursday.
ἡ Παρασκευή, Friday.
τὸ Σάββατο, Saturday.

The Months.

ὁ Ἰανουάριος, January.
ὁ Φεβρουάριος, February.
ὁ Μάρτιος, March.
ὁ Ἀπρίλιος, April.
ὁ Μάιος, May.
ὁ Ἰούνιος, June.
ὁ Ἰούλιος (Ἀλωνάρης), July.
ὁ Αὔγουστος, August.
ὁ Σεπτέμβριος, Σεφτέμβριος, September.
ὁ Ὀκτώβριος, October.
ὁ Νοέμβριος, November.
ὁ Δεκέμβριος, December.

Idiomatic and other expressions concerning time:—

The first of March, 's τὴν πρώτη Μαρτίου ; the second of March, 's ταὶς δύο Μαρτίου ; on the fifteenth of March, 's ταὶς δεκαπέντε Μαρτιόν. What day of the month is to-day ? πόσαις ἔχει ὁ μῆνας σήμερα; or πόσαις τοῦ μηνός ἔχομε σήμερα; a fortnight, δεκαπέντε μέραις ; a week to-day, σήμερα ὀχτὼ μέραις.

It is one o'clock.	εἶνε μία ὥρα.
It is ten minutes past one.	εἶνε μία καὶ δέκα.
It is a quarter past one.	εἶνε μία καὶ τέταρτο (κάρτο).
It is half past one.	εἶνε μιάμιση (ὥρα).
It is a quarter to two.	εἶνε δύο παρὰ τέταρτο (κάρτο).
It is five minutes to two.	εἶνε δύο παρὰ πέντε.
It is two o'clock.	εἶνε δυὸ ὥραις.
At three o'clock.	's ταὶς τρεῖς.

Exercise 19. —A.

Αἱ πρῶταις μέραις. Δυὸ ἐβδομάδαις. Τρεῖς μῆναις. Αἱ τέσσαραις ὥραις τοῦ ἔτους εἶνε τὸ καλοκαῖρι, τὸ φθινόπωρο, ὁ χειμῶνας, ἡ ἄνοιξι. Δέκα χιλιάδαις κάτοικοι· Μιὰ δραχμὴ ἔχει ἑκατὸ λεπτά. Οἱ τόκοι ἀναβαίνουν εἰς πεντακόσιαις σαράντα τρεῖς δραχμαὶς καὶ τριάντα τρία λεπτά. Ἕνα γρόσι ἔχει σαράντα παράδαις. Ὁ δεύτερος μῆνας τοῦ τρίτου ἔτους. Τί ὥρα εἶνε ; Ἐχτύπησαν αἱ πεντέμιση. Θὰ φύγω 's ταὶς τριάντα Αὐγούστου.

ἡ ὥρα τοῦ ἔτους, the season of the year.	τὸ λεπτόν, the centime.
	οἱ τόκοι, the interest.
τὸ καλοκαῖρι, summer.	ἀναβαίνουν εἰς, amounts to.
τὸ φθινόπωρο, the autumn.	τὸ γρόσι, the piastre (Turkish).
ὁ χειμῶνας, the winter.	ὁ παρᾶς, the para (Turkish).
ἡ ἄνοιξι, the spring.	χτυπῶ, I strike.
ὁ κάτοικος, the inhabitant.	

Exercise 19.—B.

The fourth day of the eighth week. We live in the year 1889 ('s τὰ . .). Three eighths are the half of three quarters. This is my fifth glass. What o'clock is it ? It is a quarter past eleven. How many times have you been there (ἐπήγατε 'κεῖ) ? At what o'clock (τί ὥρα) do you go to bed ? How old is he ?

(πόσων χρονῶν εἶνε ;)   He is forty years old (εἶνε σαράντα χρονῶν).
He will arrive on the eighteenth of February.   The year has
twelve months, the month thirty days, the day twenty-four hours,
the hour sixty minutes, and the minute sixty seconds.   How
much (πόσου) did you give for it ?   I gave six pounds for it
(say—for how much did you buy it ?   I bought it for six pounds).

the glass, τὸ ποτῆρι.
to go to bed, πλαγιάζω.
the minute, τὸ λεπτό.

the second, τὸ δευτερόλεπτο.
the pound (money), ἡ λίρα.

PREPOSITIONS.

All usually take the Accusative Case after them.

Ἀντί (ἀντίς), instead of.
ἀπό, of, from.
διά, on account of, during.
εἰς, at, to, in, for, by.
κατά, by.
μετά, with.

μέ, with.
παρά, than.
πρό, before.
πρός, towards.
χωρίς, δίχως, without.

ἀντίς, instead of, used with Acc. and occasionally Gen.   With
the Accusative the form ἀντίς occurs oftenest.

E.g. ἀντίς αὐτὸν ἦλθ' ὁ ἀδελφός του : his brother came instead of
him.

ἀντίς is also used in conjunction with the preposition διά (γιά).

E.g. ἐμάλλωσε ἐμένα ἀντὶς γιὰ ἐκεῖνον : he scolded me instead of
him.

ἀντίς or ἀντὶς γιά is often used with νά and the subjunctive ;
e.g. ἀντὶς γιὰ νὰ διαβάζῃ, παίζει : instead of reading he plays.

ἀπό has several distinct meanings : it is used to indicate :

(1) of place, from, *e.g.* ἔρχομαι ἀπὸ τὴ Λόντρα, I come from
London.

(2) of time, from, after, since, 's ταὶς δύο ἀπὸ τὸ γεῦμα, two
hours after dinner.

(3) in a partitive sense, some of, *e.g.* ἔπια ἀπὸ αὐτὸ τὸ κρασί, I drank some of this wine.

(4) in a distributive sense, *e.g.* καθένας ἐπῆρε ἀπὸ δύο τάλληρα, they received two dollars apiece.

(5) of material, made of, *e.g.* κοῦπα ἀπὸ μάλλαμα, a cup made of gold.

(6) of cause or origin, of, from, *e.g.* τὸ ἔλαβα ἀπὸ τὸν πατέρα μου, I received it from my father; ἀπέθανε ἀπὸ τὴ χολέρα, he died of cholera.

(7) of comparison, than, *e.g.* τοῦτο εἶνε καλλίτερο ἀπὸ κεῖνο, this is better than that.

Idioms :—

περνῶ ἀπὸ τὸ μαγαζί, I call at a shop.
ἐπέρασα ἀπὸ τὸ Μόναχον, I passed through Munich.
πᾶμε ἀπὸ 'δῶ! let us go this way.
ἀπὸ ποῦ το 'πῆρες; where did you buy it?
ἀπ' ἐδῶ καὶ μία ὥρα, an hour ago.

Δ ι ά (γιά) takes the acccusative and means :

(1) on account of, *e.g.* γιὰ τὰ χρήματα ἔγιναν ὅλα αὐτά, all that happened on account of money.

(2) during, *e.g.* ἐνοίκιασα τὸ σπῆτι γιὰ δυὸ χρόνια, I hired the house for two years.

Idioms :—

διὰ τί (γιὰ τί), why?
διὰ νά, so that.
διὰ νὰ μή, lest, so that not.
τὸ 'πούλησα γιὰ τρία τάλληρα, I sold it for three dollars.
(ὡ)μιλῶ γιὰ 'σένα, I am speaking of you.
θὰ φύγω γιὰ τὴν πόλι, I shall go away to Constantinople.
δέν μου μέλει γι' αὐτό, It does not concern me.
διὰ ποῖον το λέγετε, whom do you mean? (of whom do you say that?)

εἰς ('ς, (εἰ)σέ, σέ) takes the Acc. and means :—

(1) motion to a place, *e.g.* πηγαίνω 'ς τὴν Μαγνησίαν, I am going to Magnesia.

(2) rest in a place, *e.g.* κάθεται 'ς το σπῆτι τοῦ φίλου μου, he lives in my friend's house.

(3) time, 'ς ταὶς δεκαπέντε Ἰουλίου, on the fifteenth of July.

(4) purpose, (ἐ)καθίσαμε 'ς τὸ φαγί, we sat down to table (food).

(5) in oaths, 'ς τὸ θεύ, by God.

Idioms :—

ἰδές το 'ς τὸ φῶς, look at it in the light.
ἔκαμα ἕνα γῦρο 'ς τὸ φεγγάρι, I took a walk by moonlight.
κάθεται 'ς τοῦ Γεωργίου, he lives at George's house (τὸ σπῆτι is understood).
'ς τὴν ἀράδα, in turn.
'ς τὸ τέλος, in the end.

κατά takes the Acc. and means :—

(1) direction, *e.g.* ἐπήγαινε κατὰ τὴν προκυμαίαν, he went along the jetty.

(2) manner, *e.g.* κατὰ τύχην, by chance.

(3) definition and distinction, *e.g.* κατὰ τοὺς τόπους, according to the respective places ; κατὰ τὸν καιρόν, according to the weather.

Note.—κατά when used in the literary and polite dialect occasionally takes the Gen. and means against, *e.g.* ὡμίλησε κατὰ σου, he spoke against you.

μετά is not common in the spoken tongue.

It takes the Genitive in the expression μετὰ χαρᾶς, joyfully (with joy).

When used with the Acc. it means :—

(1) with, e.g. μετὰ 'μένα, with me ; μετὰ 'σένα, with you ; μετὰ 'κείνονε, with that one.

(2) after, e.g. μετὰ δέκα 'μέραις, after ten days. — The usual expression for this is however ὕστερα ἀπὸ δέκα 'μέραις.

μ έ is the shortened form of μετά and means :—

(1) with, in the sense of accompanying, e.g. ἐπερπατοῦσε μὲ τὸν ἀδελφόν του, he went for a walk with his brother.

(2) with, of manner, μὲ βιᾴ, with violence, haste.

(3) with, of instrument, μὲ ἐχτύπησε μὲ τὸ μπαστούνι, he struck me with the stick.

(4) in spite of, μ' ὅλο τοῦτο, in spite of all that.

π α ρ ά is used in comparisons to indicate than, e.g. καλλίτερο παρὰ τὸ ἄλλο, better than the other.

NOTE.—It is often considered a conjunction in this use. It is also used as an adverb with the accent on the first syllable to mean too, e.g. πάρα πολύ, too much.

π ρ ό, before (takes the genitive in the literary dialect).

π ρ ὸ ς, towards, for :

e.g. πρὸς ποῦ; in what direction? δεξιὰ, πρὸς τὸ τάδε χώριον, on the right, on the way to such a village ; τὸ πωλῶ πρὸς τρία φράγκα, I am selling it for three francs ; ἕνα πρὸς ἕνα, one by one.

χ ω ρ ί ς, δ ί χ ω ς, without (take Acc.), χωρὶς αὐτὸν δὲν θὰ πάω, I shall not go without him.

Exercise 20.—A.

Εἶστε ἀπ' ἐδῶ; Ὄχι, κύριε, εἶμαι ἀπὸ τὰ Μέγαρα. Ἀπὸ ποῦ ἔρχεσαι; Ἔρχομαι ἀπὸ τὸ σπῆτι. Ἐμίσεψαν ἀπὸ ἄλλον δρόμον 'ς τὸν τόπον τους. Ἀπόθανε ἀπὸ τὸ φόβο του. Θέλετε νὰ πάρετε τὸ γράμμα μαζύ σας; Ὄχι, αὔριο τὸ πρωὶ θὰ περάσω νά το πάρω. Δι'

G

αὐτὸν τὸν λόγον δὲν ἦλθα. Ἄλλην ὥραν θὰ ὁμιλήσουμε δι' αὐτὸ τὸ πρᾶγμα. Φύλαξέ το καλὰ γιὰ νὰ μὴ χαθῇ. Σὲ πολλὰ μέρη τῆς Ἀνατολῆς ἔχουνε σταφύλια ποῦ εἶνε καλλίτερα ἀπὸ τοῦτα. Σὲ πόσο καιρὸ 'μπορῶ νὰ πάω ἐκεῖ; Τὸν ἐγνώρισα 'ς τὸ ταξεῖδι. Οἱ ἐχθροὶ ἔφυγαν κατὰ τὸ φρούριον. Αὐτὸ δὲν ἔχει νὰ κάμῃ μὲ ἐκεῖνα ποῦ εἶπε αὐτός. Τᾶδα (τὰ εἶδα) μὲ τὰ μάτια μου. Δὲν 'μπορῶ νὰ διαβάσω μὲ αὐτὸ τὸ φῶς. Μὲ τὸν μῆνα ἢ μὲ τὴν ἑβδομάδα ἐνοίκιασες τὴν κάμαρα; Ποῦ πᾶς μὲ τέτοια ψύχρα; Μὲ τὸν καιρὸν θὰ ξεχάσῃ καὶ αὐτό.

μισεύω, I travel.	τὸ μέρος, the part, region.
ὁ φόβος, the fear.	ὁ ἐχθρός, the enemy.
αὔριο τὸ πρωΐ, early to-morrow morning.	τὸ φρούριον, the fort.
	τὸ φῶς, the light.
ὁ λόγος, the reason.	ἡ ψύχρα, the cold.

Exercise 20.—B.

We asked him where he was (trans. is). I worked from eight o'clock in the morning till seven in the evening. He wept for joy (say, for his joy). I recognized him by his voice. In every house there were ten soldiers. I knew that better than you. Which of the two is your brother? Let us go this way. He went by Vienna. Tell him that he may speak with me at eight o'clock. He does not do it for the sake of money. He went away (εἶνε φευγάτος) an hour ago. For how long (γιὰ πόσον καιρόν) have you hired the room? He is going to Smyrna next month (τὸν ἄλλο μῆνα). He will be here in ten minutes. They will never go with you. He does it with his own hands (say hand). You will do well to hire the room by the month. In spite of his industry (μὲ ὅλη τὴν ἐπιμέλειά του) he did not succeed. Will you lend me a thousand drachmas at four per cent. (say, for the hundred)?

until, ὥς.	I recognize, γνωρίζω.
in the morning, τὸ πρωΐ.	the voice, ἡ φωνή.
in the evening, τὸ βράδυ.	Vienna, ἡ Βιέννη.
the joy, ἡ χαρά.	to succeed, κατορθόνω.

ADVERBS.

Many adverbs of time and place are used as prepositions ; *e.g*, μαζύ, together ; μαζύ μου, with me.   Only monosyllabic pronouns, however, are thrown into the Genitive ; in other cases the adverb is used together with another preposition ; *e.g*. μαζύ μὲ τοὺς ἄλλους, with the others.

ADVERBS OF PLACE.

'πάνω, above, up, (ἐ)πάνω (ἀποπάνω). ἔλα 'πάνω, come up. εἶνε 'πάνω, he is upstairs.

Κάτω, below, down. ὑποκάτω (ἀποκάτω), used with ἀπό following as a preposition, below, beneath. ἔλα κάτω, come down. τὸ γράμμα ἤτανε ἀποκάτω ἀπὸ τὸ βιβλίο, the letter was under the book.

Ἔξω (ὄξω), out, ἀπόξω ἀπό, outside of, *e.g*. εἶνε ὄξω, he is out. ἀπόξω ἀπὸ τὸ σπῆτι, outside of the house. Idiomatic usage ; μαθαίνω ἀπ' ἔξω, I learn by heart.

Μέσα, in, inside, ἀπὸ μέσα, μέσα'ς, *e.g*. ἔλα μέσα, come in. τί εἶνε μέσα 'ς τὸ ποτῆρι; what is in the glass? εἶνε κρασὶ μέσα, there is wine in it. Κοπιάστε μέσα! please (come) in ; this way, please.

Ἐμπρός, forward, before, opposite (ὀμπρός, 'μπροστά εἰς), *e.g*. 'μπροστά σου, or 'μπροστὰ 'ς ἐσένα, before you, in your presence. 'μπροστὰ 's τὸ σπῆτι, before the house. 'μπροστὰ 's αὐτὸν ἐγὼ δέν εἶμαι τίποτε, in comparison with him I am nothing. Ἐμπρός! forward! come in! go on!

Ὀπίσω ('πίσω), behind, back, after. ἀπ' ὀπίσω ἀπό, behind, *e.g*. ἀπ' ὀπίσω ἀπὸ τὸ σπῆτι ἤτανε ἕνα περιβόλι, behind the house there was a garden. γυρίζω ὀπίσω, I return, turn back.

Μακρειά, far, distant. ἀπὸ μακρειά, from afar. Πόσο μακρειὰ εἶνε; how far is it? πολλὰ μακρειά, very far.

Κοντά, σιμά, ἀπὸ κοντά, near, κοντὰ 's, close to ; also as an adverb of time, τώρα κοντά, just now. πληγωθήκανε κοντὰ πενῆντα, nearly fifty were wounded. (κοντεύω, I am near ; κοντεύω νὰ τελειώσω, I have nearly finished ; ἐκόντεψα νὰ πέσω, I nearly fell.)

Δεξιά, to the right.

'Αριστερά (ζερβά), to the left.

'Εδῶ, here, hither.

'Εκεῖ, there, thither.

'Αναμεταξύ, between, among, e.g. ἀναμεταξύ τους δὲν ἔχουν μυστικά, they have no secrets between them.

Αὐτοῦ, there.

'Αλλοῦ, elsewhere, elsewhither.   ἀπ' ἀλλοῦ, from elsewhere ; κἄπου ἀλλοῦ, anywhere else.

Κ ἄ π ο υ, anywhere, anywhither, somewhere, &c.

Π ο υ θ ε ν ά (Πούπετα) anywhere, somewhere (in interrogative sentences), nowhere (in negative sentences).

Π ο ῦ, where.

῞Ο π ο υ, where (relative), e.g. ὅπου καὶ ἂν ἦνε, wherever he may be.

῞Ως, as far as, commonly used together with εἰς, e.g. ὡς 'ς τὸ σπῆτι, as far as the house.   ὡς also means about, e.g. ἤτανε ἐκεῖ ὡς εἴκοσι ἄνθρωποι, there were about twenty people there.

Π έ ρ α, over, beyond, is used with ἐδῶ and ἐκεῖ, over here, over there ; τὸ πέρα μέρος, the further side.

ADVERBS OF TIME.

Σήμερα (σήμερον), to-day.

Αὔριο(ν), to-morrow.

Μεθαύριο(ν), the day after to-morrow, some time.

'Εχτές (χθές), (ἐψές, ψές), yesterday.

Προχτές (προχθές), the day before yesterday, lately.

'Νωρίς (ἐνωρίς), early.

'Αργά, late.

'Ξώρας (ἐξώρας), late.

Τώρα, now.

'Ακόμη, yet.

Τότε, τότες, ἐτότες, then ; ἀπὸ τότε, since then.

Εὐτύς, (εὐθύς) ⎫
'Αμέσως ⎭ immediately.

Πάντοτε, always.

Πότε, when.

Πότε—πότε, now—now.

Ποτέ, in interrogative sentences *ever*, in negative sentences *never*. Ποτέ is often used with the genitive of the personal pronoun placed after it :

e.g. τὸν εἴδατε ποτέ σας ; have you ever seen him ? Δὲν τον εἶδα ποτέ μου. I have never seen him.

Προτῆτερα, sooner.

"Υστερα ⎫
"Επειτα ⎭ afterwards, later on.

'Φέτος (ἐφέτος), this year.

Πέρυσι, last year.

Προπέρυσι, the year before last.

Πάλι, again.

Τοῦ χρόνου, next year.

ADVERBS OF MANNER.

Most of the adverbs of manner have the termination *a* and are formed from adjectives in ος, *e.g.* ῥωμάϊκα, in modern Greek.

"Ετζι, so, thus.

Γρήγορα (γλήγορα), quickly.

Καλά, well.

Κακά ⎫
"Ασχημα ⎭ badly.

Κρυφά, secretly.

Μόλις, scarcely.

Πῶς, how ?

'Σάν, as (with Acc.).

ADVERBS OF DEGREE.

Πολλά (πολύ), much, very.

('Ο)λίγα, little.

('Ο)λιγάκι, very little, rather.

Ἀρκετά, enough, tolerably.

Μοναχά }
Μόνο   } only

Καθόλου, at all (in interrogative sentences), not at all (in negative sentences).

ADVERBS OF AFFIRMATION AND NEGATION.

Ναί   }
Ναῖσκε } yes.

Μάλιστα, certainly.

Ὄχι   }
Ὄχεσκε } no, not (in negativing a single word), *e.g.* ὄχι τοῦτο,
    not this.

Δέν, not (only to negative verbs).

Οὔτε, nor.

Οὔτε—οὔτε, neither—nor.

Τάχα }
Ἴσως } perhaps.

Exercise 21.—Α.

Τὸ σπῆτι τοῦ κυρίου Τριανταφυλλίδη εἶνε μακρειὰ ἀπ' ἐδῶ; Ὄχι, εἶνε κοντά. Ἐξώδεψε κοντὰ σαράντα λίραις. Πᾶμε ἀπὸ τὰ δεξιά. Πόσον καιρὸν ἔχετε ἐδῶ; Αὐτὸ ποῦ σας εἶπα θὰ μείνη ἀναμεταξύ μας. Ποῦ εἶνε τὸ μανδύλι; Ἐκεῖ το ἄφησες. Δὲν βρίσκω τὰ παπούτζια μου. Δέν τα 'πῆρε κανείς· θὰ εἶνε κάπου 'ς τὸ σπῆτι. Ἐγύρεψες παντοῦ; Μάλιστα, ἐγύρεψα 'ς ὅλαις ταὶς κάμεραις, ἀλλὰ δέν τα εἶδα πουθενά. Μὲ 'προσκάλεσε νὰ δειπνήσω μαζύ του αὔριον. Θέλετε νὰ φύγετε τώρα; Καθῆστε ἀκόμη ὀλίγο, δὲν εἶνε πολλὰ 'ξώρας. Τοῦ ὡμίλησα πρὸ ὀχτὼ ἡμερῶν· ἀπὸ τότε δέν τον εἶδα. Πέρνσι εἴχαμε πολλὰ φροῦτα. Κρυφὰ ἐδιάβασε τὸ γράμμα.

ἐξοδεύω, I spend. μένω, I remain. τὸ παποῦτζι, the shoe, boot.

Exercise 21.—B.

I saw her from far off.   Is he cleverer than his brother?   Far
away from here.   We have lost nearly eighty dollars.   I had
almost forgotten the affair.   He turned to the left.   Is Mr.
Manos downstairs?   What is under the plate?   Is my brother
in the office?   No, he has gone away somewhere else.   I shall
find him, wherever he may be.   To-day I have nothing to
do, to-morrow my work begins.   The wedding took place
yesterday.   I go to bed early, and get up early.   Finish your
work first (πρῶτα), then I shall speak to you.   Tell him that he
must bring me the book at once.   Have you ever heard anything
like that?   Will you go to Germany this year?   Don't go
(περπατῶ) so quickly.   What do they call (πῶς λένε) this in
modern Greek?   How will you bring that to pass?

clever, προκομμένος.	the wedding, ὁ γάμος.
the affair, ἡ ὑπόθεσι.	I take place, γίνω.
I turn, γυρίζω.	I finish, τελειόνω.
the office, τὸ γραφεῖον.	

CONJUNCTIONS AND INTERJECTIONS.

K a ί, and.   It is a common Greek idiom to coördinate two
clauses with καί, instead of subordinating one of them with
'when' or 'while.'   μὴ βροντᾷς καὶ θὰ κοιμηθῶ, make no noise
and I will sleep.   ἀκόμη δὲν εἶχα ἔβγῃ καὶ πέφτει τὸ σπῆτι,
scarcely had I gone out, when the house fell.   τὸν ἄκουσα καὶ
τὄλεγε, I heard him say so.

Καί is used to give emphasis, e.g. τί 'ξέρω καὶ 'γώ; how do I
know?   It is also used after σάν, e.g. δὲν εἶμαι πλούσιος σὰν καὶ
αὐτόν, I am not as rich as he.

ἤ, or.

ἤ—ἤ, either—or.

οὔτε—οὔτε, neither—nor.

ἀλλά, but.

ὅτι ⎫ that: e.g. μοῦ εἶπαν, πῶς (ὅτι) ἔφυγε.   They told me that
πῶς ⎭   he had gone away.

ὅτι also means 'as soon as.' ὅτι με ἐφώναξες ἦλθα, as soon as you called me I came.

Sometimes ὅτι stands instead of μόλις, just, scarcely. ποῦ εἶνε ὁ ἀδελφός σου; ὅτι ἐβγῆκε. Where is your brother? He has just gone out.

Μ'ὅλον ὅτι (μολονότι), although, is followed by the Indicative. μ' ὅλον ὅτι δέν σας γνωρίζω, θά σας δώσω τὰ χρήματα.
Although I do not know you, I will give you the money.
Λοιπόν, (well) then.

ὅ π ο υ, where, since, τώρα ὅπου μᾶς ἀπάτησε ἐκεῖνος τί θὰ κάμωμεν ; what shall we do now that he has betrayed us?
It sometimes stands for ὥστε, (so) that. τόσον ἐδούλεψε ὅπου ἀρρώστησε, he worked so much that he was ill.

Ἄ μ α
Ἄ μ α ὅ π ο υ } as soon as.

Ἀφοῦ, when, as soon as, since, (εὐθὺς ἀφοῦ).

Ἀφοῦ ἔφαγα 'σηκώθηκα καὶ ἔφυγα, when I had eaten, I got up and went away. Ἀφοῦ τον ἰδῆτε θά το πιστέψετε, as soon as you see it, you will believe it. Ἀφοῦ το θέλετε, since you wish it.

Κ α θ ώ ς, as, as soon as, e.g. καθώς μου εἶπαν, as they told me. καθὼς ἄκουσα αὐτό, as soon as I heard that.

Σ ά ν (σά) (1), as. τὰ ἀγαπῶ σὰν τὰ παιδιά μου, I love them as my own children. σάν occasionally has a prepositional force and governs the Accusative. ζοῦν σὰν τοὺς ἀγρίους, they live like savages.

(2) if (the verb following takes the Subjunctive).
σὰν ἔλθῃ, if he should come, if he comes.

(3) when. σὰν ἤμουνα νέος, when I was young.
σὰν νὰ as if, σὰν νὰ μή, as if not. σὰν νὰ μή το ἤξερε, as if he did not know.

Ἄ ν, if. ἂν ἔλθῃ, if he comes; ἂν το ἤξερα, if I knew it (or had known it).

ὅ τ α ν, when, if. ὅταν το μάθῃ, if he will learn ; ὅταν τον εἶδα, when I saw him.

NOTE.—The English *when* is often translated by τὸν καιρὸν ὅπου (the time when) or τὴν ὥραν ὅπου (the hour when).

τὸν καιρὸν ὅπου ἤτανε ὁ Πάλμερστον ὑπουργός, when Lord Palmerston was minister. Τὴν ὥρα ὅπου ἦλθα ἐγὼ, αὐτὸς ἤτανε φευγάτος, when I came, he had gone away.

Π ρ ί ν, before, commonly used with νὰ and the Subjunctive.

πρὶν νὰ στείλω τὴν ἀπάντησι, before I send the answer.

πρὸ τοῦ νά in another form instead of πρίν νά.

Ὁ π ό τ α ν, as often as, whenever. ὁπόταν ἔχετε διάθεσι, whenever you feel disposed.

Ὡ ς ὅ π ο υ, until, till. θὰ καθήσω ἐδῶ ὡς ὅπου τελειώσω, I shall stay here till I finish.

Ἀγκαλά (ἂν καλά), although.

Γιὰ νά, so that.

Γιὰ νὰ μή, so that not, lest.

Διότι ⎫
Γιατί ⎬ because.

Ὥστε, so that.

Δηλαδή, namely, viz.

INTERJECTIONS.

Α ! ὤ ! ah ! oh !

Αμποτε (νὰ) ⎫
Μακάρι (να) ⎬ would that, if only.

Ἀλλοίμονον ! Woe !

Μπᾶ ! Hilloa !

Ποῦφ ! Ugh !

Μπράβο ! Bravo !

NOTE.—The word μπράβο is very often used and sometimes means Right ! Good !

Exercise 22.—A.

Ξεύρω ὅτι με ἐγέλασαν. Ἀφοῦ ἐπέρασε ἡ Τετάρτη (τετράδη) δὲν
εἶχα πλέον ἐλπίδα νὰ ἐπιστρέψῃ. Ὡμιλεῖ σὰν νὰ ἦτο ὁ Σουλτάνος.
Σὰν ἔλθῃ ὁ Ἀλέξανδρος πέτε του νὰ μείνῃ ὡς ὅπου ἐπιστρέψω. Καθὼς
'ξημέρωσε σηκώθηκα καὶ ἔφυγα. Πρὸ τοῦ νὰ στείλῃς τὰ γράμματα
δός μοῦ τα νά τα διαβάσω. Θὰ κρατήσω τὸ ὡρολόγι του ὡς ὅπου με
πληρώσῃ. Ἀγκαλὰ εἶνε νέος ξέρει τὴν δουλειά του καλά. Ἔκαψε τὸ
γράμμα γιὰ νὰ μὴ πέσῃ 'ς τὰ χέρια του μάστορη.

'ξημερώνει, the day breaks.   ὁ μάστορης, the master.
κρατέω, I take possession of.

Exercise 22.—B.

They say that the king will arrive to-morrow. Where is your
father? He has just gone out. It is many years (ago) since
(ἀφοῦ) the theatre was burnt. He looks like an Indian. They
live like slaves. If you hear anything of it (γι' αὐτό), tell it to
me. As soon as I saw him I drew my pistol from my pocket.
Before he came to Vienna, he did not know a word of German.
As soon as he had learnt (Aorist), he wrote to his father. Put
the buttons away, so that they may not be lost.

the king, ὁ βασιλεύς.   the pistol, τὸ πιστόλι.
I burn, καίομαι.   the pocket, ἡ τσέπη.
the Indian, ὁ Ἰνδός.   I learn, μαθαίνω.
the slave, ὁ δοῦλος, ὁ σκλάβος.   the button, τὸ κομπί (κουμπί).
I draw out, βγάλλω ἀπό.

REPETITION OF ADJECTIVES AND ADVERBS.

Adjectives and adverbs are often repeated for the sake of
emphasis.

ἦλθε πρωΐ πρωΐ.   He came very early.
εἶνε κάτω κάτω.   It is away down below.
τὸ ψωμὶ εἶνε φρέσκο φρέσκο.   The bread is quite fresh.

POSITION OF WORDS.

The position of words in modern Greek is much the same as in
English. Words fall into their places naturally without the aid
of rules. A few rules have been given under the pronouns, but
one learns most from observation and practice.

IDIOMS.

ἀγαπῶ, I love.
  τί ἀγαπᾶτε; — what do you require?
  ἂν ἀγαπᾶς. — if you like.

ἀέρα, air, wind.
  αὐτὰ εἶνε λόγια 'ς τὸν ἀέρα. — (these are words to the wind) that is mere talk.

ἀκούω, I hear.
  τὸ ἔχω ἀκουστά.* — I have it on hearsay.
  δὲν τ' ἀκούω αὐτά. — I won't hear a word of it.

ἀλλάζω, I alter.
  αὐτὸ ἀλλάζει. — that is a different thing.

ἄλλος, other.
  θὰ ἔλθω χωρὶς ἄλλο. — I shall come in any case.

ἀναβαίνω, I go up.
  ὁ λογαριασμὸς ἀναβαίνει σὲ τρεῖς χιλιάδαις λίραις. — the bill amounts to £3,000.
  ἀνέβηκαν τὰ 'νοίκια. — rent has gone up.

ὁ ἄνεμος, the wind.
  ἂς πάῃ 'ς τὸν ἄνεμο. — he may go to the deuce (wind).
  ὅλη ἡ περιουσία 'πῆγε τοῦ ἀνέμου. — the whole property is squandered (scattered to the wind).

ἀνοίγω, I open.
  αὐτὸ τὸ χρῶμα ἀνοίγει. — this colour fades.
  ἤνοιξε ἡ ὄρεξίς μου. — I am hungry.

ἡ ἀπόφασι, the decision.
  τὸ παίρνω ἀπόφασι. — I know the worst (I take it as final).

ἀράδ' ἀράδα, turn.
  μὲ τὴν ἀράδα. — in turn, successively, one after the other.

ἀφανίζω, I destroy.
  εἶμαι ἀφανισμένος ἀπὸ τὴν κούρασι. — I am tired to death.
  μὲ ἀφάνισε ἡ ζέστη. — the heat is killing me.

ἀφίνω (ἀφήνω), I leave.
  ἀφίνομαι ἐπάνω σου. — I place myself in your hands.
  πόσον θὰ μ' ἀφήσῃς; — how much will you take off for me?

* Only used in this expression.

θὰ ἀφήσω τὰ γένειά μου.　I will let my beard grow.

ἄφησε ὅτι εἶνε ἀγράμματος.　not to mention that he is un-
　　　　　　　　　　　　　educated.

ἡ ἄχνη, smoke, foam.

δὲν ἔβγαλε ἄχνη.　he did not say a word.

βάλλω, I place, put.

ἀκόμη δὲ ἔβαλες γνῶσι;　have you not yet got sense?

θὰ βάζω τὰ δυνατά μου.　I will do all I can.

τὰ βάζω κάτω.　I give in (I throw down my
　　　　　　　　arms).

βάζω ταὶς φωναίς.　I call out.

δέν το βάζει ὁ νοῦς μου.　that beats me (my mind can't
　　　　　　　　take it in).

τὰ ἔβαλε μαζύ σας.　he has fallen out with you, he
　　　　　　　　has a crow to pluck with you.

βάλλω τὰ παπούτζια.　I put my boots on.

βάλ' το καλὰ εἰς τὸν νοῦν
σου.　take good heed of it.

βαθειά, deep.

κοιμούντανε βαθεία.　he was fast asleep.

βαρύς, heavy.

εἶνε ἄρρωστος βαρειά.　he is very ill.

βαριοῦμαι νὰ πάω.　I dont care to go.

δὲν βαριέσαι!　nonsense (lit. you don't trouble
　　　　　　　　yourself).

βαρὺ κρασί.　strong wine.

βαρειὰ ἀρρώστεια.　severe illness.

τὸ λουλοῦδι ἔχει μιὰ βαρειὰ
μυρωδιά.　the flower has a strong scent.

βαστῶ, I carry, hold.

βαστῶ τὴν ἀναπνοή μου.　I hold my breath.

δὲν βαστῶ εἰς τὴν ψύχραν.　I cannot bear the cold.

δὲν βαστῶ ἐπάνω μου παράδαις.　I have no money on me.

αὐτὸ τὸ χρῶμα δὲν βαστᾷ.　this colour is not fast.

δὲν θὰ βαστάξῃ ἡ καρδιά μου
νά το κάμω.　I cannot find it in my heart to
　　　　　　　　do it.

πόσον καιρὸ βαστᾷ τὸ ταξεῖδι;　how long does the journey take?

μὲ ὅλην του τὴν ἡλικίαν βασ-
τιέται καλά.　in spite of his great age he is
　　　　　　　　still active (wears well).

βαστιέται καλά.　(also), he has ample means.

τὸ βελόνι, needle.

[fall.

βελόνι δὲν ἔπεφτε κάτω.   there was not room for a pin to

βλάπτω, I hurt.

δὲν βλάφτει.   never mind !

βλέπω, I see.

δὲν βλέπω τὴν ὥρα νὰ φύγω.   I am impatient to get away (I can't see the time to go).

βλέπω ὄνειρο.   I dream.

σὲ εἶδα 's τὸν ὕπνο.   I dreamt of you.

ὁ ἰατρὸς τὸνε βλέπει.   the doctor is visiting him.

νὰ ἰδῶ.   I'll see, I shall think it over.

τὸ παραθύρι βλέπει 's τὸ δρόμο.   the window looks on the street.

ἰδὲς ἐκεῖ !   see there now !

βουλῶ.   I overturn.

τὸ σπῆτι κοντεύει νὰ βουλήσῃ.   the house is nearly falling down.

βουτῶ, I dip.

μεσ' s τὸν ἴδρο βουτημένος.   bathed in sweat.

εἶνε βουτημένος εἰς τὰ χρέη.   he is deep in debt.

βράζω, I boil.

τὸ κρασὶ βράζει 's τὸ βαρέλι.   the wine is fermenting in the cask.

βράζει ἀπὸ τὸν θυμό του.   he is boiling with rage.

βρέχει, it rains.

ὅτι βρέξῃ ἂς καταιβάσῃ.   let come what may.

αὐτὸ τὸ σπῆτι εἶνε βρυκολα-κιασμένο.   this house is haunted.

γελῶ, I laugh.

μὲ ἐγέλασες.   you have cheated me.

τὸν ἐγελοῦσε μὲ τὸ σήμερα καὶ μὲ τὸ αὔριο.   he put him off from day to day.

γίνομαι, I become.

πῶς γίνεται νὰ ......   how comes it that ...... ?

ἔγινε καλά.   he has recovered.

τί γίνεται ὁ ἀδελφός σας ;   how is your brother getting on ?

τί ἔγινε ὁ φίλος σας ;   what has become of your friend ?

γίνομαι ἄνω κάτω.   I am upset (beside myself).

τί θὰ γίνω ;   what will become of me ?

φαντάσου πῶς ἔγινα (πῶς ἔγινε ἡ καρδιά μου)   imagine what my feelings were !

τὸ καλλίτερο κρασὶ γίνεται εἰς τὴν Κύπρο.	the best wine is grown in Cyprus.
ποῦ θὰ γίνῃ ὁ γάμος;	where will the wedding come off?
ἔγινε ἔμπορος.	he has turned merchant.
δὲν ἔγιναν ἀκόμη τὰ σταφύλια	the grapes are not ripe yet.
γινωμένος.	ripe, born.

γλυτόνω, I escape, get off, rescue.

φτηνὰ τήνε γλυτώσαμε.	we got off cheap.
μόλις ἐγλύτωσε εἰς τὰς Ἀθήνας.	scarcely had he arrived in Athens.

γνωρίζω, I know, recognise.

γνωρίζεις ἀπὸ διαμάντια.	are you a judge of diamonds?
ποῦ γνωρισθήκατε;	where did you get acquainted with one another?
ξούρισε τὰ γένεια του γιὰ νὰ μὴ γνωρίζεται.	he has shaved his beard, so as not to be recognized.

τὸ γουδί, mortar.
τὸ γουδοχέρι, pestle.

τὸ γουδὶ τὸ γουδοχέρι.	always the same old story.

γράφω, I write.

δὲν ξεύρει γράμματα.	he is illiterate (cannot read and write).
ἦτο γραφτό μου.	it was my fate.
πῶς γράφεσαι;	how do you write your name?
γράφθηκαν ὀλίγοι.	a few were entered.

δείχνω, I show, teach, seem.

ἐγὼ θά του δείξω.	I will give him a lesson.
τὸ κρασὶ δείχνει σὰν νὰ ἦνε ἀνακατωμένον μὲ ἄλλο.	the wine seems as if it were mixed with another.
δείχνω (ἄγριον) πρόσωπον.	I sulk (show temper).
δείχνω καλὸν πρόσωπον.	I give a good reception to.
σὺ δείχνεις ὡσὰν νεκρός.	you look like a corpse.

δένω, I bind.

δένω βιβλίο.	I bind a book.
δένω δαχτυλίδι.	I set a ring (with jewels).
ἔδεσε καλὰ τὸν γαΐδαρόν του	he has feathered his nest (he has tied up his donkey well so that it won't run away).
τον ἔδεσα μὲ ὅρκον	I have bound him by oath.

δεξιά, to the right.

τὰ πράγματα τοῦ ἦλθαν δεξιά.   everything went well with him.

διαβάζω, I read.

διαβάζω παιδιά.   I teach children.

διαβάζω εἰς ἕνα.   I am taking lessons from so-and-so.

ὅταν ἐδιάβαζα εἰς τὰς ᾿Αθήναις.   when I was studying in Athens.

δίδω, I give.

δίδω τόπον.   I make way.

δίδω τραπέζι.   I give a dinner-party.

ὁ θεὸς νὰ μή το δώσῃ.   God forbid.

τὸ δόντι, tooth.

τὸ παιδὶ ᾿βγάζει δόντια.   the child is cutting his teeth.

αὐτὸ δὲν εἶνε διὰ τὰ δόντια σου.   that is not for you (meat for your master).

δουλεύω, I work.

δουλεύω πληγήν.   I keep the wound open, irritate a wound.

τὸ ἐργαστήρι του δὲν δουλεύει.   his shop is doing no business.

τὸ ὡρολόγι του δὲν δουλεύει.   his watch has stopped.

ἡ πληγή του δουλεύει.   his sore runs.

ἡ δουλειά, business, work.

ἔχω δουλειά.   I have work to do.

αὐτὸ εἶνε δική μου δουλειά.   that is my own affair.

πήγαινε εἰς τὴν δουλειάν σου.   go about your business.

τὸ δράμι, drachm (measure).

δὲν ἔχει δράμι μυαλό.   he has not a grain of sense.

ἐβγάζω, I take out.

ἔβγαλε τὸ ποδάρι του.   he has dislocated his foot.

βγάζω τὸ ψωμί μου.   I earn my bread.

δὲν βγάζει τίποτε.   he gains nothing (by it).

ἔβγαλε τὸν δοῦλον.   he dismissed his servant.

τὸν ἔβγαλαν.   they set him free.

θὰ σε βγάλω ψεύτην.   I'll show you are a liar, I will prove you to be mistaken.

ἔβγαλε φροῦτα.   he put fruit on the table, produced fruit.

θὰ βγάλω ἕνα δόντι.   I will have a tooth out.

δὲν το βγάζω.   I cannot understand it.

βγάζω τὰ παπούτζια.   I am taking off my boots.

ἐβγαίνω, I go out.

ἀπ' αὐτὴ τὴ δουλειὰ δὲν βγαίνει τίποτε.	nothing will come of that business.
τί ἐβγῆκε ;	what came of that ?
τὸ ροῦχο δὲν βγαίνει διὰ δύο φορεσιαίς.	the stuff wont run to two dresses (be enough for two dresses).

ἐδῶ, here.

ὁ κύριος ἀπ' ἐδῶ.	this gentleman.
ἄκουσ' ἐδῶ !	look here ! (listen here ! lit.)

εἶμαι, I am.

εἶνε ψύχρα ἢ ζέστη.	it is cold or hot.
σύ εἶσαι ;	is it you ?
ποῖος εἶνε ;	who is it ?
τὰ παιδιά σου εἶνε ;	are these your children ?
εἶνε διὰ νὰ φύγῃ.	he is on the point of setting off.
ἔστειλα νὰ μάθω πῶς εἶνε.	I sent to ask how he was.
εἶνε νὰ σκάσῃ κανείς.	it is enough to send one crazy (lit. make one burst).
εἶνε ἕνας χρόνος.	a year ago.
πῶς εἶσαι ;	how are you ?

ἐμβαίνω, μπαίνω, I go in.

αὐτὸς ὁ ἄνθρωπος μπαίνει παντοῦ.	that man interferes everywhere.
τοῦ μπῆκε εἰς τὸ κεφάλι.	he has taken it into his head.
ἐμβαίνω ἐγγυητής.	I become surety.
αὐτὸς ἐμβῆκεν εἰς τὴν δουλειάν	he set to work.
ἐμβαίνεις εἰς τὸν κίνδυνον.	you are exposing yourself to danger.
ἐμβῆκε ράφτης.	he set up as tailor.

ἡ ἔννοια, care.

ἔννοια σου !	mind your own business !

ἔξω, out.

τὸ ξεύρω ἀπ' ἔξω.	I know it by heart.
ἔξω ὁποῦ.	besides that.
ὁ ἐξωτικός.	the ghost.

ἐπάνω, above.

ἐπάνω κάτω.	about (thereabout).

ἔρχομαι, I come.

δέν μου ἔρχεται καλά.	it does not commend itself to me, it is not convenient to me.

ἔρχεσαι νὰ μ' ἀφήσῃς ἥσυχον.　be good enough to leave me in peace.

δέν μου ἔρχεται εἰς τὸν νοῦν.　it does not occur to me.

ἔλα εἰς τὸν νοῦν σου.　calm yourself (come to your senses). ⠀

ἦλθαν εἰς τὰ χέρια.　they came to blows.

ἐγὼ δὲν ἔρχομαι εἰς αὐτά.　I don't meddle with that.

τὸ ἔτος, year.

εἰς ἔτη πολλά !　long life to you ! (many years to you) answered by—

(εἰς πολλὰ ἔτη) 's πολάτη.　the same to you.

ἔχω, I have.

πῶς ἔχετε ;　how do you do ?

δέν τα ἔχω καλὰ μαζύ του.　I am not on good terms with him.

τί ἔχει νὰ κάμῃ ;　what does that matter ? what has that to do with it ?

ἔτζι τὸ ἔχομε ἐμεῖς.　it is a custom of ours.

δὲν ἔχω νὰ κάμω μαζύ σου.　I have nothing to do with you.

πόσο ἔχει αὐτό ;　how much does this cost ?

τὰ ἔχει χαμένα.　he is crazy.

δὲν ἔχω μοῦτρα νὰ.　I am ashamed to (lit. I have not the face to).

ἔχε ὑγίειαν !　good health to you ! farewell.

μὲ ποῖον τὰ ἔχεις ;　who are you angry with ?

δὲν ἔχει μάτια νὰ μὲ ἰδῇ.　he hates the sight of me.

ἔχω καιρὸν νά τον ἰδῶ.　I have not seen him for a long time.

ζουπῶ, I press.

τοῦ ἐζούπησε παράδαις.　he got money out of him.

αὐτὸς τὰ ἐζούπησε ὅλα.　he consumed everything.

ζῶ, I live.

νὰ ζῇς !　may you live ! please.

ζῇ ἡμεροδοῦλι ἡμεροφάγι.　he lives from hand to mouth.

νὰ ζοῦν τὰ μάτια μου !　bless my soul ! (bless my eyes !)

ἐμπορῶ, I can.

δὲν μπορῶ.　I am ill.

ἐμπορεῖ.　possibly.

τὸ θάρρος, courage, confidence.

μὲ ὅλον τὸ θάρρος.　without ceremony.

θέλω, I wish.

θέλει τὸ καλόν μου.	he wishes me well.
δὲν σου θέλω πλέον τίποτε.	I owe you nothing more.

ἰδιαίτερος, special.

τὸν ἐπῆρε ἰδιαιτέρως.	he took him aside.

ἰδρόνω, I sweat.

ἀπ᾽ αὐτὰ τὸ αὐτί μου δὲν ἰδρόνει.	I don't trouble myself about that.

ἴσια, just, exactly.

εἴμεθα ἴσια εἰς τὰ χρόνια.	we are the same age.
ἴσια εἰς τὴν ὥραν.	just in time.
ἴσια ἴσια αὐτὸ λέγω.	that is just what I am saying.
εἴμεθα ἴσια ἴσια.	we are quits.

καβάλα, on horseback.

τὸ ἠγόρασε καβάλα.	he bought it without looking at it (he bought a pig in a poke).

κάθε, every, each.

κάθε τι or κάθε πρᾶγμα.	everything.
κάθε δύο μέραις.	every other day.
κάθε τόσο καὶ 'λιγάκι.	every now and then.
ἀπὸ κάθε λογῆς.	of every kind.
κάθε χρόνον.	every year, yearly.

καλά, well.

καλὰ καὶ ἤμουν ἐκεῖ.	luckily I was there.
καλά σε τοὔλεγα ἐγώ.	I told you so.

καλός, good.

καλό 'ς τον!	welcome.
μία καὶ καλή.	once for all.
εἰς τὸ καλόν!	farewell, au revoir.
ἐγὼ γίνομαι καλός.	I stand surety (go bail).
καλέ, τί με λές;	good heavens, what are you telling me!

κάμνω, I make.

τί κάμνετε;	how do you do?
ἔκαμε τρεῖς μέραις νἄρθῃ.	he was three days on the way.
κάμνω καὶ χωρὶς αὐτόν.	I cannot get on without him.
τὸ ἴδιο κάμνει.	it is all the same.
δέν μου κάμνει.	that does not suit me.
δὲν κάμνει.	it is no good. [that dress?
πόσον κάμνεις αὐτὸ τὸ φόρεμα;	how much do you charge for
κάμε γρήγορα!	be quick! make haste!

καπνίζω, I smoke.
  τοῦ ἐκάπνισε νὰ φύγῃ.   it occurred to him to go away.
κἄπου, somewhere.
  κἄπου κἄπου.   now and then.
  κἄπου δέκα φοραίς.   about ten times.
καταβάζω, I bring down.
  δὲν θὰ καταιβάσῃ τίποτε.   he will not lower the price.
  θὰ του καταιβάσω μίαν.*   I will give him a box on the ear.
κατόπιν, after.
  ἔπεσε κατόπιν του.   he dogged his steps.
  μὲ παίρνει αἰωνίως κατόπιν.   he is always following me about.
κάτω, below.
  ἄνω κάτω τἄκαμες.   you have turned everything topsy-turvy.

κοντά, near.
  κοντά νὰ βασιλεύσῃ ὁ ἥλιος.   shortly before sunset.
  τὸν 'πῆρε ἀπὸ κοντά.   he ran after him.
  κοντὰ 'ς τὸν νοῦν.   of course ; obviously.
κοπιάζω, I exert myself.
  κοπιάστε !   come in, please.
κόφτω, I cut.
  αὐτὴ ἡ δουλειὰ θὰ κόψῃ ἑκατὸν δραχμαίς.   this affair will cost a hundred francs.
  δέν τον κόφτει διόλου.   that is all the same to him.
κουνῶ, I shake.
  αὐτὸ τὸ δόντι κουνιέται.   the tooth is loose.
κυττάζω, I look.
  κύτταζε τὴν δουλειά σου.   mind your business.
  κύτταξε καλά!   look out ! be on your guard !
τὸ λάθος, mistake.
  ἔχετε λάθος.   you are mistaken.
ἡ λάκκα, hole, pit.
  τὸν ἄφησαν εἰς τὴν λάκκα.   they left him in the lurch.
ἡ λάσπη, dirt.
  ἔχει πολλαὶς λάσπαις ἔξω.   it is very muddy out of doors.
  τὸ ἔκοψε λάσπη.   he has cut and run.
  λάσπη ἡ δουλειά.   it is a poor business, it is a failure.

* If δραχμήν is understood with 'μίαν' the phrase means ' I will make him take a drachma off.'

λέγω, I say.

τί θὰ 'πῇ αὐτό ;	what does that mean ?
ἄλλη ὥρα τα λέμε.	we'll talk about that another time.
λοιπόν, τα εἴπαμε.	well, that is settled.
λές;	do you think so ?
πῶς τον λένε ;	what is he called ?
ἃς 'ποῖμε ὅτι εἶνε ἔτζι.	let us suppose that it is so.
τὸ γράμμα ἔτζι ἔλεγε.	so the letter said.

τὸ λεπτόν, centime (tenth part of a Greek penny), also a minute (of time).

δὲν ἔχει λεπτόν.	he hasn't a penny.
μοῦ θέλει κᾶτι λεπτά.	he owes me a small sum.

λογῆς (τῆς). Nom. not used : kind (of), sort (of).

τί λογῆς κρασὶ ἔχεις ;	what kind of wine have you ?
λογῆς λογῆς.	all kinds.
μιᾶς λογῆς.	one kind.

ὁ λόγος, the word.

δὲν ἔχει λόγον.	it is certain (there is no need to talk about it).
ἐβγῆκε λόγος.	the rumour has spread.
δὲν παίρνει ἀπὸ λόγον.	he won't listen to reason.
αὐτὸ εἶνε ἕνας λόγος.	that is easily said.
βάζω λόγον.	I make a speech.
ἄλλα λόγια.	let us change the subject.
λόγου χάριν.	for example.
μὲ λόγον.	reasonably.

ὁ λουτρός, the bath.

μ' ἄφησεν εἰς τὰ κρύα τοῦ λουτροῦ.	he left me in the lurch.

τὸ λωρί, strap, thong, harness.

ἐδῶ παίζει λωρί.	he is playing false.

μαζεύω, μαζόνω, I collect.

μαζόνω τὰ πράγματά μου.	I am packing up.

μακρειά, far, distant.

εἶσαι μακρειά.	you are wide of the mark.

τὸ μαλλί, hair.

ἐπιάσθηκαν ἀπὸ τὰ μαλλιά.	they took hold of each other's hair (they fought like two cats).

τὸ μάτι, eye.

δὲν ἔχω μάτια νά τον ἰδῶ.   I cannot endure him.

σὲ 'πῆρε εἰς κακὸ μάτι.   he cast the evil eye on you, he took an ill-will to you.

μάτια ποῦ δὲν φαίνονται γρή-γορα λησμονοῦνται.   out of sight out of mind.

μάτι μὲ μάτι.   face to face.

μάτια μου.   my darling.

τῶδα (τὸ εἶδα) μὲ τὰ μάτια μου.   I saw it with my own eyes.

νὰ χαρῶ τα μάτια μου.   as I value my eyes (an oath).

μένω, I stay, remain.

μᾶς μένει τώρα μόνον νὰ στεί-λωμε τὸ γράμμα.   all we have to do now is to send off the letter.

μέσα, inside.

τὸν ἔβαλαν μέσα.   they imprisoned him ; also, they have taken him in, i.e. cheated him.

ἔχει τὸν διάβολον μέσα του.   he is possessed of a devil (like one possessed).

ἔλεγε μέσα του.   he said to himself.

μέσα εἰς τριάντα μέραις.   within thirty days.

τὰ μέσα.   the means (i.e. the wherewithal) ; also, the influence.

ἡ μέση, the middle.

μπαίνω 's τὴ μέση.   I interfere.

μ' ἄφησεν 's τὴ μέση.   he left me in the lurch.

μικρὸς, little.

εἶνε μικρότερος ἀπὸ μένα.   he is younger than I.

ἀπὸ μικρός.   from childhood.

μοιράζω, I divide.   [another.

δὲν ἔχομε τίποτε νὰ μοιράσωμε.   we have nothing to do with one

ποιὸς μοιράζει ;   whose deal is it ?

τὸ μούσκεμμα, the wetting.

εἶμαι μούσκεμμα.   I am wet.

ἡ μυῖα (μυῖγα), the fly.

τὸν ἔπιασε ἡ μυῖγα.   he has a bee in his bonnet.

χάφτει μυῖγαις.   he does nothing (cf. gobe-mouches).

μυρίζω, I smell, emit an odour (in passive I perceive an odour).

ποιὸς μπορούσε νά το μυρισθῇ.   who could have found that out ?

δέν μου μυρίζει τίποτε.   I smell nothing.

ἡ μυρωδιά, the smell.

τὸ 'πῆρε μυρωδιά.   he has got wind of it.

ἡ μύτη, the nose.

σήκωσε τὴ μύτη του.   he turns up his nose (he has got on the high horse).

βάζει παντοῦ τὴ μύτη του.   he interferes in everything.

'μιλᾷ μὲ τὴ μύτη.   he speaks through his nose.

τὸ νερό, the water.

τὸ ξεύρω σὰν νερό.   I have it at my fingers' ends.

αὐτὴ ἡ δουλειὰ σηκόνει νερό.   this business pays, has potentialities (raises water).

ὁ νοῦς.

ὁ νοῦς σου εἶνε πάντοτε ἐκεῖ.   you are always thinking of it.

ἔλεγα 'ς τὸ νοῦ μου.   I said it to myself.

ποῦ εἶχες τὸ νοῦ σου;   where were your thoughts (wits)?

δὲν κόφτει ὁ νοῦς του.   he is not very sharp.

τὸ νύχι, the nail.

ἀπὸ τὴ κορυφὴ ὡς τὰ νύχια.   from head to foot.   [tip-toe).

περπατεῖ 'ς τὰ νύχια.   he gives himself airs (walks on

ξεφορτόνω, I unload.

ξεφορτώσου με.   leave me alone.

ξυνίζω, I turn sour.

τὰ 'ξύνισε ὀλίγο.   he is upset a little.

ὁ καιρὸς τὰ 'ξύνισε.   the weather became unfavourable.

μοῦτρα ξυνισμένα.   a sour face.

ξυνός, sour.

μοῦ 'βγῆκε ξυνὴ αὐτὴ ἡ διασκέδασι.   that pleasure has cost me dear.

ὅλος, all.

μὲ τὰ ὅλα σου.   in earnest.

ὅλα ὅλα.   on the whole, in the main.

ὅλο κλαίει.   he keeps on crying.

μὲ ὅλους.   in a mass, in a lump.

μὲ ὅλον τοῦτο.   however, nevertheless.

μὲ ὅλον ὁποῦ.   although.

μ' ὅλον ὅτι εἶναι σοφός.   wise as he is.

ἡ ὁμιλία, speech.

ἀνοίγω ὁμιλίαν.   I begin a speech.

ὁμολογῶ, I confess, affirm.   [are talking nonsense.

δὲν 'μολογᾶς τίποτε!   you are proving nothing, you

τὸ ὄνομα, the name.

σήμερα ἔχει τὸ ὄνομά του.
to-day is his name day (*i.e.* the festival of the saint after whom he is named).

κατ᾽ ὄνομα.
by name.

τέσσαρα ὀνόματα.
four persons.

ἡ ὄρεξι, the appetite.

ἄλλη ὄρεξι δὲν ἔχω.
as if I had nothing else to do (as if I had no other taste).

κόφτω τὴν ὄρεξιν.
I take away the appetite.

ὁρίζω, I define, command, fix.

καλῶς ὡρίσατε !
welcome !

ὁρίστε.
what is your pleasure ? come in, &c.

ὅτι scarcely, just.

ὅτι ἔφυγε.
he has just gone out.

παθαίνω, I suffer.

τί ἔπαθες;
what is the matter with you ?

τὴν ἔπαθε.
he has come to grief.

παίζω, I play.

καλά μοῦ την ἔπαιξε.
he played me a nice trick.

παίρνω, I take.

παίρνω μαζύ μου.
I take with me.

παίρνω ὀπίσω.
I take back.

παίρνω ὀπίσω τὸν λόγο μου.
I take back my word.

τὸ παίρνω ἐπάνω μου.
I take it upon me.

τὸ παίρνει ἐπάνω του.
he takes too much upon himself.

παίρνω εἰς τὸ χέρι.
I cheat.

μὲ ᾽πῆρε ὁ ὕπνος.
I fell asleep.

ἀπ᾽ αὐτὰ ἐγὼ δὲν παίρνω.
I won't have that.

πάρε τὸν ἕνα χτύπα τὸν ἄλλο.
the one is as good as the other (take one and strike the other).

τὸ ᾽πῆρα ἀπόφασι.
I resolved.

ποιὸς ἐπῆρε (τὸ παιγνίδι);
who won (the game) ?

᾽πῆρε τὸ γράμμα μου.
he received my letter.

τὸ ᾽πῆρα πολὺ φτηνά.
I got it very cheap.

πόσα θά μου πάρῃς δι᾽ αὐτό;
how much will you take for that ?

παίρνω αἷμα.
I have myself bled.

παίρνω δανεικά.
I borrow money.

ἐπῆρε αὐτὸς τὴν ἐντροπήν.
he took the responsibility (lit. shame).

παρακάτω, lower.

    δὲν τὸ δίδει παρακάτω.   he will not give it for less.

ὁ πατέρας, the father.

    εἰς τὸν πατέρα σας.   go to the deuce.

πειράζω, I provoke, annoy.

    δὲν πειράζει.   it does not matter.

    εἶνε πειραγμένος.   he is angry.

περαστικός, transitory.

    περαστικά.   I hope you will soon be well again.

περνῶ, I pass.

    τοὺς ἐπέρασε ὅλους ἀπὸ τὸ σπαθί.   he put them all to the sword.

    περνῶ τὴν κλωστὴ ἀπὸ τὸ βελόνι.   I thread a needle.

    περνῶ τὸν καιρό μου.   I pass my time.

    διὰ νὰ περάσῃ ὁ καιρός.   to pass the time (to kill time).

    περνῶ ἕνα βιβλίο.   I read a book through.

    ἐπέρασε τὰ πενῆντα.   he is over (past) fifty (years old).

    πῶς περνᾷς;   how are you getting on? how d'ye do?

    ἤλπιζε νὰ περάσῃ μὲ τριάντα φράγκα ὡς τὰ Μέγαρα.   he hoped to get as far as Megara for thirty francs.

    ἐπέρασε ὁ καιρός.   the time (season) is past.

    δὲν ἐπέρασε ἕνας χρόνος.   not a year ago.

    αὐτὴ ἡ μονέδα δὲν περνᾷ πλέον.   this money is no longer current.

    μὲ πέρασε ὁ πονοκέφαλος.   my headache is gone.

    τὴν περασμένην ἑβδομάδα.   last week.

    περνῶ στενόχωρα.   I have trouble enough to get along (I am in straitened circumstances).

ἡ πετριά, the stone-throw.

    ἔχει τὴν πετριὰ ὅτι . . .   it is his crotchet that . . .

    καθένας ἔχει τὴν πετριά του.   every one has his hobby.

    ἔχει μιὰ πετριά.   he has a bee in his bonnet.

πετῶ, I fly, throw.

    πετᾷ ἀπὸ τὴ χαρά του.   he jumps for joy.

    πετᾶτε τὰ τουφέκια σας, σύρετε τὰ σπαθιά σας.   throw down your guns, draw your swords.

    μαχαίρ' ἐπέταξε.   he drew his dagger.

πέφτω, I fall.

ἔπεσε ἐπάνω του.	he fell upon him.
ἔπεσε ἀστροπελέκι.	a thunderbolt fell.
ἔπεσε τὸ σπῆτι καὶ τοὺς ἐπλά- κωσε ὅλους.	the house fell and buried them all.
ἔπεσε 'ς τὴν παγίδα.	he fell into the snare.
ἔπεσε ἀνάσκελα.	he fell on his back.
ἔπεσε κατακέφαλα.	he fell on his head.
σὲ ποιὸν ἔπεσε ὁ λαχνός;	on whom has the lot fallen?
ἔπεσε εἰς τὸ μερίδιόν του.	it fell to his share.
πέφτω ὀκνιάρης.	I turn lazy (cf. Eng. fall ill).

πηγαίνω, I go.

'πήγαινα νὰ 'πῶ.	I was (just) going to say.
'πῆγε νὰ ἀποθάνε.	he was near dying.
'πῆγε νὰ χάσῃ τον νοῦν του.	he was near losing his senses.
πηγαίνει μεσημέρι.	it is near mid-day.
δὲν σου πάει αὐτὸ τὸ καπέλο.	that hat does not suit you.
πήγαινε εἰς τὸ καλόν.	farewell.
ἔτσι πάει.	that is the way of it.

πιάνω, I take, seize.

τὸν ἔπιασε ἀπὸ τὸ χέρι.	he took his hand.
πόσα ψάρια ἔπιασες;	how many fish have you caught?
πιάνω δουλεία.	I set to work, take in hand.
μ' ἔπιασε κεφαλόπονος.	I have a headache.
σὲ πιάνει ἡ θάλασσα;	are you ever sea-sick? (does the sea affect you?)
θὰ πιάσω ἄλλη κάμαρα.	I shall hire another room.
πιάνει πολὺν τόπον.	it takes up a lot of room.
τώρα σ' ἔπιασα.	I have you there (now I've caught you).
ὅλαι ἠ θέσαις ἤτανε πιασμέναι.	all the places were taken.
πιάνω νὰ το κάμω.	I am going to do it.
ἐπιάσθηκαν.	they fell out with one another.
ὁ πνιγμένος ἀπὸ τὰ μαλλιά του πιάνεται.	the drowning man clutches at a straw.
ἔπιασαν τὰ δένδρα.	the trees have taken root.
μὲ ἔπιασεν ὁ θυμός.	I lost my temper.

πλαγιάζω, I go to bed.

ὅπως στρώσῃς θὰ πλαγιάσῃς.	as you make your bed you must lie on it.

πληρόνω, I pay.

ὁ θεὸς νά σοῦ το πληρώσῃ!	may God requite you.
τοῦ το 'πλήρωσε.	he paid him back (for it).

πλησιάζω, I approach, draw near.

πλησιάζει τὰ ἐξῆντα.	he is near sixty.

πνίγω, 1 suffocate, strangle.

ἐπνίγηκε.	he got drowned.
εἶνε πνιγμένος μέσ᾽ς τὸ χρέος.	he is deep in debt.
ἐπνίγηκε τὸ καράβι.	the ship has sunk.

τὸ ποδάρι (πόδι) the foot.

μὲ τὰ ποδάρια.	on foot.
σηκόνω εἰς τὸ πόδι.	I set on foot, set the world agog.

τὸ ποτάμι the river.

τὸν 'πῆρε τὸ ποτάμι.	he is in a sad pickle.
τὰ μάτια του ἐπήγαιναν ποτάμι.	he shed floods of tears.
ἕνα ποτάμι δάκρυα.	a torrent of tears.

τὸ πρᾶγμα, the thing.

τί πρᾶγμα εἶν᾽ αὐτό;	what is that?

ἡ προβειά, the sheepskin.

τοῦ ἐτείναξαν τὴν προβείαν.	they gave him a drubbing.

προκόπτω, I make progress.

τὸ 'προκόψαμε.	we have made a nice business of it (i.e. a mess).
εἶνε προκομμένος ἄνθρωπος.	he is a clever fellow.

προφθαίνω, I arrive, join.

δὲν ἐπρόφθασα νὰ τὸν ἰδῶ.	I did not come early enough to [see him.
δὲν 'μπορῶ νά τα προφθάσω ὅλα.	I cannot have them all finished.
δὲν θὰ προφθάσωμε νὰ τελειώσομε ἀπόψε.	we have not time to finish this evening.

πουλῶ, I sell.

ἀλλοῦ νά τα πουλήσῃς αὐτά.	tell that to the horse-marines (sell that elsewhere).

ἡ ῥάχη, the back.

σὲ τρώγει ἡ ῥάχη σου.	you are going in search of a beating (your skin itches).

ῥιχνω, I throw.

ῥίχνει τ᾽ αὐτιά του.	he puts his tail between his legs (he lets his ears drop in terror).

τὸν ἔρριξε τὸ ἄλογο.	the horse threw him.
ῥίχνει τὸ σφάλμα εἰς ἐμένα.	he throws the blame on me.
ἔρριξε κάτω τὰ μάτια της.	she lowered her eyes.
τὰ ἔρριξε ἔξω.	he throws it up, gives it up.
σέρνω, I draw.	
σύρε 'ς τὴ δουλειά σου.	go about your business.
σηκόνω, I lift.	
σηκόνω πανιά.	I hoist sail.
σηκόνω τὴν πολιορκίαν.	I raise the siege.
τὸν ἐσήκωσαν.	they took him up, deposed him.
δὲν σηκόνει χορατᾶ.	he can't take a joke.
αὐτὰ ἐγὼ δέν τα σηκόνω.	I won't stand that.
σηκόνω τὸ τραπέζι.	I clear the table.
σηκόνω πόλεμον.	I declare war.
σηκώθηκαν τὰ μαλλιά.	my hair stood on end.
σηκόνω τὸ τουφέκι.	I take up the gun.
τὸ πλοῖον σηκόνει δέκα ποδάρια νερό.	the vessel draws ten feet of water.
τώρα ἐσηκώθηκα.	I have just got up.
σηκόνομαι ἀπὸ μίαν ἀρρωστίαν.	I recover from a sickness.
σηκόνομαι ἀπὸ τὸν ὕπνον.	I awake.
σήμερα, to-day.	
σήμερα ὀχτώ.	eight days hence, this day week.
σιγανὸς, still.	
ἀπὸ σιγανὸ ποτάμι μακρειὰ τὰ ροῦχα σου.	still waters run deep (keep your clothes out of a silent river).
σκάνω, I burst.	
σκάνω ἀπὸ τὰ γέλια.	I burst with laughing.
σκάνω ἀπὸ τὸ κακό μου.	I burst with anger.
σκάσε.	get out! go to the deuce! (burst yourself).
ἡ σκάφη, trough.	
λέγω τὴν σκάφη σκάφη.	I call a spade a spade.
ὁ σκοπός, the motive.	
μὲ καλὸν σκοπόν.	well-intentioned.
δέν το εἶπε μὲ κακὸν σκοπόν.	he said it without any ill meaning.
σπάνω, I break.	
σπάνω τὸ κεφαλί μου.	I rack my brains.

τὸ σπυρί, the grain.

    δὲν ἔχει σπυρὶ μιαλό.   he has not a grain of sense.

    ἕνα σπυρί.   a trifle.

στέκω, I stand (also στέκομαι).

    στέκεται καλὰ 'ς τὸ ἄλογο.   he has a good seat on horseback.

    τὸ ὡρολόγι του 'στάθηκε.   his watch has stopped.

στέλνω, I send.

    θὰ στείλω διὰ τὸν ἰατρόν.   I shall send for the doctor.

στραβώνω, I bend.

    ἡ δουλειὰ ἐστράβωσε.   the thing goes wrong.

στρώνω, I spread.

    στρώνω τὸ κρεββάτι.   I make the bed.

    στρώνω τὸ τραπέζι.   I set the table.

    στρώθηκε 'ς τὸ χορτάρι.   he lay down on the grass.

    στρώνω τὸν δρόμον.   I pave the street.

στυλόνω, I prop up.

    στυλόνω τὰ μάτια μου.   I fix my eyes upon.

συγυρίζω, I order.

    συγυρίζομαι.   I make my toilette, dress.

τὸ συκῶτι, the liver.

    δὲν χαλνῶ τὸ συκῶτι μου δι'   I don't fret myself to fiddle-
    αὐτό.   strings over that.

ἡ συμπάθεια, forgiveness, sympathy (συμπάθειον).

    μὲ συμπάθεια.   pardon me.

σωστός, correct, exact.

    μὲ τὰ σωστά σου.   in earnest.

τελειόνω, I finish.

    ἐτέλειωσα.   ready.

τὸ τέρι (ταῖρι) the equal.

    δὲν ἔχει τέρι.   he is beyond compare.

τεριάζει (ταιριάζει), I fit.

    δὲν τεριάζει.   it does not fit.

    τί τεριάζει;   what fits?

ὁ τόπος, the place.

    κρασὶ τοῦ τόπου.   wine of the country.

τραβῶ, I draw.

    τραβῶ χέρι.   I give up, I withdraw.

    τράβα!   go on!

    τραβῶ καπνόν.   I smoke.

    τραβοῦμαι and τραβιοῦμαι.   I withdraw.

τρελλαίνω, I make (a person) mad.

τὴν τρελλαίνεται.   he is madly in love with her.

τρέχω, I run.

τρέχουν τὰ μάτια του.   his eyes stream (with tears).

αὐτὸς ὁ λόγος μοῦ τρέχει εἰς τὸ   I have the word on the tip of my
στόμα.   tongue.

τί τρέχει ;   what is up? what is going on?

ὁ τρόπος, the way, manner.

τί τρόπος εἶν' αὐτός ;   what sort of behaviour is that?

τρώγω, I eat.

τρώγει τὰ λόγια του.   he eats his words.

ἔφαγε ξύλο.   he got a beating.

αὐτὸ τὸ ψωμὶ δὲν τρώγεται.   this bread is not fit to eat.

μοῦ ἔφαγε τὰ αὐτιά.   he talked my head off.

αὐτὸ πλέον δὲν τρώγεται !   that wont do any longer ; that
is too much.

τρώγεται μὲ τὰ ῥοῦχά του.   there is no pleasing him.

τυφλός, blind.

τυφλὸς δρόμος.   blind alley.

φαίνομαι, I seem.

πῶς σας φαίνεται ;   How does it seem to you? what
is your opinion?

ἤτανε ἄρρωστος, ἀλλὰ δέν του   he was ill, but he does not appear
φαίνεται.   so.

ποῦ σου ἐφάνη !   what an idea !

τὸ φαρμάκι, the poison.

πόσα φαρμάκια ἔπια !   how many a bitter pill I have
had to swallow ! what I have
had to put up with !

τὸ φασοῦλι, the bean.

φασοῦλι φασοῦλι γεμίζει τὸ   many a little makes a mickle,
σακοῦλι.   (bean upon bean fills the bag).

φεύγω, I go away.

ὅπου φύγῃ φύγῃ.   every one for himself (let him
flee who can.)

ἡ χαλάστρα, the breach.

μοῦ ἔκαμε χαλάστρα.   he has upset my plans.

χαλνῶ, I spoil.

χαλνῶ ἕνα φράγκο.   I change a franc.

τὰ ἐχαλάσαμε.   our friendship is broken off.

ὁ καιρὸς ἐχάλασε.	the weather has broken.
'χάλασε τὸ στομάχι μου.	my stomach is out of order.
χάλασε ἡ καρδία μου.	my heart is breaking.
ἐχάλασαν τὸν ἐχθρόν.	they have put the enemy to flight.
πολὺ ἐχάλασες ἀπὸ ἐκεῖνο ὁποῦ ἤσουν.	you have changed much from what you (once) were.
ἐχάλασα τὴν νηστείαν.	I have broken my fast.
τὸ κρασὶ ἄρχισε νὰ χαλάσῃ.	the wine is beginning to turn.
χάνω, I lose.	
τὰ χάνω.	I lose my head.
δι' αὐτὸ χάνομαι.	I am dying for it, I must have it.
τὸ χέρι, the hand.	
τῶνα χέρι νίπτει τἄλλο.	one must give and take (one hand washes the other).
εἶνε 'ς τὸ χέρι του.	the affair lies in his hands.
δὲν ἔχω 'ς τὸ χέρι.	I have no money in hand, I am out of money.
πέντε χέρια.	five times.
ὁ χρόνος, the year.	
κακὸ χρόνο νἄχῃ!	bad luck to him.
πόσων χρόνων εἶνε;	how old is he?
τοῦ χρόνου.	next year.
χωρίζω, I separate.	
δέν τον χωρίζω ἀπὸ ἀδελφόν.	I treat him as a brother.
χωρέω, χωρῶ, hold, have room for.	
τοῦτο δέν το χωρεῖ ὁ νοῦς μου.	my mind can't take that in.
τὸ ψωμί, the bread.	
βγάζω τὸ ψωμί μου.	I earn my bread.
ἐφάγαμε ψωμὶ καὶ ἁλάτι μαζύ.	we have eaten bread and salt together (i.e. we are old friends).
ἡ ὥρα, the hour.	
τί ὥρα εἶνε;	what o'clock is it?
κατὰ τὴν ὥραν.	for the present.
ὥραν τὴν ὥραν.	from minute to minute.
ὥραις ὥραις.	from time to time.
πᾶσαν ὥραν.	at any time.
κακὴ ὥρα νὰ τὸν εὕρῃ.	plague take him!
ὥρα καλή.	good-bye.

VOCABULARY.

VOCABULARY.

A.

able, to be, (ἐ)μπορῶ
about, nearly, (ἐ)πάνω κάτω
about, concerning, περί, γιά
about four o'clock, περὶ ταῖς τέσσεραις
above, ἐπάνω
absent, be, λείπω
accept, δέχομαι
accident, δυστύχημα
accompany, συνοδεύω
account, bill, ὁ λογαριασμός
accustom, συνηθίζω
accustomed, συνηθισμένος
acid, ὀξύς
acknowledge, ὁμολογῶ
acorn, τὸ βαλανίδι
acquaintance, knowledge, ἡ γνῶσι
add, προσθέτω
address, ἡ διεύθυνσις
adjoining, next, δίπλα
admire, θαυμάζω
advantage, ὠφέλια
advantageous, beneficial, ὠφέλιμος
advice, ἡ συμβουλή
advise, συμβουλεύω
advocate, (n.), ὁ δικηγόρος
affair, τὸ πρᾶμα
afraid, be, φοβοῦμαι, σκιάζομαι
after, ὕστερα (ἀπὸ)
afternoon, τὸ ἀπόγευμα, μεταμεσήμβρια
afterwards, ὕστερα, ἔπειτα, κατόπιν
again, πάλι, ἀκόμη μιὰ φορά

agent, ἐπίτροπος, πράκτωρας
agree, make an agreement, συμφωνέω, -ῶ
agreement, ἡ συμφωνία
ague, ὁ πυρετός, ἡ ζέστη
(go) ahead, forward, ἐμπρός
aim (n.), ὁ σκόπος
aim at, σκοπεύω
air, ὁ ἀέρας
alight, καταβαίνω
all, ὅλος
Almighty, ὁ Παντοκράτωρ
almond, τὸ ἀμύγδαλον
almond-tree, ἡ ἀμυγδαληά
almost, κοντά, παρ' ὀλίγο
  I almost fell, ἐκόντεψα νὰ πέσω
alms (beggar's cry), ἐλεήσατέ με
alone, μόνος, μόναχός(μου, σου, &c.)
along, παρά
also, ἐπίσης
alter, ἀλλάζω
although, ἀγκαλά, ἂν καί
always, πάντοτε
ambassador, πρεσβύς
among, μεταξύ
amount, τὸ ποσόν
amuse, entertain, διασκεδάζω
amusement, ἡ διασκέδασι
anchor, ἄγκυρα, σίδερο
ancient, παλαιός, ἀρχαῖος
angel, ὁ ἄγγελος
anger, ὁ θυμός
angry, get, θυμόνω

I

animal, τὸ ζῶον
answer (n.), ἡ ἀπάντησι
answer (v.), ἀπαντάω, -ῶ
antiquity, ἡ ἀντίκα, τὸ ἀρχαῖο
anxious, ἀνήσυχος
anxiety, ἡ ἀνησυχιά, ἀνησυχία ἡ
   φροντίδα
any (with neg.), κανένας
any, have you? ἔχεις ἀπ' αὐτό;
appear, φαίνομαι
appetite, ἡ ὄρεξι
apple, τὸ μῆλο
apple-tree, ἡ μηληά
approach, πλησιάζω
apricot, τὸ βερύκοκκον
April, ὁ 'Απρίλιως
apron, ἡ ποδιά
Arab (n.), ὁ 'Αράπης
Arabian (a.), 'Αραβικός
arm (n.), τὸ χέρι
army, ὁ στρατός
arrange, σιάνω
   ,, (set in order), βάλλω εἰς
   τάξι
arrest (v.), βάλλω s φυλακή
arrival, ἡ ἄφιξις
arrive, φθάνω
art, ἡ τέχνη
artichoke, ἡ ἀγγινάρα
artist, ὁ τεχνίτης
as, σάν, ὡς
as (since), ἀφοῦ, ὅπως, ἐπειδή
as far as, ἕωι
as soon as, ἅμα, ἀφοῦ
(be) ashamed, 'ντρέπομαι
ashes, ἡ στάχτη
ask, (ἐ)ρωτάω, -ῶ
ask for, ζητάω, -ω, γυρεύω
askew, λοξός
asleep, be, κοιμοῦμαι
ass, τὸ γαϊδοῦρι
assure, βεβαιονω
at, εἰς
at all, καθόλου, διόλου, μπίτι
attend, προσέχω
attentive, προσεκτικός
August, ὁ Αὔγουστος
aunt, ἡ θεία (ἡ θειά)
Autumn, ὀπώρα
avaricious, φιλάργυρος

await, καρτερέω, -ῶ, περιμένω
awake (v.), 'ξυπνάω, -ῶ
awake (a.), ἔξυπνος
axe, ὁ μπαλτᾶς

B.

baby, ὁ μπεμπές, τὸ μωρό
back (backbone), ἡ ράχι
back, behind, ὀπίσω
bad, κακός
bag, ἡ σακκοῦλα, ἡ βαλίτσα
(go) bail for, ἐγγυάομαι, -ῶμαι
bake, ψήνω
bakehouse, ὁ φοῦρνος
baker, ψωμᾶς
balcony, τὸ μπαλκόνι
ball, ἡ μπάλλα, τὸ τόπι
ball (dance), ὁ χορός
bandit, ὁ κλέφτης
banish, ἐξορίζω
bank, ἡ μπάγκα, ἡ τράπεζα
banker, ὁ μπαγκιέρης, τραπεζίτης
baptise, βαφτίζω
barber, ὁ μπαρμπέρης, ὁ κουρεύς, κουρέας
bargain, ἡ συμφωνία
barley, τὸ κριθάρι
barrel, βαρέλι
basket, τὸ καλάθι, τὸ κοφίνι, τὸ
   πανέρι, τὸ ζιμπήλι
bath, τὸ μπάνγιο, τὸ λουτρό
bath, take a, κάμνω μπάνγιο
battle, ἡ μάχη
bay-tree, ἡ δάφνη
beam, flash, ἡ ἀχτῖνα (ἀκτῖνα, ἀκτῖδα)
bean, τὸ φασοῦλι
bear, carry, βαστάω, -ῶ, φέρω
beard, τὰ γένεια
beast, τὸ ζῶον
beat, χτυπάω, -ῶ
beautiful, ὡραῖος, ὄμορφος
beauty, ἡ καλλονή
because, γιατί, διότι
become, γίνω, γίνομαι
bed, τὸ κρεββάτι
(go to) bed, πλαγιάζω
bedclothes, τὸ στρωσίδι, τὰ ρούχα
bee, ἡ μέλισσα
beef-tea, broth, τὸ ζουμί

beer, ή μπίρα
before, πρὶν νά
before, πρότερον, προτήτερον
before (place), ἐμπρός, ἐμπροστά, ὀμπρός
beg, ζητέω, -ῶ, ἐλεημοσύνην
beggar, ὁ ζητιάνος
begin, ἀρχίζω
behave oneself, φέρομαι
behaviour, τὸ φέρσιμο
behind, (ὀ)πίσω
believe, πιστεύω, θαρρῶ, νομίζω
bell, τὸ κουδούνι
bellows, τὸ φυσερό
belly, ἡ κοιλιά
beloved, ἀγαπημένος
belt, ἡ ζώνη
bench, τὸ σκαμνί
bend, στραβόνω
beneath, κάτω (ἀπὸ), ἀπυκάτω
benefit (n.), ἡ ὠφέλεια
besides, ἐκτός, παραπάνω
bet, wager (n.), τὸ στοίχημα
bet, wager (v.), στοιχηματίζω
betrothal, αἱ ἀρραβῶναις
betrothe, ἀρραβωνίζομαι
better, καλλίτερος
all the better, τόσο τὸ καλλίτερο
between, μεταξύ
beyond, πέρα ἀπύ (adv.) παραπέρα
Bible, ἡ ἁγία γραφή
big, μεγάλος
bill of fare, ἡ λίστα, ὁ κατάλογος τῶν φαγητῶν
billiards, τὸ μπιλλιάρδο
bird, τὸ πουλί, τὸ πουλάκι
birthday, τὰ γεννητούρια
biscuit, rusk, τὸ παξιμάδι, τὸ μπισκότο
bishop, ὁ δεσπότης, ὁ (ἐ)πίσκοπος
(little) bit, κομμάτι
bite, δαγκάνω, τρώγω
bitter, πικρός
black, μαῦρος
black (of boots, v.), λουστράρω, λουστρόνω
blacking, ἡ μπογιά
bless, εὐλογίζω, -ω
blind, τυφλός, στραβός
blonde, ξανθές

blood, τὸ αἷμα
blotting-paper, τὸ στουπόχαρτι
blow (v.), φυσάω, -ῶ
blow up, πετάω (-ῶ) ’s τὸν ἀέρα
blow with a fist, ἡ γροθιά
blue, μαβής
blunder (v.), φταίω, φταίγω
blush, reddon, κοκκινίζω
boat, ἡ βάρκα, τὸ καΐκι
boatman, ὁ βαρκάρης
body, τὸ κορμί, τὸ σῶμα
bold, γενναῖος
bone, τὸ κόκκαλο
book, τὸ βιβλίο
bookbinder, ὁ βιβλιοδέτης
boot, τὸ παπούτζι, τὸ στιβάλι
born, γεννημένος
borrow, δανείζομαι, παίρνω δανεικά
both, καὶ οἱ δυό
bottle, ἡ μπουτίλια
boundary, τὰ ὅρια
bourse, τὸ χρηματιστήριον
box, τὸ κουτί
boy, τὸ παιδί, τὸ ἀγόρι
brain, τὸ μυαλόν
brandy, τὸ κονιάκ
bread, τὸ ψωμί
break, σπάνω
breast, τὸ βυζί
brick, τοῦβλον
bricklayer, ὁ χτίστης
bride, ἡ νύφη
bridegroom, ὁ γαμπρός
bridge, τὸ γεφύρι
bridle, τὸ καπίστρι
brigand, ὁ κλέφτης
bring, φέρω
broad, φαρδύς, πλατύς
bronze, ὁ μπροῦντζος, τὸ χάλκωμα
brook, τὸ ρυάκι, τὸ ρεῦμα
broom, ἡ σκούπα
broth, τὸ ζουμί
brother, ὁ ἀδελφός
brother-in-law, ὁ γυναικάδελφος, ὁ ἀνδράδελφος, ὁ γαμβρός
brown, μελαγχροινός, κόκκινος
brush (n.), ἡ βούρτσα
brush (v.), βουρτσίζω
bud, μάτι
bug, κοριός

build, χτίζω
  (who) built this house? ποιὸς ἔκαμε
    αὐτὸ τὸ σπῆτι;
burial, τὸ θάψιμο
burn, καίω
bury, θάπτω
bush, ὁ βάτος
(be) busy, ἔχω δουλειά
butcher, ὁ κασάπης, ὁ κρεοπώλης
butter, τὸ βούτυρο
butterfly, ἡ πεταλούδα
buy, ἀγοράζω
buy food, (ὀ)ψωνίζω
by, διά. ἀπό. μέ

C.

cab, carriage, ἡ καρότσα, ἡ ἅμαξα
cabbage, τὸ λάχανο
cabman, ὁ ἁμαξᾶς
café, τὸ καφενεῖον
calculate, λογαριάζω
calf, τὸ μοσχάρι
call (name), λέγω
call out, φωνάζω
(what is this) called? πῶς ὀνομάζεται
    αὐτό; πῶς τὸ λένε;
calm (n.), ἡ ἡσυχία, ἡ γαλήνη (at
    sea)
calm (v.), ἡσυχάζω
calm (a.), ἥσυχος, γαληνός (at sea)
can, (ἐ)μπορῶ
can (n.), ὁ τενεκές
candle, τὸ κηρί
cape, headland, τὸ ἀκρωτήρι
captain, ὁ λοχαγός: of a ship, ὁ
    πλοίαρχος
card, τὸ χαρτί
(play) cards, παίζω χαρτιά
care, ἡ προσοχή
care, take, προσέχω
careful, προσεκτικός
careless, ἀπρόσεκτος
caress, cajole, χαϊδεύω
carnival, ἡ ἀπόκρεως
carpenter, ὁ μαραγκός
carpet, τὸ χαλί
carriage, ἡ ἅμαξα, ἡ καρότσα
carry, φέρω

case, in any, χωρὶς ἄλλο
cask, τὸ βαρέλι
castle, τὸ παλάτι, τὸ κάστρο, ὁ πύργος
cat, ὁ γάτος, ἡ γάτα
catch, πιάνω
catholic, ὁ δυτικός (ὁ φράγκος)
cauliflower, τὸ κουνουπίδι
cedar, ἡ κέντρος
cemetery, τὸ νεκροταφεῖον, ἡ μάνδρα
centime, τὸ λεπτόν
certain, βέβαιος
certainty, ἡ ἀσφάλεια
chain, ἡ καθένα, ἡ ἀλυσίδα
chair, ἡ καρέκλα
chalk, ἡ κιμωλία, τὸ τεμπεσίρι
change (n.) (small money), λιανά,
    ψίλα
change (money) (v.), χαλάζω, ἀλλάζω
charcoal, τὸ κάρβουνο
charity, ἡ ἐλεημοσύνη
cheap, εὐθυνός, φτηνός
cheat (v.), γελάω, -ῶ
cheek, τὸ μάγουλο
cheese, τὸ τυρί
chemist's shop, τὸ φαρμακεῖον
cherry, τὸ κεράσι
cherry-tree, ἡ κερασιά
chest (of the body), τὸ στῆθος
chicken, τὸ κοττόπουλον
child, τὸ παιδί, τὸ παιδάκι
chill, τὸ κρύο
chin, τὸ γένειον
choke, πνίγω (pass. πνίγομαι)
cholera, ἡ χολέρα
Christian, ὁ χριστιανός
Christmas, τὰ χριστούγεννα
church, ἡ ἐκκλησία (ἡ ἐκκλησιά)
cigar, τὸ ποῦρο
cigarette, τὸ σιγάρο: (ready made) τὸ
    σιγαρέττο
cistern, ἡ δεξαμενή, ἡ στέρνα
citizen, ὁ πολίτης
city, ἡ πόλις
clean (a.), παστρικός, καθαρός
clean (v.), παστρεύω, καθαρίζω
clear, λαμπρός
clerk, γραμματεύς
climate, τὸ κλίμα
climb, ἀναβαίνω
cloak, τὸ πανοφόρι

clock, τὸ ὡρολόγι
cloth, ἡ τσόχα, τὸ πανή
clothes, ἡ φορεσιά
cloud, ἡ καταχνιά, ἡ συννεφιά, τὰ σύννεφα
cloudy, συννεφής
coal, τὸ κάρβουνο, ὁ γαιάνθρακας
coarse, χονδρός
coast, τὸ παράλι
coat, τὸ ρούχο
cock, ὁ πετεινός
coffee, ὁ καφές
coffee-house, τὸ καφενείον
coin, ὁ παρᾶς, τὸ νόμισμα, ἡ μονέδα
coins (ancient), τὰ μαρτσέλια
cold, catarrh, τὸ συνάχι
cold, to be, κρυόνω, κρυαίνω
cold, κρύος
(it is) cold, κάμνει κρύο, κάμνει ψύχρα
(it is) colder to-day than yesterday, κάμνει μεγαλείτερα ψύχρα ἀπὸ χτές
collar, τὸ κολάρι
collect, συλλέγω
collection, συλλογή
colour, χρῶμα
column, ὁ στῦλος, ἡ κολόννα
comb (n.), τὸ χτένι
comb (v.), χτενίζω
come, ἔρχομαι
come in, ἐμπρός! μέσα!
  (please) come in, κοπιάσατε μέσα
comedy, ἡ κωμῳδία
command (v.), ἡ διαταγή
command (n.), διατάσσω
commercial, ἐμπορικός
common (ordinary), πρόστυχος
companion, ὁ σύντροφος
company, ἡ συντροφιά : (military), τὸ τάγμα
compass, ἡ μπούσσολα
compel, oblige, ὑποχρεόνω
compensate, indemnify, ἀποζημιόνω
complain, παραπονοῦμαι, κάμνω παράπονα
condition, ἡ κατάστασι(s)
congratulate, συγχαίρω
conquer, νικάω, -ῶ
console, comfort, παρηγορέω, -ῶ
consul, ὁ πρόξενος
consulate, τὸ προξενεῖον

consult, συμβουλεύομαι
consumption, phthisis, ἡ φθίσι
content, εὐχαριστημένος
conversation, ἡ ὁμιλία, ἡ κουβέντα
cook (n.), ὁ μάγειρος, ἡ μαγείρισσα
cook (v.), μαγειρεύω
copper (n.), ὁ χαλκός, τὸ χάλκωμα
copy, ἀντιγράφω
cord, σχοινί
cork, plug, τὸ στούπωμα
corn (wheat), σιτάρι
corn (on the foot), ὁ κάλος
corner, ἡ γωνία
corpse, τὸ λείψανον, τὸ πτῶμα
correct, σωστός
cost (v.), κοστίζω
cottage, hut, τὸ καλύβι
cotton, cotton wool, τὸ βαμβάκι
(of) cotton, βαμβακερός (βαμβακερνός)
cough (n.), ὁ βῆχας
cough (v.), βήχω
count, μετράω, -ῶ (μετρέω, -ῶ)
country, land, ἡ χώρα
  I am going into the country, θὰ πάω 's τὴν ἐξοχήν
courage, τὸ θάρρος
court, ἡ αὐλή
cousin, ὁ ἐξάδελφος. ἡ ἐξαδέλφη
cover, σκεπάζω
coverlet, τὸ σκέπασμα
cow, ἡ ἀγελάδα
crab, ὁ κάβουρας
credit, ἡ πίστωσι
crew, τὸ πλήρωμα
criminal, ὁ κακοῦργος
crops, τὰ γεννήματα
cross, ὁ σταυρός
crown-prince, ὁ διάδοχος
cruel, rude, coarse, ὠμός
crumb, ἡ ψίχα
cry out, φωνάζω
cry (weep), κλαίω
cudgel, γδέρνομαι
cuff, μανικέτι
cup, ἡ φλιντζάνι, φιλτζάνι
cupboard, τὸ ἀρμάρι. τὸ δουλάπι
cure, ἰατρεύω, κάμνω καλά
curiosity, ἡ περιέργεια
(be) current (of coin), περνάω, -ῶ
curse, βλασφημέω, -ῶ

cursed, execrable, καταραμένος·
curtain, κορτίνα
cushion, μαξιλλάρι
custom, ή συνήθεια
customer, ό μουστερῆς, πελάτης
cut, κόφτω, κόβω

D.

damage, βλάφτω
damp, ύγρός, βρεμμένος
dance (n.), ό χορός
dance (v.), χορεύω
danger, ό κίνδυνος
daring, bold, τολμηρός
dark, σκοτεινός
   it is dark, είνε σκοτάδι
date (day of the month), ή μερομηνιά
daughter, ή θυγατέρα
day, ή (ή)μέρα
day before yesterday, προχτές
dead, (ά)πεθαμμένος
deaf, κουφός
dealer, ό πραγματευτής
dear, άκριβός
death, ό θάνατος
debt (n.), χρέος
decanter, τὸ μπουκάλι
December, ό Δεκέμβριος
decide, κρίνω
decision, judgment, ή άπόφασι, ή κρίσι(s)
deed, ή πρᾶξις
deep, βαθύς
delay (v.), άργέω, -ῶ
departure, άναχώρησις
depth, τὸ βάθος
deputy, βουλευτής
describe, περιγράφω
desert (n.), ή έρημία, τὰ έρημα
despise, περιφρονέω, -ῶ
devil, ό διάβολος
diarrhœa, ή διάρροια
die (v.), (ά)ποθαίνω : (of an animal), ψυφῶ
differ, διαφέρω
difference, διαφορά
difficult, δύσκολος
dig, σκάφτω

digest, χωνεύω
digestion, ή χώνεψι
dine, γευματίζω, τρώγω
dining-room, ή τραπεζαρία, ή σάλα
dinner, γεῦμα
dinner-napkin, ή πετσέτα
direction, ή διεύθυνσι
director, ό διευθυντής
dirt, mud, ή λάσπη
dirty, βρώμιγος
discover, έκκαλύφτω
disgrace, shame, ή έντροπή
disguise, άλλάζω
disgust, ή άηδία
dish, τὸ πιάτο
dismiss, διώχνω
disorder, άταξία
disposition, ή διάθεσι
ditch, τό αὐλάκι, ό ὀχετός
divide, χωρίζω
do, κάμνω
   (how do you) do, πῶς είσθε : τί κάμνετε ;
   (what am I to) do ? τί νὰ κάμω ;
doctor, ό ίατρός (γιατρός)
dog, τὸ σκυλί, ό σκύλος, (f.) ή σκύλα, τὸ σκυλάκι
doll, ή κοῦκλα
dollar, τὸ τάλληρον
donkey, ό γάϊδαρος, το γαϊδούρι, τὸ γομάρι
door, ή πόρτα
doubt (n.), ή άμφιβολία
doubt (v.), άμφιβάλλω
dove, pigeon, τὺ περιστέρι
down, κάτω
dozen, ή ντουζίνα, ή δωδεκάς
drag, draw, σέρνω
drawer, τὸ συρτάρι
drawers, τὸ σώβρακο
dream (n.), τὸ ὔνειρο
dream (v.), βλέπω 's τὸν ὔπνον
dress, τὸ φόρεμα
drink, πίνω
drive, take a, πηγαίνω μὲ τὴν ἅμαξα
drop, ή σταλίτσα
drown, άποπνίγω
druggist, apothecary, ό φαρμακοποῖος
druggist's shop, ή σπεζαριά, τὸ φαρμακεῖον

drunk, μεθυσμένος
drunkard, ὁ μπερῆς
drunkenness, ἡ μέθη
dry (a.), στεγνός, ξηρός
dry (n.), στεγνόνω
duck, ἡ πάπια
dumb, βουβός
dust, powder, ἡ σκόνη
duty, τὸ χρέος, τὸ καθῆκον
dye (v.), βάφω
dye (n.), ἡ μπογιά
dysentery, ἡ δυσεντερία
dwarf, ὁ νάννος

E.

each, ὁ καθένας, κάθε
ear, τὸ αὐτί
early, (ἐ)νωρίς, πρωΐ
earn, gain, κερδίζω, παίρνω
earth, ἡ γῆ
earthquake, ὁ σεισμός
east, ἡ ἀνατολή
Easter, ἡ Λαμπρή
easy, εὔκολος
eat, τρώγω
edge, rim, τὸ χεῖλος
education, ἡ ἀνατροφή
eel, τὸ χέλι, τὸ ἐγχέλι
egg, τὸ αὐγό
either...or, ἤ...ἤ
election, ἡ ἐκλογή
electric, ἠλεκτρικός
else, ἄλλως
embassy, ἡ πρεσβεία
embroidery, τὸ κέντημα
emperor, ὁ αὐτοκράτορας
empress, ἡ αὐτοκρατόρισσα
empty, ἄδειος
empty one's glass, ἀδειάζω τὸ ποτῆρι
end (n.), τὸ τέλος
end (v.), τελειόνω
endure, βαστάω, -ῶ, ὑποφέρω
enemy, ὁ ἐχθρός
energetic, προκομμένος
England, ἡ Ἀγγλία
English, Ἀγγλικός, Ἰγγλέζικος
Englishman, ὁ Ἄγγλος, ὁ Ἰγγλέζος
enough (adj.), ἀρκετός

enough (adv.), μπάστα, ἀρκετά
it is) enough, φτάνει
entertain (as a guest), τραττάρω, πεοιποιοῦμαι
entrance, ἡ εἴσοδος
envelope, ὁ φάκελλος
environs, τὰ περίχωρα
envy, ὁ φθόνος
equal, ἴσος
estate, κτῆμα
Europe, ἡ Εὐρώπη
evening, ἡ ἑσπέρα, τὸ βράδυ
(good) evening, καλησπέρα (σου, σας)
(this) evening, ἀπόψε
(in the) evening, τὸ ἑσπέρας
every, κάθε, ὁ καθένας
exact, accurate, σωστός
(six o'clock) exactly, σωστὰ 's ταὶς ἕξι
examine, ἐξετάζω
excavation, ἡ ἀνασκαφή
except, παρά, ἐκτός
exception, ἡ ἐξαίρεσι
excuse (v.), συγχωρῶ
exert oneself, κοπιάζω
exit, ἡ ἔξοδος
expend, ἐξοδεύω
expense, τὰ ἔξοδα
explain, ἐξηγέω, -ῶ
express, ἐκφράζω
extinguish, σβύνω
extra, χωριστά, παραπάνω
extravagant, σπάταλος
eye, τὸ μάτι
eyebrow, τὸ φρύδι

F.

face, τὸ πρόσωπον, τὰ μοῦτρα
factory, ἡ φάμπρικα
fade, ἀνοίγω
faint, λιγοθυμέω, -ῶ, λιποθυμέω, -ῶ
fainting-fit, ἡ λιγοθυμιά, ἡ λιποθυμία
faith, ἡ πίστι
faithful, πιστός
fall, πέφτω
fall ill, ἀρρωστέω, -ῶ
false, lying, ψεύτικος
falsehood, lie (n.), τὸ ψέμμα (ψεῦμα)
(speak) falsely, lie, λέγω ψέμματα

family, ἡ οἰκογένεια
famous, περίφημος
fan (n.), ἡ βεντάλια, τὸ ριπίδι,
far, μακράν, μακρυά, ἀλάργα
fare, τὸ ἀγώγιον, (by sea) ὁ ναῦλος
fashion, mode, ἡ μόδα, ὁ συρμός
fast (adv.), γρήγορα, ὀγλήγορα
fast (v.), νηστεύω
fasting (a.), νηστικός
fat, stout, παχύς, χονδρός
fate, ἡ τύχη, τὸ γραφτό
father, ὁ πατέρας
fault, sin, κρῖμα
feather, τὸ φτερό
February, ὁ Φεβρουάριος
feel, αἰσθάνομαι
female, θῆλυς
fetch, πηγαίνω νὰ φέρω
fever, ὁ πυρετός
fickle, ἄστατος
fiddle, τὸ βιολί
field, τὸ χωράφι
fig, τὸ σῦκο
fight (v.), πολεμέω, -ῶ
fight (n.), ἡ συμπλοκή
figure, ἡ φιγούρα
fill, γεμίζω
find, βρίσκω
fine (a.), λεπτός, φίνος
finger, ὁ δάχτυλος
finish, τελειόνω, σώνω
fir, ἡ πεύκη
fire (n.), ἡ φωτιά
(the) fire has gone out, ἔσβυσε ἡ φωτιά
fire (conflagration), ἡ πυρκαϊά
fire-brigade, οἱ πυροσβέσται
(at) first, πρῶτα, τὸ πρῶτον
fish, τὸ ψάρι
fisher, ὁ ψαρᾶς
fist, ὁ γρόθος
fix, στερεόνω
flag, banner, ἡ σημαία
flame, ἡ φλόγα
flank (of a person), ἡ πλευρά
flatter, κολακεύω
flax, τὸ λίνον
flea, ὁ ψύλλος
flee, φεύγω
fleet (n.), ὁ στόλος
floor, τὸ κατάστρωμα

florin, τὸ φιορίνι
flour, τὸ ἀλεύρι
flower, τὸ λουλούδι
flute, τὸ φλάουτο
fly (n.), ἡ μυῖγα, μυῖα
fly (v.), πετῶ
fog, ὁμίχλη
fold, διπλόνω
follow, ἀκολουθέω, -ῶ
folly, ἡ ἀνοησία
food, τὸ φαγί, ἡ τροφή
fool, ὁ λουρδός
foot, τὸ πόδι, τὸ ποδάρι
forbid, ἐμποδίζω, ἀπαγορεύω
force, power, ἡ δύναμι
force (v.), ἀναγκάζω
forehead, τὸ κούταλο
foreign, ξένος, ἐξωτερικός
forest, τὸ δάσος
forgive, συγχωρέω, -ῶ
fork, τὸ πηροῦνι
former, περασμένος, πρῴην
forsake, ἀφήνω
fortress, τὸ φρούριον
fortune, ἡ τύχη
fortune (wealth), ἡ περιουσία
fowl, ἡ κύττα, τὸ κυττόπουλο
fox, ἡ ἀλεποῦ
free, ἐλεύθερος
freedom, ἡ ἐλευθερία (ἐλευθεριά)
freight, fare, τὸ ἀγώγιον
French, Γαλλικός
Frenchman, ὁ Γάλλος (Φραντσέζος)
fresh, φρέσκος
Friday, ἡ παρασκευή
friend, ὁ φίλος, ἡ φιληνάδα
(he is a) friend of mine, ἔχω φιλίαν
    μὲ αὐτόν
friendship, ἡ φιλία
fright, ὁ φόβος
(to) frighten, τρομάζω
frog, ὁ βάτραχος
from, ἀπό
(in) front, ἐμπρόσθε(ν), μπροστά
fruit, ὁ καρπός, τὰ φροῦτα
full, γιομάτος, γεμάτος
functionary, ὁ ὑπάλληλος
fur, ἡ γούνα
furniture, τὰ ἔπιπλα
further on, παραπέρα

G.

gain (n.), τὸ κέρδος
gain (v.), κερδίζω
game (play), τὸ παιγνίδι
game (food), τὸ κυνήγι
garden, τὸ περιβόλι, ὁ κῆπος
garlic, τὸ σκόρδο
garter, ὁ καλτσοδέτης
gate, ἡ πόρτα
gem, τὸ πετράδι, ἡ πετρίτσα
gently, slowly, σιγὰ σιγά, ἀγάλια
  ἀγάλια
German (n.), Γερμανός (f. Γερμανίδα)
German (a.), Γερμανικός
Germany, ἡ Γερμανία
get up, σηκόνομαι
girl, τὸ κορίτσι
give, δίδω
give back, ἐπιστρέφω
glad, εὐχαριστημένος
glance, ἡ ματιά
glass, τὸ γυαλί
glass (for drinking), τὸ ποτῆρι
glass (of window), τζάμι
glove, τὸ γάντι
go, πηγαίνω
go on! ἐμπρός!
go away, φεύγω
going on, what is! τί τρέχει;
go out, βγαίνω
goat, τὸ γίδι, ἡ κατσέκα
god, ὁ θεός
godfather, ὁ νουνός, ὁ κουμβάρος
gold, μάλαμμα, χρυσό
golden, μαλαμματένιος, χρυσινός
good, kind, καλός
goodbye, ἀντίο, ὥρα καλή
goodbye (say), leave (take one's),
  ἀποχαιρετάω
Good Friday, ἡ Μεγάλη Παρασκευή
goodness, kindness, ἡ καλοσύνη
goose, ἡ χήνα
government, ἡ κυβέρνησι
grammar, ἡ γραμματική
grandchild, ὁ ἔγγονος
grandfather, ὁ παππούς
grandmother, ἡ μαμμή
grape, τὸ σταφύλι
grass, τὸ χορτάρι

grateful, εὐχάριστος
grave, ὁ τάφος
grease (n.), τὸ πάχος
Greece, ἡ Ἑλλάδα (Ἑλλάς,
Greek (n.), ὁ Ἕλλην(ας)
Greek (a.), Ἑλληνικός
green, πράσινος
greet (v.), χαιρετίζω, -άω, -ῶ
greeting, ὁ χαιρετισμός (τὰ χαιρετίσ-
  ματα)
grief, ἡ λύπη
grocer, ὁ μπακάλης
(on the) ground, χάμου, κατάχαμα
grow, μεγαλόνω
guard, be on one's, beware, φυλά-
  γομαι
guardian, ὁ φύλακας
guide, ὁ ὁδηγός, ὁ ἀγωγιάτης
gnitar, cithern, ἡ κιθάρα
gun, τὸ γκόμμι
gun, τὸ τουφέκι
gunpowder, ἡ σκόνη, ἡ πυρίτιδα
gunshot, ἡ τουφεκιά
gutter, channel, τὸ αὐλάκι, ὁ ὀχετός

H.

habit, custom, τὸ ἔθιμον, ἡ συνήθεια
hail (n.), τὸ χαλάζι
(it) hails, πέφτει χαλάζι
hair, τὰ μαλλιά, ἡ τρίχα
half (n.), τὸ μισό
half (a.), μισύς
hall, saloon, ἡ σάλα
hall door, ἡ μεγαλόπορτα
ham, τὸ χοιρομέρι
hammer, τὸ σφυρί
hand (n.), τὸ χέρι
handkerchief, τὸ μανδύλι
happy, εὐτυχής
hard, σκληρός
hare, ὁ λαγός
harm (v.), βλάφτω
harvest, τὸ ἀλώνι
hasten, βιάζομαι
hat, τὸ καπέλο
hats off, κάτω τὰ καπέλα
hat off, to take the, βγάλλω τὸ
  καπέλο

hate (n.), τὸ μῖσος

hate (v.), μισῶ

hay, τὸ χορτάρι

head, τὸ κεφάλι

health, ἡ (ὑ)γεῖα

hear, ἀκούω, ἀκούγω

heart, ἡ καρδιά

heat, ἡ ζέστη

heaven, ὁ οὐρανός

heavy, βαρύς

heel, ἡ φτέρνα

heel (of stocking), τὸ τακούνι

height, τὸ ὕψος

hell, ἡ κόλασι

help, βοηθῶ

hen, ἡ κόττα

here, ἐδῶ

here! here I am! (answer by a waiter), ἔφθασα (from φθάνω, I arrive)

herring, ἡ ἀρίγγα

hide, skin, ἡ πέτσα, τὸ πετσί

hide (v.), κρύβω

high, (ὑ)ψηλός

high-way, βασιλικὸς δρόμος

hinder, prevent, ἐμποδίζω

hire (v.), ἐνοικιάζω

history, ἡ ἱστορία

hold, κρατέω, -ῶ

hole, ἡ τρύπα, τροῦπα

holiday, ἡ ἑορτή, ἡ φέστα, ἡ ἀργία

holy, ἅγιος

Holy Thursday, ἡ μεγάλη Πέφτη

home, inland, ἐσωτερικός

home, at, 's τὸ σπῆτι

(is he at) home? εἶνε μέσα;

honey, τὸ μέλι

honour, ἡ τιμή

hope (v.), ἐλπίζω

hope (n.), ἡ ἐλπίδα

horn, τὸ κέρας

horse, τὸ ἄλογο, ὁ καβάλλης

(on) horseback, καβάλλα

horse-boy, ὁ ἀγωγιάτης

hospital, τὸ νοσοκομεῖον

hot, ζεστός

hotel, τὸ ξενοδοχεῖον

hotel-keeper, host, ὁ ξενοδόχος

hour, ἡ ὥρα

house, σπῆτι

householder, ὁ νοικοκύρης

how! πῶς;

how much! πόσος;

humble, χαμηλός

hung up, κρεμασμένος

hunger, ἡ πεῖνα

hunter, ὁ κυνηγός

hurry, be in a, βιάζομαι

hurt (v.a.), βλάφτω, ζημιόνω

hurt (be in pain), πονέω, -ῶ

husband, ὁ σύζυγος, ὁ ἄντρας

hush! σίγα

hut, τὸ καλύβι

I.

ice, ὁ πάγος

ice-cream, τὸ παγωτό, ἡ γλασάδα

idea, ἡ ἰδέα

if, ἄν, ἅμα

if he should come, τυχὸν νὰ ἔλθῃ

ill, ἄρρωστος, ἀσθενής

ill, I feel, μου ἔρχεται τὸ κακό

ill-use, abuse (v.), κακαμεταχειρίζομαι

illegal, παράνομος

illegitimate, ψεύτικος

illness, ἡ ἀρρωστιά

immediately, ἀμέσως

(he will come) immediately, τώρα ἔρχεται

impatient, ἀνυπόμονος

important, σπουδαῖος

impossible, ἀδύνατος

improvement, ἡ καλλιτέρευσι

impudent, αὐθάδης

in, μέσα (εἰς), εἰς

incessant, ἀκατάπαυστος

inconvenience (v.), πειράζω

indeed, certainly, βέβαια, μάλιστα

indifferent, ἀδιάφορος

indisposed, κακοδιάθετος

indisposition, ἡ κακοδιαθεσία

infant, τὸ μωρό

infect, to (with a disease), κολλάω, κολλῶ

infectious, κολλητικός

inform, εἰδοποιέω, -ῶ

information, ἡ πληροφορία

(be) informed, πληροφοροῦμαι

ingratitude, ἡ ἀχαριστία
inhabit, κατοικέω, -ῶ
inhabitant, ὁ κάτοικος
inherit, κληρονομέω, -ῶ
injury, ἡ βλάβη, ἡ ζημία
ink, τὸ μελάνι
inn, τὸ ξενοδοχεῖον, ἡ ταβέρνα, ἡ λοκάντα
(wayside) inn, τὸ χάνι
innocent, ἀθῷος
insane, τρέλλος
inscription, ἡ ἐπιγραφή
instead of, ἀντίς
instrument, ἡ μηχανή
insult (v.), προσβάλλω, πειράζω
insurance, ἀσφάλεια
international, διεθνής
interrupt, διακόφτω
interruption, ἡ διακοπή
intolerable, ἀφόρητος
introduce, παρουσιάζω
invent, find out, ἐφευρίσκω
invention, ἡ ἐφεύρεσι, τὸ ἐφεύρεμα
investigate, ἐξετάζω
invite, προσκαλέω, -ῶ
iron (n.), ὁ σίδηρος
iron (a.), σιδηρένιος
iron (v.), σιδερόνω
island, τὸ νησί
Italian (n.), ὁ Ἰταλός
Italian (a.), Ἰταλικός
Italy, Ἰταλία
ivory, τὸ φίλτισι

J.

jam, τὸ γλύκισμα
January, ὁ Ἰανουάριος
jealous, ζηλιάρης
Jew, ὁ Ἑβραῖος, ἡ Ἑβραία
jewel, τὸ στολίδι
join, ἐνόνω
joke (n.), ὁ χωρατᾶς
joke (v.), χωρατεύω
journey, τὸ ταξίδι
(have you done this) journey ! ἔκαμες αὐτὸν τὸν δρόμο;
joy, ἡ χαρά
judge, δικαστής

jug, pitcher, τὸ κουμάρι
July, ὁ Ἰούλιος
jump, spring, πηδάω, -ῶ
June, ὁ Ἰούνιος
just, δίκαιος
just (exactly), ἴσα, ἴσια, σωστά
justice, τὸ δίκαιον, δικαιοσύνη

K.

keep (hold), κρατέω, -ῶ
keep (guard), φυλάγω, φυλάω
keep (one's word), βαστῶ (τὸν λόγον)
kettle, ὁ τέντζερες, ἡ τζαῖάρα
key, τὸ κλειδί
kick, κλοτσῶ
kidneys, τὰ νεφριά
kill, σκοτόνω
kind (a.), καλός
kind (description), τὸ εἶδος
king, ὁ βασιλέας (βασιλεῦς)
kiss (n.), τὸ φίλημα
kiss (v.), φιλέω, -ῶ
kitchen, τὸ μαγειρειό
knee, τὸ γόνατο
knife, τὸ μαχαῖρι : (pen-knife), ἡ σουγιά
knife-thrust, ἡ μαχαιριά
knit, πλέκω
knock, χτυπάω, -ῶ
knot (n.), ὁ κόμπος
know, ξέρω, ἐξεύρω
know, recognize, γνωρίζω
known, familiar, γνωστός

L.

labour, ἡ δουλειά
ladder, ἡ σκάλα
lady, ἡ κυρία, ἡ κυρά
lake, ἡ λίμνη
lamb, τὸ ἀρνί, τὸ ἀρνάκι
lame, κουτσός
lamp, ἡ λάμπα
land, ἡ γῆ
language, ἡ γλῶσσα
lantern, τὸ φανάρι
large, μεγάλος

last (v.), βαστῶ, φθάνω
last (a.), τελευταῖος
lastly, at last, 's τὸ τέλος
late, ἀργά
late (dead), μακαρίτης
laugh, γελάω, -ῶ
law, ὁ νόμος
lawyer, ὁ δικηγόρος
lay, put, βάζω
lay the table, σ-ρῶσε τὺ τραπέζι
lazy, τεμπέλης
lead (v.), ὁδηγέω, -ῶ, φέρνω
lead, τὸ μολύβι, τὸ βολύμι
lead pencil, τὺ μυλυβδοκόνδυλον, τὸ
    μολύβι
leaf, τὸ φύλλο
learn, μαθαίνω, μανθάνω
learn by heart, μαθαίνω ἀπ' ἔξω
leather, τὸ πετσί, ἡ πέτσα
leave, ἀφήνω
left, ἀριστερός, ζερβός
leg, τὸ πόδι, τὸ ποδάρι
lemon, τὸ λεμόνι
lemonade, ἡ λιμονάδα
lend, δανείζω
length, τὸ μῆκος
Lent, Σαρακοστή
less, ὀλιγότερον
lesson, τὸ μάθημα
let (of a house) (v. , ἐνοικιάζω
let, to be, ἐνοικιάζεται
letter, τὸ γράμμα, ἡ ἐπιστολή
letter of the alphabet, τὺ γράμμα, τὺ
    στοιχεῖον
lettercase, τὸ πορτοφόλιο
liar, ὁ ψεύτης
liberty, ἡ ἐλευθεριά
library, ἡ βιβλιοθήκη
lie, (n.) τὸ ψέμμα
lie down, πλαγιάζω
life, ἡ ζωή
lift up, σηκόνω
light. τὸ φῶς
light (weight, ἐλαφρός
lightens, it, ἀστράφτει
lightning, ἡ ἀστραπή
like (a.), ὅμοιος, παραπλήσιος
like (v.), ἀγαπῶ
(do you) like it, σ' ἀρέσει αὐτό;
likely, πιθανός

lime, ὁ ἀσβέστης
line, ἡ γραμμή
linen, canvas, τὸ λινάρι
linen from the wash, τὰ ἀσπρόρρουχα
linen (soiled), τὰ ροῦχα
lion, τὸ λεοντάρι
lip, τὸ χεῖλος
listen, ἀκούω
little, μικρός, ὀλίγος
live, ζῶ, ζάω
live (at), κάθομαι
lively, ζωηρός
liver, τὸ συκώτι
living, ζωντανός
load (v.), γεμίζω
load (n.), τὸ φόρτωμα
lobster, τὸ ἀστάκι
lock (n.), ἡ κλειδαριά
lock (v.), σφαλίζω
London, ἡ Λόντρα, τὸ Λονδίνον
long, μακρύς
(a) long time, πολὺν καιρόν
long for, γυρεύω, ζητέω, -ῶ
look (v.), κυττάζω
look out ! βάρδα, ἐμπρός
looking-glass, ὁ καθρέπτης
lose, χάνω
lottery, τὸ λαχεῖον
love (n.), ἡ ἀγάπη
love (v.), ἀγαπῶ
low, χαμηλός
luck, ἡ τύχη
luggage, τὰ πράμματα
luggage-porter, ὁ χαμάλης
luggage-ticket, ἀπόδειξις ἀποσκευῆς
lunch, mid-day meal, τὸ πρόγευμα

M.

machine, ἡ μηχανή
mad, τρελλός
Madonna, ἡ Παναγία
maiden, τὸ κορίτσι
maid-servant, ἡ δούλα, ἡ ὑπηρέτρια
make, κάμνω
male, ἀρσενικός
man, ὁ ἄντρας, ὁ ἄνθρωπος
manner, way, τρόπος
many, πολλοί

map, ὁ χάρτης
marble, τὸ μάρμαρο
March, ὁ Μάρτιος
mare, ἡ φοράδα
mark (n.), σημαῖον, σημάδι
market, ἡ ἀγορά, τὸ (μ)παζάρι
marketing, go, ψουνίζω
marriage, ἡ (ὑ)παντρειά
married, παντρεμμένος (ὑπανδρευμένος)
marry, (ὑ)παντρεύομαι
mask, ἡ προσωπίδα, ἡ μουτσοῦνα
mason, ὁ χτίστης
mass, multitude, τὸ πλῆθος
mass, service, ἡ λειτουργία
master, builder, carpenter, &c.), ὁ
    μάστορης
mat, ἡ ψάθα
match, τὸ σπίρτο
matter, it does not, δὲν πειράζει
mattress, τὸ στρῶμα
May, ὁ Μάϊος
mayor, ὁ δήμαρχος
meadow, τὸ λιβάδι
meal, τὸ ἀλεύρι
mean (v.), σημαίνω
meaning, ἡ ἔννοια
means, medium, τὸ μέσο
measles, ἡ κοκκινάδα, ἡ ἴλερι
measure, τὸ μέτρο
measure, μετρέω, -ῶ
meat, τὸ κρέας
medicine, τὸ γιατρικό, τὸ φάρμακον
mediterranean, μεσόγειος
meet, ἀνταμόνω, ἀπαντάω, -ῶ
meeting, ὁ σύλλογος
melt, λυόνω
mend, διορθόνω, φτειάζω: (of clothes),
    μπαλλόνω
mention (v.), ἀναφέρω
merchandise, τὸ ἐμπόριον
merchant, ὁ ἔμπορος
merry, καλόκαρδος
metal, τὸ μέταλλο
methylated spirit, σπίρτο καμινέτο
mid-day, τὸ μεσημέρι
midnight, τὸ μεσονύκτι
middle, centre, τὸ μέσο
mile (league), τὸ μίλι
milk (n.) τὸ γάλα
milk (v.), ἀμέργω

mill, ὁ μύλος
miller, ὁ μυλωνᾶς
mind, ὁ νοῦς
mine, τὸ μεταλλεῖον
minister (of state), ὁ ὑπουργός—(diplo-
    matic) ὁ πρέσβυς
minute (n.), τὸ λεπτύ
miracle, τὸ θαῦμα
mirror, ὁ καθρέπτης
misery, misfortune, ἡ δυστυχία
miss (unmarried woman), ἡ δεσποσύνη,
    ἡ δεσποινίς
mistake, τὸ λάθος
misunderstand, παρανοέω, -ῶ
mix, shuffle, ἀνακατόνω
model, τὸ παράδειγμα
moderate, μέτριος
modern, νέος, νεώτερος, σημερινός
moment, ἡ στιγμή
Monday, ἡ Δευτέρα
money, ὁ παρᾶς, οἱ παράδες, τὰ χρή-
    ματα, τὰ λεπτά
monk, ὁ καλόγερος
month, ὁ μῆνας
moon, τὸ φεγγάρι, ἡ σελήνη
moral, ἠθικός
more, περισσότερος
morning, ἡ πρωΐα, τὸ πρωΐ
morning, in the, τὸ πρωΐ, σύνταχα
mosquito, midge, τὸ κουνοῦπι
mosquito net, ἡ κουνουπιέρα
mother, ἡ μητέρα, ἡ μάννα
mother-in-law, ἡ πενθερά (πεθερά)
mother tongue, ἡ μητρικὴ γλῶσσα
mount, ἀναβαίνω
mountain, τὸ βουνό
mouse, ὁ ποντικός, τὸ ποντικάκι
moustache, τὸ μουστάκι
mouth, τὸ στόμα
move, κουνέω, -ῶ, σαλεύω
much, πολύς
mud, ἡ λάσπη
mule, τὸ μουλάρι
murder, ὁ φόνος
music, ἡ μουσική
musician, ὁ μουσικός
muslin, ἡ μουσελίνα
must (n.), μοῦστο
must (v. impers.), πρέπει
mustard, τὸ σινάπι, ἡ μουστάρδα

N

nail, τὸ καρφί
nail (of the finger). τὸ νύχι
naked, γυμνός
name, τὸ ὄνομα
name, what is your ? πῶς σε λένε :
narrow, στενός
nation, τὸ ἔθνος
national, ἐθνικός
native, ἐντόπιος
native country, ἡ πατρίδα
natural, φυσικός
nature, ἡ φύσι
near, κοντά, σιμά
necessary (it is), εἶνε ἀνάγκη
necessitate, ἀναγκάζω
necessity, ἡ ἀνάγκη
neck, ὁ λαιμός
need, require, χρειάζομαι
needle, τὸ βελόνι
negro, ὁ ἀράπης
neighbour, ὁ γείτονας
neither...nor, οὔτε...οὔτε
nephew, ὁ ἀνεψιός
nest, ἡ φωλεά
net, τὸ πλεμμάτι, τὸ δίχτι
never, δέν...ποτέ
new, καινούριος
new year's day, ἡ πρωτοχρονιά
news, ἡ εἴδησι
newspapers, ἡ ἐφημερίδα (ἡ ἐφημερίς)
nice, καλός, νόστιμος
niece, ἡ ἀνεψιά
night, ἡ νύχτα
night, at, τὴν νύχτα
no, ὄχι
noble, εὐγενής
noise, shout, ἡ φωναίς
noon, τὸ μεσημέρι
north (n.), ὁ Βορρᾶς
north (a.), Βόρρειος
nose, ἡ μύτη
not, δέν
not yet, ἀκόμη
note. τὸ γραμματάκι, ἡ σημείωσις
nothing, τίποτα
notice, ἡ σημείωσις
novel, romance, τὸ μυθιστόρημα

November, ὁ Νοέμβριος
now, τώρα
number, ὁ ἀριθμός
nurse, ἡ παραμάνα, ἡ νταντά
nut (walnut), τὸ καρύδι : (hazel nut),
τὸ φουντούκι

O.

oak, ἡ δρῦς, τὸ δέντρον, ἡ βαλανιδιά :
(evergreen). τὸ πουρνάρι
oath, ὁ ὅρκος
oats, τὸ βρόμι
oblige, κάμνω χάριν. See also 'com
pel'
oblique, λοξός
observation, ἡ παρατήρησι
observe, παρατηρέω, -ῶ, σκοπεύω
occupied (of a place). πιασμένος
October, ὁ Ὀκτώβριος
offer, προσφέρω
office, counting-house, τὸ γραφεῖον
often. συχνά
oil, τὸ λάδι
old, παλαιός
old man, ὁ γέρος
old woman, ἡ γρηά, ἡ γερόντισσα
older than I, μεγαλείτερος ἀπὸ μένα
olive (n.), ἡ ἐλῃά
olive-tree, ἡ ἐλῃά
omnibus, τὸ λεωφορεῖον
onion, τὸ κρομμύδι
only, μόνον
open (a.), ἀνοιχτός
open (v.), ἀνοίγω
opera, ἡ ὄπερα [τὸ μελόδραμα]
opinion, ἡ γνώμη
opium, τὸ ἀφιόνι
opportunity, ἡ εὐκαιρία
opposite, ἀπέναντι, καρσί
opposite, δίπλα
opposite the house, δίπλα's τὸ σπῆτι
he lives hard by, κάθεται ἀπὸ δίπλα
oppressive, βαρύς
orange, τὸ πορτογάλλι : (mandarin), τὸ
μανταρίνι : (bitter), νεράντζι.
orange-tree, ἡ πορταγαλλιά
order, badge, το παράσημον
order, regulation, ἡ τάξι

(give) order for, παραγγέλλω (aor.
παράγγειλα, παρήγγειλα)
ornament, τὸ κόσμημα
orphan, τὸ ὀρφανό
outside (also, get out), ἔξω, ὄξω
out, he has gone out, ἐβγῆκε ἔξω
over, πάνω
over a hundred pounds, παρεπάνω
ἀπὸ ἑκατὸν λίραις
overcoat, τὸ πανωφόρι
owl, ἡ κουκκουβάγια
own (a.) [ἰ]δικός (μου, σου, &c.)
ox, τὸ βῶδι
oyster, τὸ στρίδι

P.

pack, μαζόνω
packet, τὸ πακέτο, τὸ δέμα
pain (n.), ὁ πόνος
pain (be in), πονέω, -ῶ
paint (n.), τὸ χρῶμα, ἡ μποϊά
paint (v.), ζωγραφίζω
painter, ὁ ζωγράφος
pair, τὸ ζευγάρι
palace, τὸ παλάτι
pale, ὠχρός: (of colours), ἄνοικτος
paper, τὸ χαρτί
Paradise, ὁ Παράδεισος
parasol, ἡ ὀμπρέλλα
pardon, I beg your pardon, μὲ συμπάθεια! νά με συγχωρῆτε! συγγνώμη
parents, οἱ γονεῖς
Paris, τὸ Παρίσι
parrot, ὁ παππαγάλλος
part, τὸ μέρος
parting (of the hair), ἡ χωρίστρα
partridge, ἡ πέρδικα
pass (of time), περνάω, -ῶ
passport, τὸ διαβατήριον, ὁ τεζκερές
past (a.), περασμένος
patch (v.), μπαλλόνω
patience, ἡ ὑπομονή
pattern, model, τὸ δεῖγμα
pay (n.), ὁ μισθός, τὰ λεπτ
pay (v.), πληρόνω
payment, ἡ πληρωμή
pea, τὸ πιζέλι
peace, ἡ εἰρήνη

peach, τὸ ῥοδάκινον
pear, τὸ ἀπίδι : (wild) τὸ ἀχλάδι, τὸ
ἀγραπίδι
pear-tree, ἡ ἀπιδιά, (wild) ἡ ἀχλαδιά
pearl, τὸ μαργαριτάρι
peasant, ὁ χωρικός, ὁ χωριάτης, fem.
χωριάτισσα
peculiar, odd, περίεργος, παράξενος
pen, τὸ κονδύλι, ἡ πέννα
penknife, ἡ σουγιά
people, οἱ ἄνθρωποι, ὁ κόσμος
pepper, τὸ πιπέρι
perfume, ἡ μυρωδιά
permission, ἡ ἄδεια
permit, ἐπιτρέπω
permitted, it is not, δὲν ἐπιτρέπεται
persevere, βαστῶ
person, man, ὁ ἄνθρωπος, τὸ πρόσωπον
pet, ἀγαπητός, χρυσό
photograph (n.), ἡ φωτογραφία
photograph (v.), φωτογραφίζω
photographer, ὁ φωτογράφος
photography, ἡ φωτογραφία
pianoforte, τὸ πιάνο
pick (n.), ὁ κουζμᾶς, ὁ καζμᾶς
picture, ἡ εἰκῶνα, ἡ ζωγραφία
piece, τὸ κομμάτι
pig, τὸ γουρούνι
pigeon, τὸ περιστέρι
pilgrim, ὁ χατζής
pill (n.), τὸ καταπότι
pillow, τὸ μαξιλάρι
pilot, ὁ ναυηγός
pin, ἡ καρφίτσα
pine, ἡ πεύκη
pink, gilly-flower, τὸ γαρόφαλλο
pipe (to smoke), τὸ τσιμπούκι : nar-
ghileh, ὁ ναργιλές, ὁ ἀργιλές
pipe (water), ὁ σωλῆνας
pistol, τὸ πιστόλι
pitch, τὸ κατράνι (κατράμι)
pity (v.), λυποῦμαι
pity, what a, τί κρίμα
place, ὁ τόπος, τὸ μέρος
plague, ἡ πανούκλα, ὁ λοιμός
plain, ὁ κάμπος
plan, τὸ σχέδιον
plank, τὸ σανίδι
plant (n.), τὸ φυτόν

plate, τὸ πιάτο
play. παίζω
pleasant. εὐχάριστος
please, ἀρέσω : do you like that?
σ'ἀρέσει αὐτό ;
if you please, σὲ παρακαλῶ.
pleasure, ἡ χάρι, ἡ εὐχαρίστησι(s)
pleasure. what is your? ὁρίστε
plough, τὸ ἀλέτρι
plum, τὸ δαμάσκηνον
pocket, ἡ τσέπη
point, peak, ἡ μύτη
poison (n.), τὸ φαρμάκι
poison (v.), φαρμακόνω
police, ἡ ἀστυνομία
policeman, ὁ κλητῆρας
polite, εὐγενής
pomade, ἡ πομάτα
poor, φτωχός : (wretched), καϋμένος
pope, ὁ παπᾶς
poplar, ἡ λεύκη
pork. τὸ χοιρινό
port, ὁ λιμένας, τὸ πόρτο, ἡ σκάλα
porter, ὁ χαμάλης
position, situation, ἡ θέσι
possible, δυνατός
(it is) possible, (ἐ)μπορεῖ
post, ἡ πόστα, τὸ ταχυδρομεῖον
postage-stamp, τὸ γραμματόσημον
postman, ὁ διανομεύς
postpone, ἀναβάλλω
pot, vessel, τὸ ἀγγεῖον
potato, ἡ πατάτα
pound (livre), ἡ λίτρα, of weight ; ἡ
λίρα (ἀγγλική), of money
pour out, χύνω
powder, ἡ σκόνη
power, ἡ δύναμις, ἡ μπόρεσις
praise, ἐπαινέω, -ῶ
pray, προσεύχομαι
prefer, προτιμάω, -ῶ
prepare, ἑτοιμάζω
prescription, ἡ συνταγή
present (n.), τὸ δῶρον
present (v.), χαρίζω
pretty, ὤμορφος
prevent, ἐμποδίζω
price, ἡ τιμή
prick, pierce, κεντάω, -ῶ
pride, ὑπερηφάνεια

priest, ὁ παπᾶς
prince, ὁ πρίγκηπας ὁ πρίγκηψ)
princess, ἡ πριγκηπίσσα
print (v.), τυπόνω
prison, ἡ φυλακή
probable, πιθανός
profit, τὸ κέρδος
progress, ἡ προκοπή
promise n.), ἡ ὑπόσχεσι(s)
promise (v.), ὑπόσχομαι, τάζω
pronounce, προφέρω
pronunciation, ἡ προφορά
proper, regular, τακτικός
property, ἡ περιουσία
proprietor, ὁ ἰδιοκτήτης
proud, ὑπερήφανος
prove, ἀποδεικνύω, -ῶ
proverb, adage, ἡ παροιμία
provide, προμηθεύω
province, ἡ ἐπαρχία
Prussia, ἡ Πρωσσία
Prussian, ὁ Πρῶσσος
public, δημόσιος
publish, δημοσιεύω
pull, τραβάω, -ῶ, σέρνω
pulse (pulsation), ὁ σφυγμός
pump, ἡ τλοῦμπα
punctually, σωστὰ 's τὴν ὥραν
punish, τιμωρέω, -ῶ, παιδεύω
punishment, ἡ τιμωρία
pure, καθαρός
purgative, τὸ καθάρσιον, τὸ καθαρτικόν
purse, τὸ πουγγί
push (v.), σπρώχνω
put on (a coat, shoes), βάλλω, ντύνομαι

Q.

quail, τὸ ὀρτύκι
quarrel (v.), μαλλόνω
quart (litre), ἡ λίτρα
quarter, ἕνα τέταρτο (κουάρτο)
quay, ἡ προκυμαία
queen, ἡ βασίλισσα
queer, περίεργος
question, ἡ ἐρώτησι
quickly, γρήγορα, ὀγλήγορα
quiet. ἥσυχος

R.

rabbit, τὸ κουνέλι
rabies, hydrophobia, ἡ λύσσα
race, τὸ γένος
radish, τὸ ῥαδίκι
railway, ὁ σιδηρόδρομος
railway carriage, τὸ βαγόνι
rain, ἡ βροχή
rains, it, βρέχει
raise, σηκόνω
raisin, ἡ σταφίδα
rare, σπάνιος
rash, αὐθάδης
rat, ὁ μεγάλος ποντικός
raven, ὁ κόρακας
raw, ἀνέψητος, σκληρός
razor, τὸ ξουράφι, τὸ ξυράφι
reach, φθάνω, φτάνω
read, διαβάζω
ready, ἕτοιμος
ready money, μετρητά
real, actual, πραγματικός
reap, θερίζω
reason, ὁ λόγος
receipt, ἡ ρετζέτα
recommend, συσταίνω
red, κόκκινος
reed, rush, ὁ κάλαμος, τὸ καλάμι
reflect, συλλογίζομαι
regiment, τὸ σύνταγμα
registered, συστημένος
regret (v.), λυποῦμαι
rejoice, χαίρω, χαίρομαι
relative (kinsman), συγγενής
religion, ἡ θρησκεία
remain, μένω
remain here, κάτσε 'δῶ
remembrance, τὸ μνημονικόν
renew, ἀνανεώνω, 'ξαναρχίζω
renown, ἡ φήμη
rent, hire, τὸ (ἐ)νοῖκι, τὰ ἐνοίκια
repair, διορθόνω, φτειάζω
repent, μετανοέω, -ῶ
repentance, ἡ μετάνοια
reply (n.), ἀπόκρισις
reprove, scold, μαλλόνω
republic, δημοκρατία
reputation, good, τιμή
request (v.), παρακαλέω, -ῶ

require, ask for, ζητέω, -ῶ, γυρεύω
rescue, σώζω
resemble, ὁμοιάζω (takes μέ after)
reservoir, ἡ δεξαμενή
resin, ἡ ρετσίνα
resined wine, τὸ ρετσινάτο, τὸ ρετσίνο
rest, ἡσυχάζω
restaurant, ξενοδοχεῖον
return, ἐπιστρέφω, γυρίζω
revenge, ἡ ἐκδίκησι
(au) revoir, καλὴν ἀντάμωσιν
reward (for thing lost), τὰ εὑρετίκια
rheumatism, ὁ ρευματισμός
ribbon, ἡ κορδέλλα
rice, τὸ ρύζι
rich, πλούσιος
riches, ὁ πλοῦτος (τὰ πλούτη)
ride, καβαλλικεύω
ride, go for a, βγαίνω μὲ ἄλογο
ridiculous, γελάσιμος
right, σωστός : (of an account, rightly added up), δίκαιος
right hand, δεξιός
right hand, on the, δεξιά
ring (v.), χτυπάω, -ῶ (τὸ κουδοῦνι,, κουδουνίζω
ring (n.), τὸ δαχτυλίδι
ripe, καμωμένος, γεννωμένος
rise, σηκόνομαι
rising, the sun is, ὁ ἥλιος βγαίνει
risk, κίνδυνος
river, τὸ ποτάμι, ὁ ποταμός
road, ὁ δρόμος
roast (v.), ψήνω
roast (a.), ψημένος, ψητός
roast beef, τό ψητὸ βωδινό
roast meat, τὸ ψητό, τὸ ρόστο
rob, κλέφτω
robber, ὁ κλέφτης, ὁ ληστής
rock, ἡ πέτρα
roof, ἡ στέγη, ἡ ὀροφή
room, ἡ κάμαρα, τὸ δωμάτιον
room, space, τόπος
root, ἡ ρίζα
rope, τὸ σχοινί
rose, τὸ τριαντάφυλλο, τὸ ρόδο, ἡ ρόζα
rot (v.), σαπίζω
rotten, σάπιος
rough, τραχύς
round, στρογγυλός

round about, τριγύρω εἰς
row, paddle, λάμνω
row (n.), ἡ σειρά
royal, βασιλικός
rub (v.), τρίβω
rubbish, τιποτάνιο πράγμα
ruin, καταστρέφω
ruins, τὰ ἐρείπια, τὰ χαλαστά
ruler (for lines), ἡ ῥῆγα
run, τρέχω
Russian (n.), ὁ Ρῶσσος
Russian (a.), Ρωσσικός
rustic, χωριατικός

S.

sacrifice, θυσιάζω
sack, ὁ σάκκος
sad, λυπημένος
saddle, ἡ σέλλα: (pack-saddle), τὸ σουμάρι
safe, σωστός
sail, τὸ πανί
sailor, ὁ ναύτης
saint, ἅγιος
salad, ἡ σαλάτα
salt (n.), τὸ ἁλάτι
salt (v.), ἁλατίζω
salted, ἁλατισμένος
same, ἴδιος
sample, τὸ δεῖγμα
sand, ἡ ἄμμος
sap, juice, τὸ ζουμί
sardine, ἡ σαρδέλλα
sate, χορτάζω
sated, χορτασμένος
satisfied, εὐχαριστημένος
Saturday, τὸ Σάββατο
sauce, ἡ σάλτσα
saucer, τὸ πιατάκι, ἡ πιατέλλα
savage, ἄγριος
save, σώζω
save, economize, οἰκονομέω, -ῶ, κάμνω οἰκονομίαν
Saviour, ὁ Σωτῆρας
saw, τὸ πριόνι
scales, weighing instrument, ἡ ζυγαριά
scamp, ὁ κατεργάρης, ὁ μασκαρᾶς
scarce, σπάνιος

scarcely, μόλις
scarf, τὸ βέλο
scent, ἡ μυρωδιά
scholar, student, ὁ μαθητής, ἡ μαθήτρια
school, τὸ σχολεῖον (τὸ σκολειό)
science, ἡ ἐπιστήμη
scissors, τὸ ψαλίδι
screw, ἡ βίδα
sculptor, ὁ γλύφτης
sea, ἡ θάλασσα
(are you) seasick? σᾶς πιάνει ἡ θάλασσα;
seal, signet, ἡ βοῦλα
season, ἡ ὥρα
seat oneself, κάθομαι
second (of time), τὸ δευτερόλεπτον, ἡ στιγμή
secret (n.), τὸ μυστικό
secretary, ὁ γραμματεύς
see, βλέπω (γλέπω)
I have not seen him for two days
   ἔχω δύο μέραις νά τον ἴδω
seed, ὁ σπόρος, τὸ σπέρμα
seek, γυρεύω
seem, φαίνομαι
seethe, βράζω
seize, πιάνω
seldom, σπάνια
sell, πουλάω, -ῶ (πουλέω, -ῶ)
send, στέλνω
sense, ὁ νοῦς
sentry, ὁ σκοπός
separate, χωρίζω
sermon, κήρυγμα, διδαχή
serpent, τὸ φίδι
servant, ὁ δοῦλος, ἡ δούλα, ὁ ὑπηρέτης, ἡ ὑπερέτρια
service, ἡ ὑπηρεσία
set, βάλλω
set on fire, ἀνάφτω
severe, austere, αὐστηρός
sew, ράφτω
shadow, ἡ σκιά
shake, κουνέω, -ῶ
shame, ἡ ἐντροπή
share, divide, μερίζω
sharp, κοφτερός, ἀκονισμένος
sharpen, ἀκονίζω
shave, ξουρίζω, ξυρίζω
shawl, τὸ σάλι

sheep, τὸ πρόβατον
sheet, τὸ σινδόνι
shelter, τὸ σκέπασμα
shepherd, ὁ τσοπάνης, ὁ βλάχος
shine, ὑαλίζω
ship, τὸ πλοῖον, τὸ καράβι
shirt, τὸ (ὑ)ποκάμισο
shoe, τὸ παποῦτζι
shoemaker, ὁ παπουτζῆς
shoot (v.), τραβῶ τὸ τουφέκι
shop, τὸ μαγαζί, τὸ μπακκάλι
shore, τὸ παράλι
short, κοντός
shoulder, ὁ ὦμος
shout, φωνάζω
shovel, τὸ φτυάρι
show, δείχνω, ἀποδείχνω
shut (v.), κλείω, σφαλνάω, -ᾶ, κλειδόνω
shut (a.), κλειστός
shy, feel, be ashamed, 'ντρέπομαι
sick, ἄρρωστος, ἀσθενής, ἀδύνατος
(be) sick (vomit), ξερνῶ
side, τὸ μέρος, ἡ πλευρά
(on this) side, ἀπὸ τοῦτο τὸ μέρος, ἀπ'
αὐτὴ τὴ μεριά
sigh, ἀναστενάζω
sight, τὸ βλέψιμο
silence, σώπα!
(be) silent, σιωπῶ
silk (n.), τὸ μετάξι
silken, silk (a.), μεταξωτός
silly, λουρδός
silver (n.), τὸ ἀσήμι, ὁ ἄργυρος
silver (a.), ἀσημένιος, ἀργυροῦς
simple, ἁπλός
sin, ἡ ἁμαρτία
since (conj.), ἀφοῦ
since (adv.), ἀπὸ τότε
sincere, εἰλικρινής
sing, τραγουδέω, -ῶ
singer, ὁ τραγουδιστής, ἡ τραγουδίσ-
τρια
sink, βυθίζω
sir, Mr., master, gentleman, ὁ κύριος
sister, ἡ ἀδελφή, τὸ ἀδέλφι
sister-in-law, ἡ γυναικαδέλφη, ἡ ἀνδρ-
αδέλφη
sit, κάθομαι
site, situation, ἡ θέσι
size, μέγεθος

skill, ἡ μαστοριά
skilled workman, ὁ τεχνίτης
skin (n.), τὸ πετσί, ἡ πέτσα, τὸ δέρμα
skin, flay, γδέρνω
skull, cranium, τὸ κρανίον
sky, ὁ οὐρανός
sleep (n.), ὁ ὕπνος
sleep, fall asleep (v.), κοιμοῦμαι
sleeve, τὸ μανίκι
slip, 'ξεγλιστρῶ
slipper, ἡ παντούφλα
slow, ἀργός
sly, πανοῦργος
small, μικρός
smallpox, ἡ εὐλογιά
smart (v.), πονάω, -ῶ
smell, μυρίζω
smell (n.), ἡ μυρωδιά, bad smell, ἡ
ἀποφορά
smile, χαμογελῶ
smith, ὁ σιδηρουργός, ὁ γύφτος
smoke (n.), ὁ καπνός
smoke (v.), φουμάρω, καπνίζω
sneeze, φτερνίζομαι
snow, τὸ χιόνι
(it) snows, χιονίζει, πέφτει χιόνι
snuff, ὁ ταμβάκος
so, ἔτζι
so much, τόσος
so that, ὅπου νά, ὥστε
soap, τὸ σαπούνι
society, ἡ ἑταιρία
sock, ἡ κάλτσα
soda, ἡ ποτάσσα
soft, μαλακός
softly (of sound), χαμηλά
soiled, λερωμένος
soldier, ὁ σολδᾶτος, ὁ στρατιώτης
sole (of a shoe), ἡ σόλα
son, ὁ υἱός
son-in-law, ὁ γαμπρός
song, τὸ τραγοῦδο
soon, μετ' ὀλίγο
sorrow, ἡ λύπη
(be) sorry, λυποῦμαι
sorry, I am, μοῦ κακοφαίνεται
sorry, λυπημένος
soul, ἡ ψυχή
soup, ἡ σοῦπα
sour, ξεινός

south (n.), ὁ νότος
southerly, southern, νότιος
sovereign (pound), ἡ λίρα (Ἀγγλική)
spade, shovel, τὸ φτυάρι
Spain, ἡ Ἱσπανία
Spanish, Ἱσπανικός
speak, ὁμιλάω, -ῶ
specimen, τὸ δεῖγμα
spectacles, τὰ ματογυάλια
speech, ἡ ὁμιλία, ὁ λόγος
spider, ἡ ἀράχνη
spirit, πνεῦμα
spirit for lamp, τὸ σπίρτο καμινέτο
splendid, λαμπρός, ἐξαίρετος
splinter, ἀπόσχισμα
spoil, χαλνάω, -ῶ
sponge, τὸ σφογγάρι
spoon, τὸ κουτάλι, τὸ κουταλάκι
sport, hunting (n.), τὸ κυνῆγι
sprain, τὸ στρέμμα
spread, ἑξαπλόνω
spring (of water), ἡ βρῦσι
spring (season), ἡ ἄνοιξι
squander, σπαταλέω, -ῶ
square, τετράγωνος
squeeze, σφίγγω
squint, ἀλλοιθωρίζω
squinting, ἀλλοίθωρος
stable, ὁ σταῦλος
stag, τὸ λάφι
stage (of theatre), ἡ σκηνή
stagger, σκοντουφλάω, -ῶ
staircase, ἡ σκάλα
stand, στέκομαι, στέκω
stand still (v.), σταματάω, -ῶ
star, ὁ ἀστέρας, τὸ ἄστρο
start, φεύγω
starving, πεινασμένος
state, ἡ πολιτεία
station, ὁ σταθμός
steady, σταθερός
statue, ἄγαλμα
steal, κλέφτω
steam, ὁ ἀτμός
steamboat, τὸ βαπόρι, τὸ ἀτμόπλοιο
stench, ἡ ἀποφορά, ἡ βρῶμα
step, pace, τὸ βῆμα
stick, τὸ μπαστούνι
still, ἀκόμη
stink, βρωμάω, -ῶ

stinking, βρώμιγος
stirrup, ἡ σκάλα
stocking, ἡ κάλτζα
stomach, τὸ στομάχι
stone, ἡ πέτρα, precious stone, ἡ
    πετρίτσα
stop, stand, σταματάω, -ῶ, στέκομαι,
    τελειόνω
stop (imperative), στάσου
stopper, cork, τὸ στούπωμα
store-room, cellar, ἡ ἀποθήκη
storm, ἡ φορτοῦνα, ἡ τρικυμία
story (of a house), τὸ πάτωμα
(on the upper) story, 's τὸ ἐνάνω
    πάτωμα
stove, ἡ θερμάστρα
straight on, ἴσια, ἴσα
stranger, ξένος
strap, thong, τὸ λουρί
straw, chaff, τὸ ἄχυρο(ν)
strawberry, τὸ φράουλο
stream, τὸ ρεῦμα
street, ὁ δρόμος, ἡ ὁδός
strength, power, ἡ δύναμι
strike, κτυπάω, -ῶ
string, τὸ σπαγάτο, ὁ σπάγγος
string of an instrument, chord, ἡ
    χορδή
strong, ὑγιής, γερός, δυνατός
strong-box, chest, ἡ κάσσα
student, ὁ μαθητής
study, σπουδάζω
stuff, material, cloth, ἡ τσόχα
stumble, σκοντουφλάω, -ῶ
stupid, κοντός
suburbs, τὰ περίχωρα
succeed, ἐπιτυχαίνω
such, τοιοῦτος, τέτοιος
sudden, ἔξαφνος
suffer, ὑποφέρω
suffice, φθάνω (φτάνω)
sugar, ἡ ζάχαρι
suits (it), ἔρχεται
sulphur, τὸ τιάφι
sum, amount, τὸ ποσόν
summer, τὸ καλοκαῖρι
sun, ὁ ἥλιος
sunset, the sun is setting, ὁ ἥλιος
    βασιλεύει
sunrise, ἡ ἀνατολὴ τοῦ ἡλίου

Sunday, ἡ Κυριακή
support (n.), ἡ ὑποστήριξις
support (v.), ὑποστηρίζω
surgeon, ὁ χειρουργός
suspend, hang, κρεμάω, -ῶ
swallow (v.), καταπίνω
swallow (n.), χελιδόνι
swear, ὁρκίζομαι (take an oath)
sweat, ὁ ἵδρος
sweat (v.), ἱδρόνω
sweep (v.), σαρόνω
sweet, γλυκύς
sweetheart, ἡ ἐρωμένη, ἡ ἀγαπημένη
swell, φουσκόνομαι
swim, κολυμπάω
(can you) swim? ξέρεις κολύμπα;
Swiss, ὁ Ἐλβετός
Switzerland, ἡ Ἐλβετία
sword, τὸ σπαθί
sympathy, ἡ συμπάθεια
symptom, τὸ σύμπτωμα, τὸ σημάδι

T.

table, τὸ τραπέζ.
tail, ἡ οὐρά
tailor, ὁ ῥάφτης
tailoress, ἡ ῥάφτρια
take, παίρνω, λαμβάνω
take, I shall take you there, θά σας
    πάω ἐκεῖ
take off (clothes), take out (tooth),
    βγάλλω
talk, discourse, ὁ λόγος
tall, μεγάλος
tame, ἥμερος
tar, τὸ κατράνι
taste, τὸ γκοῦστο
tax, tribute, ὁ φόρος
tea, τὸ τσάι
teach, learn, μαθαίνω, διδάσκω
teacher, ὁ δάσκαλος
tear (n.), τὸ δάκρυ
tear (v.), σχίζω
tease, vex, πειράζω
telegram, (τὸ τηλέγραμμα) τὸ τηλε-
    γράφημα
telegraph (v.), τηλεγραφέω, -ῶ
telegraph-clerk, ὁ τηλεγράφος

tell, λέγω
terrible, τρομερός, φοβερός
test, try, δοκιμάζω
testament, ἡ διαθήκη
thank (v.), εὐχαριστῶ
thank you, σᾶς εὐχαριστῶ
theatre, τὸ θέατρο(ν)
then, τότε
there, ἐκεῖ, ἐκεῖ πέρα
there is, there are, ἔχει (with acc.)
there he is, νά τον
there they are, νά τους
thermometer, τὸ θερμόμετρον
thick, χονδρός
thief, ὁ κλέφτης
thimble, ἡ δαχτυλήθρα
thin, λεπτός
thing, τὸ πρᾶγμα (τὸ πρᾶμα)
think (meditate), συλλογίζομαι
thirst, ἡ δίψα
(I am) thirsty, διψῶ
thought, ἡ σκέψι, ὁ συλλογισμός
thread, ἡ κλωστή
through, ἀπὸ μέσα
throw, ῥίχνω (ῥίχτω)
throw away, πετάω, -ῶ
thunder, ἡ βροντή
(it) thunders, βροντᾷ
Thursday, ἡ Πέφτη, Πέμπτη
ticket, τὸ μπιλλιέτο
ticket of admission, τὸ εἰσιτήριον
tie (v.), δένω
tie it fast, δὲς τὸ καλά
tied, δεμένος
tiger, ἡ τίγρις
tile, τὸ κεραμίδι
time, ὁ καιρός
time (so many times), ἡ φορά, ἡ βολά
time-table, τὸ δρομολόγιον
tin can, ὁ τενεκές
tire, κουράζω
tired, κουρασμένος
tobacco, ὁ καπνός
to-day, σήμερα, σήμερον, σήμερις
toe, δάχτυλος τοῦ ποδαριοῦ
together, μαζύ
toil, labour, ὁ κόπος
tolerate, ὑποφέρω
tomato, ἡ ντομάτα
tomb, ὁ τάφος

to-morrow, αὔριο(ν)

(day after) to-morrow, μεθαύριον (used of any indefinite near future time)

to-morrow morning, αὔριο τὸ πρωΐ

tongue, ἡ γλῶσσα

too, too much, παραπολύ, more commonly omitted, e.g. it is too little, εἶναι ὀλίγο

tooth, τὸ δόντι

torment, βασανίζω

tortoise, ἡ χελώνη

torture, suffering, τὸ βάσανο

torture (v.), βασανίζω

touch, ἐγγίζω

towel, ἡ πετσέτα

tower, ὁ πύργος

town, ἡ πόλι(s)

train, τὸ τραῖνο

tramway, τὸ τράμι, τὸ τραμβαΐ

transcribe, ἀντιγράφω

translate, μεταφράζω

travel, ταξιδεύω

treat (v.), (entertain), τραττάρω

tree, τὸ δένδρο (δέντρο), τὸ κλαρί

tremble, τρέμω

trench, ὁ λάκκος, τὸ χαντάκι

trial (in court), ἡ δίκη

trip, τὸ ταξίδι

trousers, τὸ πανταλόνι

true, ἀληθινός, βέβαιος

trumpet, ἡ σαλπίγγα

trunk, τὸ μπαούλο

truth, ἡ ἀλήθεια

try (test), δοκιμάζω, (do one's best) προσπαθέω, -ῶ

tumbler, τὸ ποτήρι

tune (v.), χορδίζω

Turk, ὁ Τοῦρκος

Turkey, ἡ Τουρκία

turkey, ὁ γάλλος, τὸ γαλλόπουλο

Turkish, Τούρκικος (Τουρκικός)

turn, γυρίζω

turn, drive (of a mill), τραβῶ

turn upside down, revolutionize, γυρίζω ἄνω κάτω, ἀνακατόνω

twilight, τὸ λυκαυγές

U.

ugly, ἄσχημος

umbrella, ἡ ὀμπρέλλα

uncle, ὁ μπάρμπας, ὁ θεῖος

unclean, ἀκάθαρτος

uncleanness, ἡ ἀκαθαρσία

under, κάτω (ἀπό)

understand, καλαβαίνω, καταλαμβάνω, ἐννοέω, -ῶ

undo, χαλνῶ

undress oneself, 'γδύνομαι

unhappy, δυστυχής

uniform (n.), ἡ στολή

unknown, ἄγνωστος

unluckily, δυστυχῶς

unpleasant, δυσάρεστος

until, ἕως, ὡς

unusual, σπάνιος

unwell, κακοδ.άθετος

up, (ἐ)πάνω

uphill, ἀνήφορος

upon, (ἐ)πάνω (εἰς), εἰς

upon the table, 's τὸ τραπέζι

use, make use of, μεταχειρίζομαι

useful, χρήσιμος

V.

vacation, ἡ παῦσις, αἱ διακοπαί

vaccination, inoculation, ὁ ἐμβολιασμός, τὸ ἐμβολίασμα

valley, ἡ κοιλάδα

varied, ποικίλος

vase, τὸ ἀγγεῖον

veal, τὸ βιδέλο, τὸ μουσχάρι

veil, τὸ βέλο

vein, ἡ φλέγα, ἡ φλέβα

velvet, ὁ κατιφές

venture, τολμάω, -ῶ

vermicelli, ὁ φιδές

vermicelli soup, ἡ σούπα φιδέ

vernacular, ἡ καθομιλουμένη

very, very much, πολύ, πολλά

vest, τὸ γελέκι

victory, ἡ νίκη

Vienna, ἡ Βιέννη

village, τὸ χωριό

vine, τὸ ἀμπέλι: (trellised), τὸ κλίμα

vinegar, τὸ ξεῖδι

vineyard, τὰ ἀμπέλια

virtue, ἡ ἀρετή

visit (n.), ἡ ἐπίσκεψι

visit (v.), ἐπισκέπτω
voice, ἡ φωνή
volume, ὁ τόμος
vomit, ξερνάω, -ῶ
vote (v.), ψηφίζω
voyage, τὸ ταξίδι

W.

wages, ὁ μισθός, τὸ μηνιαῖον, τὰ λεπτά
wait for, await, προσμένω, καρτερέω
wait till I mount, στάσου ν᾽ἀναβῶ
wait upon (a sick person), περιποιοῦμαι, κυττάζω
waiter, τὸ παιδί
waken, ᾽ξυπνάω, -ῶ
walk (n.), ὁ περίπατος
walk (v.), περιπατέω, -ῶ. σιργιανίζω
walking-stick, τὸ μπαστούνι, ἡ κάνια
wall, τὸ τεῖχος, τὸ ντουβάρι
walnut, τὸ καρύδι
want, χρειάζομαι
war, ὁ πόλεμος
warm (a.), ζεστός
warm (v.), ζεσταίνω, oneself ζεσταίνομαι
wash, πλύνω, πλένω
washerwoman, ἡ πλύστρα
waste, χαλνάω, -ῶ
watch, clock, τὸ ὡρολόγι
watch, keep awake, ἀγρυπνέω, -ῶ
watchman, guard, sentinel, ὁ σκοπός
water, τὸ νερό
water-pipe, ὁ σωλήνας
water-closet, τὸ ἀναγκαῖον, ὁ ἀπόπατος
wax, τὸ κηρί
wax-candle, ἡ σπερματσέτα
way, ὁ δρόμος
weak, ἀδύνατος
weakness, ἡ ἀδυναμία
weapon, τὸ ὅπλον
weather, ὁ καιρός
wedding, ὁ γάμος
Wednesday, ἡ Τετράδη, Τετάρτη
weep, κλαίω, κλαίγω
weight, τὸ βάρος
welcome, καλῶς ὥρισες (ὡρίσατε)!
well (a.), καλά
(get) well soon! περαστικά σας

well (n.), τὸ πηγάδι
west, δυτικός
wet, βρεμμένος, βρεγμένος
what difference does that make to me? τί με νοιάζ͑ι; τί με μέλει
wheat, τὸ σιτάρι
wheel, ὁ τροχός
when? πότε;
where? ποῦ;
whistle, pipe (v.), σφυρίζω
white, ἄσπρος
whitsuntide, ἡ πεντεκοστή
why? γιατί (διατί);
widow, ἡ χήρα
wife, ἡ σύζυγος
wild, ἄγριος
will, purpose, ἡ θέλησι
wind, ὁ ἄνεμος, ὁ ἀέρας
window, τὸ παραθύρι, ἡ παράθυρα
window-pane, τὸ τζάμι
wine, τὸ κρασί
wing, φτερό
wink (v.), γνέφω
winter, ὁ χειμῶνας
wish, will (v.), θέλω, ἐπιθυμίω, -ῶ
wish (n.), ἡ ἐπιθυμία
(to) wit, δηλαδή
wither, μαραίνομαι
without, χωρίς, δίχως, ἄνευ
wolf, ὁ λύκος
woman, ἡ γυναῖκα
wonder, θαυμάζω
wood, τὸ ξύλο
wooden, ξυλένιος
wool, τὸ μαλλί
word, ἡ λέξι(ς)
work (v.), δουλεύω, ἐργάζομαι
work (n.), ἡ δουλειά, ἡ ἐργασία
workman, ὁ ἐργάτης
workwoman, ἡ ἐργάτρια
world, ὁ κόσμος
worm, τὸ σκουλήκι
worry oneself (v.), νοιάζομαι
worth, ἡ ἀξία
(be) worth, ἀξίζω
(it is not) worth while, δὲν ἀξίζει
wound (v.), πληγόνω
wrangle, μαλλόνω
wreath, τὸ στεφάνι
write, γράφω

writing, τὸ γράψιμον
writing-paper, τὸ χαρτὶ τοῦ γραψί-
μοτος
wrong, ἄδικος

Y.

yard (25 inches—cubit), ἡ πήχη
(πῆχυς) : (39½ inches, metre), τὸ
μέτρον
yarn, ἡ κλωστή
year, ὁ χρόνος (plur. τὰ χρόνια), τὸ
ἔτος
year, this, ἐφέτος

(last) year, πέρυσι
(next) year, τοῦ χρόνου
yellow, κίτρινος
yes, ναί
yes, indeed ! μάλιστα, βέβαια
yesterday, (ἐ)χθές, (ἐ)ψές
yesterday evening, 'ψὲς τὸ ἑσπέρας
yolk (of an egg), ὁ κρόκος
young (a.), νέος
younger, μικρότερος

Z.

zeal, ἡ σπουδή
zealous, πρόθυμος

RICHARD CLAY AND SONS, LIMITED, LONDON AND BUNGAY.

DAVID NUTT, 270-271 STRAND.

Allen (Thomas William). Notes on Greek Manuscripts in Italian Libraries. 1890. 12mo. xii, 62 S. Cloth, 3s. 6d. net.

Prof. Ludwich in the *Berl. Phil. Wochenschrift:* "Den Inhaltsangaben fehlt es zwar hin und wieder an Genauigkeit, z. B. auf S. 17, wo unter No. 164 die Mitteilung vermiszt wird, dasz der Kodex auch die Hymnen des Proklos enthält ; trotzdem aber wird dasz handliche, hübsch ausgestattete Büchlein manchem Philologen sich als ein brauchbarer Führer erweisen, der z. B. für die Bibliotheca Estensis in Modena viel zuverlässiger ist als der dortselbst handschriftlich existierende Katalog. Wer sich für Subskriptionen, Schreibernamen, Datierungen, Besitzernamen u. dergl. interessiert, findet hier einen reichen Vorrat beisammen. Auch die Vorrede enthält allerlei nützliche Winke über italienische Bibliotheken."

Aristotle. Analecta Orientalia ad Poeticam Aristoteleam edidit D. Margoliouth. 144, 104 pp. Cloth. 1887. 10s. 6d. net.

CONTENTS : Historiae Analectorum adumbratio—Symbolae orientales ad emendationem Poetices—Specimen versionis latinae Poetices Avicennae—Poetica Aristotelis *Arabice* interprete Abu Bashar—Definitio tragoediae *Syriace*—Poetica Avicennae, ex libro Sanatationis *Arabice*—Excerptum ex commentario Fakhru-ddini in Fontes Sapientiae *Arabice*—Poetica Barhebraei, ex Butyro Sapientiae, *Syriace*.

Headlam (Walter, M.A.). On Editing Aeschylus : a Criticism. 8vo. 162 pp. Sewed, 6s.

Wilson (J. Cook). On the Interpretation of Plato's Timaeus. Critical studies with special reference to a recent edition. 145 S. 8vo. Sewed. 1889. 6s.

Berl. Phil. Wochenschrift: "Die Exegese des Timäus erfährt manche dankenswerte Förderung."

Schrumpf (G. A.). A First Aryan Reader, consisting of specimens of the Aryan languages which constitute the basis of Comparative Philology, viz. : Indic, Erānic, Armenian, Hellenic, Albanian, Italic, Teutonic, Keltic, Baltic, Slavonic. Continuous text with transliteration, translation, and explicit commentary. 12mo. 212 pp. Cloth. 1890. 7s. 6d.

Mgr. de Harlez in the *Muséon :* "Excellent petit livre donnant des spécimens du sanscrit védique et classique ; de l'éranien représenté par le vieux persan, l'avestique et le pehlevi, l'arménien, le cypriaque, l'albanais, l'italique latin, ombrien et osque, le celtique, le lithuanien, le vieux slave et le gothique.

" Pour chacune de ces langues l'auteur nous donne des aperçus historiques, des textes transcrits, traduits, expliqués et de nombreuses notes tant historiques que philologiques ou littéraires.

" M. Schrumpf s'est enquis aux meilleures sources de ces sciences et s'est ainsi assuré l'exactitude des explications et des renseignements. Ce petit ouvrage très intéressant se recommande aux lecteurs qui désirent se faire une idée générale de ces différents idiomes."

DAVID NUTT.

Classical Review. Vols. I—V. Royal 8vo, double columns.
Upwards of 500 pages. Vol. I., II., each 12s. 6d. Vols. III.—V., each
15s.

Adams (Rev. H. C). **The Greek Text of the Gospels,**
with Prolegomena, Notes, and References. New Edition. 8vo. Cloth,
10s. 6d.

Separately, sewed.
St. Matthew, 5th ed., 1886. 2s. 6d. | St. Luke, 3rd ed., 1879. 2s. 6d.
St. Mark, 3rd ,, 1874. 2s. | St. John, 2nd ,, 1873. 2s. 6d.

Athanasius (S.), on the Incarnation. Edited for the
use of Students, with introduction and notes, by the Rev. A. ROBERTSON.
8vo. 1882. (xii. 89 pp.) Cloth, 3s.

Athanasius (S.), on the Incarnation. Translated by
the Rev. A. ROBERTSON. 8vo. 1884. Sewed, 1s. 6d. Cloth. 2s. 6d.

King (Rev. C. W.). **The Gnostics and their Remains,**
Ancient and Mediaeval. Second Edition. 8vo. 1887. (xxiii. 466 pp.,
14 full-page chromolithographed plates and 19 woodcuts in the text.)
Cloth. £1 1s.

This edition contains one-third more text and illustrations than the first
edition published in 1864.

Simonides (K.). Ὀρθοδόξων Ἑλλήνων θεολογικαὶ γραφαὶ
τέσσαρες. 8vo. 1859. (xviii. 220 pp.) Sewed. Published at 10s. 6d.
reduced to 4s.

Contains polemical writings against the Roman Church on the Nature and
Office of the Holy Ghost by Nicolas, Bishop of Methona: Gennadius,
Archbishop of Constantinople; Gregory, Archbishop of Thessalonica; and
Georgius Coressius.

Aristophanis Comœdiæ quatuor (Equites, Nubes, Vespæ,
Ranæ) rec. et copiosa annotatione critica instruxit F. H. M. BLAYDES.
8vo. 1882. Cloth, 12s.

Du Cange (Car. du Fresne, Dom.) Glossarium mediæ
et infimæ Latinitatis, auctum a Monachis Ordinis S. Benedicti, cum supple-
mentis integris, D. P. Carpenterii, Adelungii, aliorum suisque digessit G.
A. L. HENSCHEL. Sequuntur Glossarium Gallicum, Tabulæ, Indices
auctorum et rerum, Dissertationes. Editio nova aucta pluribus verbis
aliorum Scriptorum a LEOP. FAVRE. 10 vols. 4to. 1884-88. Ordinary
paper £10 : or in cloth, 2s. 6d. per volume extra.

DAVID NUTT.

Homer's Odyssey. Edited with marginal references, various reading, notes and appendices by the Rev. H. HAYMAN, D.D. 3 vols. 8vo. Cloth.

Vol.	I.	Books	I.—VI.	1866 (ciii. 240 clii.) 14s.
,,	II.	,,	VII.—XII.	1873 (exxxvi. 292, xli. pp.) 14s.
,,	III.	,,	XIII.—XXIV.	1882 (clii. 596, xi. pp.) £1 4s.

Platonis Opera omnia, recognoverunt J. G. BAITER, J. C. ORELLI, et A. G. WINCKELMANN. Accedunt variæ lectiones, scholia et nominum index. 4to. 1842. (viii. 1073 pp.) Sewed, £1 15s.

Platonis Opera omnia, recognoverunt J. C. BAITER, J. C. ORELLI, et A. G. WINCKELMANN. Editio in usum scholarum. 21 parts in 4 vols. 16mo. Bound. £1 16s.

The Parts are sold separately, at the affixed prices, in paper covers.

Pars 1. Euthyphro, Apologia Socratis, Crito. Ed. V. 1s.
,, 2. Phaedo, item incertorum auctorum Theages et Erastae. Ed. IV. 1s. 6d.
,, 3. Theaetetus. Ed. II. 1s. 6d.
,, 4. Sophista. Ed. II. 1s.
,, 5. Euthydemus et Protagoras. 1s.
,, 6. Hippias minor. Cratylus. Ed. II. 1s.
,, 7. Gorgias et Io. Ed. II. 1s. 6d.
,, 8. Philebus. Ed. II. 1s.
,, 9. Meno. Alcibiades I. Ed. II. 2s.
,, 10. Alcibiades II., Charmides et Laches. 1s.
,, 11. Lysis, Menexenus, Hipparchus.

Pars 12. Politicus et Minos. 1s. 6d.
,, 13. Res Publica. Ed. VI. Cloth, 5s.
——on writing paper with very wide margins for annotations. Sewed, 9s. Cloth, 10s. 6d.
,, 14. Leges et Epinomis. 2s.
,, 15. Timaeus et Critias. Ed. II. 1s. 6d.
,, 16. Parmenides. Ed. II. 1s.
,, 17. Symposion. Ed. II. 1s.
,, 18. Phaedrus. 1s.
,, 19. Hippias maior, item Epistolae.
,, 20. Dialogi spurii: Axiochus. De Justo. De Virtute. Demodocus. Sisyphus. Eryxius. Clitophon.
,, 21. Scholia.

Parts 11, 19, 20, and 21 are only sold in the sets.

Poetae Scenici Graeci, ex recensione et cum Prolegomenis GUIL. DINDORFII. Fifth entirely new edition, printed with *Greek Inscription Type.* Imp. 8vo, cloth. £1 4s.

Poetae Scenici Graeci, ex recensione et cum Prolegomenis GUIL. DINDORFII. 5th Oxford Stereotyped Edition. Imp. 8vo (748 pp.), cloth, £1 1s.

DAVID NUTT.

Hoskier (Herman C.). A full Account and Collation of the Greek Cursive Codex Evangelium 604 (with Two Facsimiles) [Egerton 2610 in the British Museum]. Together with two Appendices containing

(A) The Collation of a Manuscript in his own possession. (B) A reprint with corrections of Scrivener's list of differences between the editions of Stephen 1550 and Elzevir 1624, Beza 1565 and the Complutensian, together with fresh evidence gathered from an investigation of the support afforded to the various readings by the five editions of Erasmus, 1516, 1519, 1522, 1527, 1535, by the Aldine Bible 1518, by Colinæus 1534, by the other editions of Stephen of 1546, 1549, 1551, and by the remaining three Bezan editions in folio of 1582, 1588-9, 1598 and the 8° editions of 1565, 1567, 1580, 1590, 1604. (C) A full and exact comparison of the Elzevir editions of 1624 and 1633, doubling the number of the real variants hitherto known, and exhibiting the support given in the one case and in the other by the subsequent editions of 1641, 1656, 1662, 1670, and 1678. (D) Facsimile of Codex Paul. 247 (Cath. Eps. 210), with correction of previous descriptions. (E) Report of a visit to the Phillips MSS., with corrections of and supplement to previous information concerning them, and collations of parts of some of them. (F) Report of a visit to the Public Library at Bâle, with Facsimile of Erasmus' second MS. Evan. 2, and a collation of Codex Apoc. No. 15. (G) Report of a visit to the Public Library at Geneva, with corrections of Cellerier's collation of Evan. 75, as supplied to Scholz. (H) Report of a visit to the Library of Harvard College, Cambridge, Mass. U.S.A., with information concerning the sacred Greek codices there. (I) Some further information concerning Codex 1ª, an Evangelistary at Andover, Mass. U.S.A. (J) Note on 1 Tim. iii. 16.

Royal 8vo, 280 pages, bound in Buckram, price 21s.

Professor O. v. Gebhardt in the *Theologische Literaturzeitung.* — "So macht die Collation im Grossen und Ganzen den Eindruck der Zuverlässigkeit, zumal, dank der schon gerühmten Gewissenhaftigkeit des Verf.'s, der Gedanke an Flüchtigkeitsfehler gar nicht aufkommen kann. Und wenn wirklich eine oder die andere Lesart Misstrauen erregt, wie Mt. 1, 23 ἴξει (st. ἔξει) oder 2, 7 σιξεταστε ('sic, certè'), so kann dadurch der günstige Gesammteindruck nur wenig abgeschwächt werden. . . . glänzend ausgestattete Buch, durch welches sich der Verf. den Dank aller derjenigen verdient hat, welche auf dem Gebiete der neutestamentlichen Textkritik arbeiten."

"A piece of very honest, careful, and valuable work."
PROF. SANDAY, *Academy.*

"Every theological library and every original student of the N.T. will find it important to possess this work."

"A valuable contribution to textual criticism."—*Classical Review.*

"Ein solches Maas von Sorgfalt ist nun freilich überhaupt noch nicht dagewesen. Sind mit einer Genauigkeit angegeben, welche die bisher bekannten Angaben weit hinter sich lassen."